BLOWBACK

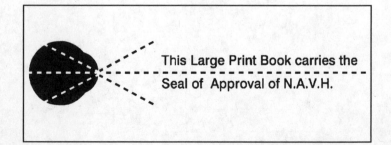

A VANESSA PIERSON NOVEL

BLOWBACK

VALERIE PLAME
AND SARAH LOVETT

THORNDIKE PRESS
A part of Gale, Cengage Learning

GALE
CENGAGE Learning·

Detroit • New York • San Francisco • New Haven, Conn • Waterville, Maine • London

GALE
CENGAGE Learning

LIBRARY OF CONGRESS CATALOGING-IN-PUBLICATION DATA

Plame, Valerie.
    Blowback : a Vanessa Pierson novel / by Valerie Plame and Sarah Lovett.
      pages ; cm. — (Thorndike Press large print thriller)
      ISBN 978-1-4104-6231-2 (hardcover) — ISBN 1-4104-6231-5 (hardcover)
    1. Women intelligence officers—Fiction. 2. Undercover operations—Fiction.
    3. Large type books. I. Lovett, Sarah, 1953– II. Title.
    PS3623.I58586B58 2013b
    813'.6—dc23   2013025553

Published in 2013 by arrangement with Blue Rider Press, a member of Penguin Group (USA) LLC, a Penguin Random House Company

Printed in Mexico
1 2 3 4 5 6 7 17 16 15 14 13

*To my parents, Sam and Diane Plame,
whose unwavering love made everything
else possible.*

— VALERIE

*To my daughter, Pearl —
your resiliency, fierce loyalty, and faith
astound me.
I love you with all my heart.*

— SARAH

ONE

The quick slap of a runner's stride against asphalt broke the late-afternoon hush of Vienna's Prater Garten. Vanessa Pierson tensed, catching a flash of blue and white in her peripheral vision. Lean legs encased in a warm-up suit, slightly scuffed running shoes, rhythmic breathing — an athlete training for Vienna's annual marathon? She exhaled as he passed, but the knot behind her solar plexus tightened, her body's message that she'd moved way beyond normal operational adrenaline.

But there'd been nothing normal about this op from the beginning.

Her Iranian asset had sent her a private message embedded within the careful content of the e-mail that prompted this meeting. He'd used the code they'd agreed on the last time they met in person. A phrase that told her the meeting was so urgent it warranted the risk entailed. "Although my conference schedule is extremely busy, I'm hoping to visit the Klimt paintings in the Belvedere Palace."

And now you're forty-two minutes late, Arash.

Fear for him whispered through her. What if he'd been detained, arrested —

She forced her mind away from the worst-case scenarios. Screwed-up Agency commo plans were legendary — the most intricate and carefully arranged meetings blown by someone forgetting whether to move the clock forward or back by one hour or two.

She'd played tourist for the last ninety minutes, strolling the main avenue, circling the park's ornate lake to feed the raucous ducks, the burn phone in her pocket pressing against her hip. Only one person had the number: Chris Arvanitis, her boss at the counterproliferation division, the only one at CIA Headquarters who still had her back.

Now, retracing her steps, she followed the path to the amusement park, where the Riesenrad, the Giant Wheel, spun ponderously against a low gray sky. When Arash arrived, he would head toward their landmark.

They hadn't had any contact since their last meeting in Copenhagen, almost two years ago. For a few minutes they'd walked through Tivoli Gardens, the last gleam of sunset reflecting off the lake. As a swan stretched its gray wings, sending ripples over the water's metallic shimmer, she'd pressed a flash drive into his damp palm, squeezing his hand gently. To calm him, she quietly joked, "For one of your colleagues at Natanz who enjoys the soft porn of *Game of Thrones*. Leave it where it will be used often and shared."

He had offered a faint smile, but the skin around his dark eyes tightened and Vanessa read the spike of fear. He knew better than to ask what the drive contained — he would put the pieces together easily enough, even before the story burned through the international press and the virus contained on the flash drive irrevocably changed the nature of covert war. Knowing she would not see him again soon, if ever, she'd walked away without looking back. Almost whispering the silent request: *Be very careful, Arash Farah. Stay safe, my friend.*

The Riesenrad groaned to a halt just as the lights sparked on in the amusement park, a small rainbow glowing against fading sunlight. A handful of laughing teenagers stumbled from a carriage on the huge wheel, and a small, screaming boy of about four tugged desperately on his mother's arm. But Vanessa focused on the solitary male pedestrians within sight. No Arash, but a pale, dark-haired man turned away from her gaze abruptly.

The first glimmer of the icy panic rose. A panic that had dogged her since the shit storm from Prague and Jost Penders's disappearance.

Even when the pale man waved to an elderly woman shepherding twin boys of about ten, the fear remained, irrational now.

She reined herself in, but all her instincts pushed her to move. Turning in slow motion, scanning the amusement park and the green tree-shaded park beyond, marking: the teenage neopunk fan, noise leaking from his earbuds; the tourist family; the fraught woman with the noisy toddler.

A group of college students brushed past her on their way to the biergarten, voices rising over the groan of gears and piped music. She sidestepped them, abruptly brought back to ground.

She would give Arash ten more minutes.

"Komm schon! Vorwärts! Venez-vous! Come on!" The barker at the faded shooting gallery beckoned, calling out in assorted tongues, *Come on, pretty lady, three shots for a euro!*

She flashed a smile that didn't reach her eyes — the open booth offered an easy view of the Hauptallee; at the same time, its proximity to the Riesenrad meant Arash would spot her quickly. She stepped up. *"Nur drei?"*

"Ordnung, drei, ja," the barker offered with a dodgy wink. He took her money and handed her a scuffed target rifle.

Pushing strands of her dark bobbed wig behind one ear, Vanessa set the butt of the rifle squarely to her right shoulder. She took a breath and began the slow squeeze on the trigger. Four shots, four targets blown apart.

The barker fanned his forehead with his hand and whistled.

She powered through her next shots, annihilating four new marks, refusing another go — *"Nein, nein"* — abandoning the target rifle on the counter of the faded green booth.

Even if it was a timing mix-up, Arash should have been there by now. She had to move and — *damn,* the screaming toddler was dragging his mother her way.

Vanessa pivoted toward the main avenue, with its green canopy of chestnut trees, catching a glimpse of her distorted image in the mirror of the adjacent fun house, her jeans, boots, and jacket melding together, her slender body twisted to a freakish cipher.

Still the child screamed, a sound capable

of shattering glass.

"Sie gewinnen!" The barker thrust a huge red plush panda into Vanessa's arms just as she saw a familiar figure in a black overcoat in the near distance: Arash walking briskly along the Hauptallee, the recognizable hitch in his stride, his coat flapping slightly in the breeze, a tuft of blue-black hair falling over his high forehead, five-o'clock shadow emphasizing his softening jawline.

Relief at the sight of him surged through her, its intensity catching her off guard.

Vanessa handed off her prize to the tearful child. She barely registered the mother's surprised thanks because she was already moving to meet Arash. She quickened her pace to reach him while he was still on the main avenue.

Abruptly, a small shock ran through her body — the burn phone in her pocket vibrating.

Arash was no more than ten meters away, and he pulled up straighter when he saw her. His step lightened.

With her fingers pulling the phone quickly from her pocket while she tensed reflexively, she glanced down to read one word: Ephesus.

Abort, Vanessa thought — code to call off the operation.

No fucking way. Headquarters didn't have eyes on this op, so why were they calling her off? Why was Chris calling her off? Had something gone seriously wrong? Or was it overcaution on the side of Headquarters?

But she was too damn close now to abort. Arash had always brought her solid intel. She shoved the phone back into her pocket, pressing forward even as Arash slowed for an instant. Had he seen her hesitate?

She strode the last few paces, close enough to read his face — strain, exhaustion, the flush of urgency. But still he managed a twisted half-smile.

She slipped her arm through his and whispered, "Am I glad to see you. Now look happy, I'm your girlfriend."

Arash gripped her hand, almost stumbling as he tried to match his step with hers. "I didn't know if you'd still be here."

"I'll always wait for you as long as I can — but what happened? Why are you late?"

He shook his head. "The Sepah watch me; they watch us all. I had to wait until I could get away."

Sepah — literally, "army" — was the term used by many Iranians to refer to Iran's Revolutionary Guard without expressing loyalty to the Regime. "Are you positive you weren't followed?"

"Yes."

But he'd hesitated a second before answering.

"I was very careful. I did everything you taught me."

"All right, that's good." But she pictured Arash as he hurried toward the meet: vigilant, pausing anxiously to glance into shop windows, looking for familiar reflections, stepping inside shops to force a shadow to pass and backtrack, all of it along a route he'd no doubt studied on a map. What must have been a very rusty and rushed surveillance-detection routine. Was that enough? Was she putting him in harm's way?

As if he sensed her doubts, he tightened his grip. "Yes, it's good. When I found out they were sending me here, I knew we had to meet, whatever the risks."

"Then tell me what you've got, because we don't have much time."

"What I've got . . . it's very important," he said, slowing almost imperceptibly. "How much will your government pay?"

"The usual transfer to your account." She shook her head, impatient now, steering him away from the avenue, into the park and the neat rows of chestnut trees. It wasn't like him to ask about money. "You know there's

14

no time for renegotiation, not right now." She eyed him sharply. "Arash, tell me what you know that's so important."

"Do you remember your promise? If anything happens to me, you will take care of my family."

"Of course I remember. And I promise, I swear, I will keep them safe."

They were following a neat gravel path. She knew the small yellow pavilion in the near distance offered privacy as well as a vantage point. They would be able to see but not be seen.

"You have been looking a long time for the weapons facility that you suspect Bhoot, your ghost, is operating."

Vanessa tensed internally at the mention of Bhoot. She'd been hunting the phantom-like arms dealer and nuclear proliferator for three years, since the first rumors of his existence began surfacing in international intelligence communities. She'd come close to a new lead last year in Prague. "Bhoot?" She forced herself to breathe normally. "Yes. We've been looking for an Iranian weapons facility linked to him."

"Well, I have seen it," Arash said, his voice gone flat.

She shivered — but not from the deepening chill in the air.

They passed a handful of families and couples sprawled on blankets. Ahead, an aspiring boy director with a camera called out directions in French to his group of jaded friends.

Vanessa leaned her body against Arash, keeping her voice low. "You've been to this facility yourself?"

"Yes. And I heard what they are planning —"

"You saw Bhoot, the ghost?"

"Not yet — but there are rumors he will be there —" He shook his head, speaking so rapidly now that he stuttered.

She clutched his hand even more tightly. Over the next seconds, as his story began to unfold, she tried not to betray her primary emotion — dark elation. She had a hundred questions to ask him, but she knew her immediate priority was to memorize the geo-coordinates that would mark the facility's location. But even as he agreed, something caught her attention.

She tipped her head to identify the fragments of a sound, the wrongness of it: a high-pitched whine growing louder. An engine revving up?

A black-and-silver motorcycle, roughly a hundred meters away, slalomed over grass, tearing a path through the chestnut trees.

Her body quickened as adrenaline surged. The bike accelerated — a Suzuki, showering divots on a man and a woman entwined on a blanket. They bolted up, and the woman cursed loudly in German.

The driver, thick-shouldered and masked in black, skidded into a half-turn, dodging low-hanging branches. *Forty meters away now.* Headed for Vanessa and Arash.

"The pavilion," Vanessa hissed, pushing Arash toward it.

The bike swerved past the group of teenagers beneath the trees.

Vanessa got a first look at the biker's gloved right hand.

"Gun!" Running now, she pulled Arash with her until he matched her stride. She felt the motorcycle closing the distance.

Five meters to reach the pavilion. Too far to make it —

Arash stumbled over a tree root, and she grabbed for his jacket, pushing him down, sheltering him.

The Suzuki pulled even with them, splattering dirt, the helmeted driver braking as he looked their way — almost close enough that Vanessa could see their reflections in his helmet shield.

He aimed a black pistol —

Vanessa's fingers contracted reflexively,

cutting into her palm. She cursed the rule that kept NOCs from carrying guns without express permission.

But he didn't fire!

A toy gun?

Abruptly, the biker peeled into a hard right turn, raining turf in his wake.

A sick joke?

A rapid rush of relief mixed with outrage surged inside Vanessa as the Suzuki disappeared in the shadows of the trees, the whir of the engine fading quickly.

The reprieve brought her to her feet. "Stay down," she told Arash. She scanned the area around them. She had to get him away from there, to a safe house, if possible.

Later, she wouldn't be sure what caught her eye. The glint of metal through the far trees? The slightest motion in the distance where the ground rose slightly and a sniper could take a shot?

Instinctively, she turned toward Arash.

He was halfway to his feet.

She felt the rush of air between them — heard a small, hard snap.

A piece of tree bark slapped her cheek as she reached out for Arash — *"No!"*

Saw the fear and confusion in his eyes.

Almost instantly there was a second hiss of air, a second snap of sound, and Arash's

18

head jerked back and his body seemed to hover for an instant before he crumpled to the ground.

Vanessa dropped to her knees next to him. The bullet had hit him between the eyes. A shudder ran through her as his death registered viscerally. Then shock shut her down, leaving only the instinct for survival. Was she still in the shooter's sights?

She had to get away from there as quickly and as invisibly as possible. But first she searched Arash's pockets for anything that would give her more information about the facility — he'd been seconds away from verbally giving her the coordinates to memorize. She found nothing.

She rose numbly to her feet, turning from the few gathering onlookers. As she forced herself to walk intently through the dark-limbed trees toward the park boundary, the world jerked back to life, harsh voices, sirens. The *polizei* would show soon; Interpol and Europol soon after.

When she believed she was alone, she slipped the scarf from her neck and tied it over her head. She slowed for a few strides as disparate emotions overpowered the shock. But she pushed them back and kept moving. Already she could hear the sound of traffic from the main boulevard. She'd moved deliberately toward the shooter's location, knowing the shooter was gone — but trying to gather as much info as possible. She passed the knoll she would have chosen to take her shot.

Was he just ahead of her? Why hadn't he killed her, too?

As she walked quickly under the last of the tree canopy, she heard sirens.

She reached the boulevard, stepping into twilight. She hesitated, looking toward the noise. The city's inhabitants and tourists were strolling the avenue, enjoying a pleasant September evening.

But not the man leaving the park less than a half-block away.

He was more shadow than substance beneath a gray overcoat and fedora. Judging from the people around him, he stood under six feet tall. Was he stocky? Probably not, because the overcoat looked padded at the shoulders and long in the sleeves, while his gloved hands seemed disproportionately large. As he moved, he scanned the area intently, and she noted the high cheekbones and sharp Slavic angles of his face. At a guess, she'd tag him for Eastern European.

He turned away from the intersection, moving with other pedestrians, staying close to the park boundary. A satchel hung heavily

over his left shoulder. Black, ubiquitous —
half of Europe carried one. It wasn't long
enough to contain a full rifle. But a pro
could assemble and disassemble a customized rifle in a matter of seconds. He
wouldn't leave it behind.

Vanessa followed, keeping to the shadows
as they skirted the park.

He didn't look back, but Vanessa sensed
his wariness, almost kindred with her own.
If she was right about his sniping position,
he'd fired from a distance of about three
hundred meters. A windless day made it an
easy shot for a decent sniper — except it
was dusk, and the falling light made the shot
more difficult.

Is that why he'd missed her?

The question raced through her mind
even as she walked in a numb haze, still
fighting against the shock of Arash's murder.

No way to be tracking a target.

As he approached a busy intersection, she
moved to close the distance between them.

Just as he turned his head and looked back
at her.

She hesitated, letting her mind overpower
her instinct to keep tracking him.

He timed it perfectly, waiting for the light
to change, moving toward the trolley stop
just as the queue surged forward.

In a matter of seconds, he vanished.

Had he joined the quick rush of pedestrians who jumped the trolley?

Was he still ahead of her, halfway down a gloomy side street?

But what the hell could she do? She was a NOC — a non-official cover officer. If she let herself get caught up in an international imbroglio involving the assassination of a high-level Iranian target in Austria, the CIA would disavow any knowledge of her. End of story.

Her job demanded she stay undercover and avoid getting caught. An asset's life depended on it. So could her own.

She stopped with a shudder, and Arash's face filled her mind. She saw him falling, saw the dark hole in his head.

Barely aware of the curious glances of a few passersby, she clutched her jacket tightly, fighting free fall, working to regain control. She had to get out of Vienna as quickly as possible.

In this instant she had only one purpose: get Arash's intel to Headquarters.

She pivoted back toward the park and then away, drawn north. She knew Vienna. She'd visited as a child. It was part of her world map.

The street address of the safe house came

to her. *Not far from here.* She pushed back from the edge and forced herself to move through the falling darkness.

Two

Vanessa stared almost blindly past the officer sent by Vienna Station and looked at the TV, where a CNN reporter spoke solemnly: ". . . this time of heightened tension, Iran's minister of defense has issued a public statement blaming Israel and America for today's assassination of a prominent Iranian nuclear engineer, a member of the Iranian delegation to the IAEA conference in Vienna, Austria, who was gunned down in that city's landmark Prater . . ."

Vanessa muted the rest of the sound bite, a repeat, to refocus on the officer, who struck her as untested and much younger than her own twenty-nine years. "Go on."

"Obviously not a good idea for you to fly out of Vienna, so you've got a throwaway alias to get you as far as Prague." He pushed a black plastic wallet across the coffee table. "Canadian, twenty seven, European history student on a year's study leave in Vienna."

Prague — the site of her last screwup, and things had only gotten worse since then . . .

"The Chief of Station is talking to the head of BVT," he said. "We have our scanners tuned to police channels; we're running all the traps."

Distracted, she nodded, already impatient to get her eyes on available CCTV footage. It was possible they'd caught a view of the shooter on one of the myriad public and private security cameras in Vienna. If so, she could find him.

"We haven't heard a report on the weapon —"

"Sniper rifle, guessing semiauto for accuracy on a long shot, maybe three hundred meters out, and the bullet was definitely sonic," she said, flinching internally as she remembered the distinct snap of the passing bullet. "He carried the rifle out with him. I'll need to see the ballistics report ASAP."

She stared at the wallet as she turned it in her fingers and then flipped it open, studying the Canadian driver's license and her own plain-faced photo. The portrait was unflattering but effectively forgettable. When the hell was it taken? She couldn't remember. Pulling up in the straight-backed chair, she silently read and reread the stats. It took three times the usual effort to commit everything to memory. She tried out the name she would use for the next few hours on her way to Prague: Tia Harris.

She glanced again at the monitor, then away from the footage of paramedics carrying the body of Arash to a waiting emergency vehicle. She couldn't stand the images — couldn't bear the sense of guilt. What if she had obeyed Chris's order to abort the meet? *Would Arash still be alive?*

The pale officer cleared his throat. "We'll be getting hourly updates —"

Vanessa stood abruptly, the first taste of bile burning deep in her throat. She left him midsentence and walked steadily to the bathroom even as her breathing quickened. Inside, she slid the bolt and turned the rusting faucet to full force.

She pressed her back against the cold tiles. She slid heavily to the floor. *Useless as a fucking sack of flour.*

She felt her cheek against the tile floor. Her heart crashed against her ribs at a rate that had to be lethal. Somewhere inside herself, she recognized this self-assault. It wasn't the first — the first panic attack had come when she was nineteen, right after her father's death. But she couldn't allow it —

not ever again, Christ.

She didn't know how much time had passed before she heard a knock at the door and a distant voice: "Are you all right? Do you need anything?"

She didn't trust herself to answer. It took all her strength to push herself off the floor. Her borrowed shirt, now sweat-soaked, clung to her back. She reached out, found the old porcelain handle, and flushed the toilet.

Finally she used her arms to steady herself so she could make it to the mirror. She blinked against the light, barely recognizing the sad, wild-eyed woman in the glass. Tentatively, she touched a finger to her left cheekbone, where the sniper's passing bullet had sent ricocheting bark. The skin was pink and tender, and definitely beginning to bruise.

Another tentative knock.

She took a shaky breath. She couldn't keep him waiting much longer.

Quickly, she splashed water on her face, dampening her hair. She used the single small towel, doing her best to rub herself dry.

She stepped out without meeting his eyes. And gave him no opening. Instead, nodding sharply at the wad of bills in his right hand, she snapped her fingers impatiently. "I'll count them." Her voice sounded hard, but at least it worked.

While he waited — eyeing her warily, she knew — she skimmed through the stack. "Seven hundred euros."

He filled in a line of the inventory sheet and held out the clipboard.

Scrawling her signature, Vanessa glanced impatiently at the muted television images playing behind him. She aimed the remote and jumped channels for the umpteenth time. From CNN to a local Austrian station to the BBC.

"Here, your ticket on the night train to Prague."

Vanessa pulled the ticket from between his fingers, slipping it into the pocket of the khakis supplied by Vienna Station. She pushed the euros into her wallet and pocketed that, too, as her companion spelled out the last set of instructions — where and when she would meet her Prague contact.

She was hoisting the dark blue backpack when she noticed the grainy, obviously amateur footage on the screen — a dark-haired woman in faded jeans and a jacket stumbling away from a man's body and disappearing through the trees. It took her an instant to register what she was seeing.

Vanessa fumbled to unmute the TV: "... a student came forward with this footage he'd shot during the attack, and authorities are interviewing witnesses, urgently searching for this mystery woman who left the scene shortly after the Iranian scientist was killed . . ."

"Wait," the officer said, squinting at the screen. "Is that —"

Shit.

Vanessa stared at the unfolding scene the way you watch a train wreck. The kid with the camera had caught her on film only seconds after Arash was shot. He hadn't caught her face, thank God, only the barest profile as she searched the body and then made her exit. Still, it was worse than bad.

THREE

After driving almost six hours straight, Pauk pulled off between Passau and Nuremberg and parked in a gravel lot next to the last of a half-dozen cars at a roadside pub-and-petrol. A place where he would not be noticed or remembered.

A dozen patrons were scattered at the bar and more at a few of the tables inside the large room. Both pool tables were busy, and two flat-screens broadcast soundlessly.

He used the bathroom, comforted to find soap if not clean towels, and then he ordered coffee and a cheese and sausage sandwich from a fat barkeep.

The barkeep idly asked if he was passing through, then took his money, didn't bother him after that.

Both monitors displayed sporting events, but breaking news got play.

He ate quickly, was almost done with the sandwich when he found himself staring at a video of the Prater on the closest flat-screen. Amateur. Grainy. But good enough that he could see the brunette woman he had failed to kill.

For the second time that day, something about her roused a dark place deep inside him — *but why?* Did she resemble someone he'd known? Had he seen her somewhere before? The mere questions threw him — because he was a man who never forgot a face, a gesture, any detail about anyone he encountered in his life.

The sight of her in Vienna had shaken him so much he'd fired twice to kill the Iranian. Who was she? His mentor hadn't warned him about the woman. Nor had he given orders to kill anyone but the traitor.

Inside his car again, engine running, he sent a text message in French — one of their shared languages — to the man he worked for exclusively. The man who had saved his life nineteen years ago in Chechnya. The one man he would gladly die for.

one problem solved. there may be an-other

FOUR

"Next!"

The rumpled, middle-aged traveler in front of Vanessa rolled his bag up to the female customs agent at Dulles's International Arrivals Building.

Vanessa nudged her carry-on impatiently to the painted red line. The soft leather bag and its basic contents were given to her by her contact when she had arrived in Prague, along with her full-cover alias and passport, and the message "You'll be debriefed at safe house Stag."

She let her fingers slide over the U.S. passport in her jacket pocket. "Make sure you thank the tech guys," the Prague inside officer had offered coolly, pocketing Tia Harris's Canadian driver's license. "They were up all night getting your visa stamp close to perfect."

She found herself staring now at the snaking queues of noncitizens, travelers carrying a collective sense of nervous exhaustion. Inevitably, her thoughts turned to Arash's wife and daughter.

She knew the odds were high that Yassi Farah might already be in the custody of the Revolutionary Guard. But Vanessa didn't believe it. She'd walked Arash and Yassi through the emergency protocols at least a dozen times. While Yassi had never made any effort to mask her distrust of "the American spy," she was tough and smart — a natural at tradecraft. And she'd backed Arash's decision to become an Agency asset — for complex reasons having to do with her hatred of Iran's regime, dollars in a U.S. bank account, and the potential of defection.

And Arash would have made sure his wife could deliver vital intelligence if the worst happened.

She pictured Yassi's delicate features and sharply intelligent eyes and felt certain she was already on the move with her daughter.

"Next!"

Vanessa stepped past the painted line, offering up her passport to the uniformed agent. She resisted the urge to touch her cheekbone. She'd done a decent job of masking the bruise with makeup.

"Welcome to the U.S.A., Ms. Gray.

Where's home?"

Vanessa hoped her practiced smile covered the fraction of an instant her mind blanked.

Damn — she thought she'd finally shaken off the haze that lingered through most of the eight-and-a-half-hour flight from Prague. The haze that came with complete exhaustion — the shock of traumatic events, the mind's obsessive replay, the endless turning of details. Had she missed something that could have saved Arash's life?

She sensed the other woman's rising curiosity. *Claire Gray. U.S. Citizen.* Pushing away other thoughts, summoning her energy and her voice. "New York City's home now, but I do a lot of business in D.C." *Partial truths.*

"Where's family?"

Pennsylvania. She pictured her mother in her bright yellow kitchen.

"Connecticut," she said, lying automatically. "Waterbury area."

"Oh, it's pretty around there this time of year; the fall colors are so spectacular. Anything to declare?"

Vanessa blinked. *I've burned through identities to the point I can hardly remember who I am? I've graced CNN in a wig? I'm at least partially responsible for a good man's death?*

"Nothing, thanks. Traveling light."

FIVE

She walked quickly from the terminal into the gray twilight of the Virginia evening, ignoring the pain from too-tight shoes and the glances from men attracted by the physical package — young, blond, lithe, and nicely sexy.

But one man wearing black sunglasses standing in the shadows smoking a cigarette caught her attention.

David Khoury, ops officer, counterterrorism. He'd gotten her text from Prague: coming into IAD can u run traps? A message she never should have sent. It was out of bounds. And it revealed her level of desperation.

He turned, moving ahead of her, six feet tall, taut and lean, slowing only to stab out his cigarette in a receptacle of sand. She caught the lines of exhaustion on his face, felt a deep pang of concern, but was almost instantly pulled back to the questions racing through her mind.

Who ordered the hit?

Was Bhoot involved?

Was Arash's intel valid?

If she'd followed orders, would Arash still be alive?

She followed Khoury toward the daily parking garage, by-passing the cab queue.

By the time she turned onto the covered walkway, he had disappeared. No one ahead, just row after row of parked cars trapped in the gloom. The click of her heels against concrete and the hush of her roller bag's wheels echoed eerily through the closed space.

But twenty paces later he reached out to pull her into the dark corner of a stairwell.

She inhaled, a sharp, startled breath, as he pressed his lips to hers. Her roller bag toppled with a clatter. He'd taken off his sunglasses. He tasted of cigarettes, and his day-old beard scraped her chin. His hands were warm against the small of her back, and she pressed against him, absorbing his heat. They kissed again, this time neither of them breathing until they had to.

When he eased his hold enough to meet her eyes, a complexity of emotions played over his features, but she couldn't pin them down before voices rang through the garage and he released her and she stepped back sharply. Khoury turned his face to the shadows, and she busied herself by reaching down to right her bag while a handful of people passed by.

Meeting like this was a serious protocol breach, and, given the dog-eat-dog environment at Headquarters, a serious risk he'd taken for her benefit.

As soon as they were alone she shook her head, shifting restlessly. "This is too crazy, meeting here. I shouldn't have asked."

"We've done crazy before." His face lit up unexpectedly, and he grinned at her. Thick dark-brown hair, square-jawed, handsome as hell, but the slightly crooked front tooth and the faded scar on his chin from a childhood dare made him look like a kid.

She couldn't help but smile. "You're right, we have."

He stepped onto the walkway, guiding her into the endless rows of parked cars, speaking quietly, soberly now. "A body turned up in Stockerau, an industrial district —"

"About thirty kilometers outside Vienna, I know," she said, hearing how abrupt she sounded.

But Khoury took no umbrage. "Early twenties, wearing cheap leather gear like your bike jockey from the Prater. A small-time Austrian-Chechen punk, executed with two close-range shots to the head. If your hit man was cleaning up loose ends, he used the 9×19-millimeter 7N21 cartridge — a high-velocity Russian round used by some of their special forces."

"I saw the shooter leaving the park," Vanessa said flatly.

Khoury tensed. "Can you identify him?"

"It was dusk and he was roughly twenty-five meters away . . ." But she nodded. "It's enough. What I saw, I won't forget."

"Does he know that?" Khoury asked. "If you're burned —"

"I'm not burned." Heat surged through her body. "He killed my asset. He gunned him down in cold blood."

In the abrupt silence that followed her words, she heard her own question. Khoury heard it, too, because he said, "Your asset was dead the moment he landed in Vienna."

"I was ordered to abort the op, David. But I went ahead."

For an instant he cut his gaze away before he said, "You did the right thing; you got the intel."

She wished she could believe that absolutely.

Neither of them spoke again while he walked her to a small, dark sedan parked in a corner of the structure, away from the full glare of industrial lights. He lifted a compact carry-on bag from the trunk, replaced it with her bag, and pushed it closed.

She reached out, touching his arm. "You know I have one more question you haven't answered yet."

Evading her eyes, he shook his head almost imperceptibly.

"David."

"It wasn't their hit. That's the word from my assets — somebody else had a message to send."

She went still. Khoury was Lebanese American, and his sources were linked to Hezbollah and Hamas, so, in turn, to Iran. His access was part of his value to Headquarters, part of why he'd been so heavily recruited by the Agency. Now he was confirming what her instincts had already told her.

She worked to keep her voice cool. "Your assets — have they heard anything to connect this hit to Bhoot?"

He had inherited his mother's green-flecked hazel eyes, and they narrowed now with wariness. "I know where you want to go with this, but you're so fixated on bringing down Bhoot, it blinds you to other possibilities."

"But it makes sense; this is the way he works — he eliminates anyone, anything standing in his way."

"Then you should be even more careful, Vanessa, because you were in the fucking line of fire in Vienna." He spoke roughly, in a voice she'd never heard him use.

She took a step back. "I don't expect this from you. You're the one person in my life . . ."

His eyes met hers, and she saw the quick, dark dilation of his pupils. His fingers grazed her cheek. "I don't want to wake up next time and hear they got you —" His voice broke off.

"I know." She nodded. "That's how I feel each time you walk away."

He reached for her hand, placing the small set of keys in her palm. "Take the car." He stood, staring at her intently, hesitating too long before he said, "I'm on a flight back to Cairo in less than two hours."

"You look like you haven't slept for weeks, David," she whispered, acutely aware of the strain etched on his face. "Something's going on; something's wrong."

"It's nothing, just the usual work shit that always blows over."

"Then tell me."

His fingers brushed lightly through her

hair, but then, as if sensing she was focusing too closely on him, he pulled his hand away. "Next time."

"When is next time going to be?" She asked the question softly, knowing it was impossible to answer.

"Soon."

"Khoury —"

But he intended to change the subject, and he said, "You might want to wear that brunette wig when you talk to the DDO. Your YouTube clip's been running on CNN today. Every segment."

She resisted for a moment, wanting to force him to confide in her, but she knew how stubborn he was — *anta aa-need*, according to his mother.

So she relented. "How much shit am I in?"

He cocked his head, and his mouth twisted into a smile. "Up to your neck?"

She smiled, too, but she felt the distance between them. "At least it isn't over my head."

"Listen," he said, abruptly serious. "I watched that fucking video a hundred times. Somebody let you live."

As he walked away, she thought again about the risk he'd taken to meet her. Relationships between ops officers who shared the same cover were commonplace. It was so much easier to fall in lust and love with someone when they knew what you did for your day job, so much easier to live with someone who hadn't heard the lies that came before the partial truths.

But relationships between NOCs and "inside" officers (like Khoury, who ostensibly was a political officer at the embassy in Cairo) were forbidden. Love affairs gone bad did not breed trust in the field. If Chris and the seventh-floor management became aware of her relationship with David Khoury, at the least they could both be forced to come "inside." Or they could be fired. Either was a fate she would hate. They would end up blaming each other, and maybe worse.

So how had they let their affair go this far?

The question pushed her back to training days at the Farm during an interrogation simulation. The metal hut locked in heat and humidity and the stink of a dozen "prisoners." The hood snuffed out all but the faintest light.

Heavy footsteps of guards coming back. Vanessa snapped out an internal command that carried the echo of her father — *They push you, push the hell back!*

The footfalls faded. But she couldn't breathe with the stupid hood. And then, a *not* unfamiliar tickling wave of euphoria lifted her out of herself, and her mind caught up. *Her hands were free, weren't they?* Her mouth pulled into a taut little smile.

She raised the edge of the hood and blinked into dusty light — and found herself staring straight at another prisoner who had pulled his own hood up. For a moment his dark eyes sparkled with a manic gleam. Then he winked and she winked back. Kindred souls.

They yanked their hoods back down just in time. The guards were back, taunting and shoving. Later she had introduced herself more formally to David Khoury.

Now he was almost out of sight, on his way back to Cairo, his post at the U.S. embassy, and she felt a sense of foreboding and the fleeting and impossible impulse to call him back.

Under the intensity of her gaze, he turned briefly, just a glance, barely a nod. And then he was gone.

For a moment, his last words echoed silently — *Somebody let you live.*

Six

At 17 Rue de la Bûcherie, above Librairie du Mille Ciels, Pauk climbed the familiar, narrow staircase quickly, soundlessly.

At the crest of the second landing, instead of continuing up the last flight to his attic rooms, he paused to listen to the faint, flat whine of televised voices, a *fútbol* match, coming from inside his landlady's apartment.

In one hand he held a plain brown sack, and he took care not to crinkle or disturb the paper in any way. He knocked once, then again.

At least a minute passed before he heard the scratch and click of the metal locks.

The door opened and the old woman peered out at him with her milky eyes. The most she could see were shadows, and yet her wrinkled face seemed to literally crack into a smile. *"Vous êtes de retour! Bonjour!"*

In return, he held up the sack and gave it

a shake. *"Coeur et foie."*

"Ah, coeur . . ." In a voice of gravel and phlegm, Madame Desmarais admonished him to hurry inside and close the door before the cats escaped.

He obeyed, eyes watering from the stench of cat piss and shit, waiting by the door until she limped her way back to the loveseat. Cats scattered as she turned and dropped onto the faded blue cushions. He shook the bag again for the animals' benefit. Half a dozen multicolored felines clustered around him, squalling and mewling at the scent of bloody organs. A pied piper of sorts, he lured them toward the tiny kitchen, all the while his eyes flickering to the television screen, where — during a break in the France versus Pakistan game — a segment suddenly featured Terek Stadium in Grozny, Chechnya.

His throat clenched as he was sucked back almost twenty years — only to see a boy, weak and spindly and crying like a baby, dragged by an old man with iron claws down a filthy, crumbling staircase. The boy struggled, fighting to run back to the apartment where his mother lay sick and close to death, but the old man was strong, and he forced the boy the rest of the way to the icy, stinking street.

Gray world, filthy snow, bombs, tanks, and rubble.

At the makeshift orphanage, they locked him in a closet so he couldn't run away. When he managed to escape, he ran back to find his mother, but she was gone and strangers occupied what had been his home.

Months later the rebel fighters, the Wahhabi, found him hiding in a ditch filled with raw sewage and freezing rain. Some of them laughed; others shook their heads and said he was an orphan crazy from war. But one day, a rebel put a long and battered rifle in his hands and showed him how to use it.

So then, for the cause and for Allah, they told him to kill one of the Russian soldiers from the camp far across the creek. Whichever one he wanted!

He had no idea if Allah cared or not — or if He even existed — but the rifle gave him a purpose and the faintest sense that he belonged to something.

It took him three days lying prone in the snow and then mud. He shit and pissed his pants. He didn't move. Lay there frozen in the rough weeds. Watching through the scope: one soldier, then another and another. He didn't know which one to kill. By the third day the Russians began to move gear to their trucks. He picked out the biggest soldier who might be easier to hit because of his size. He held him in his scope, squeezed the trigger, and put a hole in his heart.

When the Russians went berserk and crazy for revenge, he didn't know what to do or where to run or hide. If not for the man who pulled him from the weeds, he would have been dead.

The man took him to a room where it was dry and too warm. On the first day he just sat silently and kept the distance between them. On the next day he brought a ball — shiny and smooth, black and white — unlike any ball Pauk had seen in his life. The man asked him in broken Chechen, "How old are you? Twelve? Thirteen?"

The man was a resistance fighter, too, but he came from far away and spoke strange words in a quiet voice. He moved slowly. Even when he made the ball dance and spin and obey, still he moved slowly.

When he finally sat across from Pauk, the boy saw the man's dark eyes were different — his left eye slashed with tiny shards of blue —

A woman's voice cut into his memories: *"Merde!"*

Pauk blinked, openmouthed, to see Madame jerk forward in her seat. *"Connard!"*

This is Paris, Madame's apartment — where he was jolted by the cries of the fat tabby.

He took the final few steps to the kitchen, where he selected the sharpest knife and a cutting board. He poured out the chicken parts, arranging them neatly with the tip of the knife. He worked, dicing the organs with precision to the rhythm of the steady drip of water from the faucet. Whenever the cats jumped up on the small, cluttered counter, he gently shooed them away.

In between slices, he opened the cabinet above the sink. Soundlessly sliding the collection of empty canning jars to one side, he slipped the knife blade into the barely visible seam at the back of the shelf. The trick panel released.

He took a passport from his pocket and set it on top of a pile of a dozen others — the identities he used for jobs. Unremarkable men, all in their early thirties, hailing from countries such as Switzerland and France and Canada and the UK.

He kept the tools of his trade locked in a broken freezer, chained shut, in the same private one-car garage where he parked the Fiat. Three retractable hunting knives; his Snayperskaya Vintovka Dragunov — the same model of "short stroke" semiautomatic

Russian-made Dragunov sniper rifle he used to make his first kill as a boy in Chechnya; boxes of 7.62×54R rounds; extra "cans," or suppressors; and a Leopold Mark IV scope.

For the garage, he paid cash every month and had the payment delivered to the same box. He and the owner had never met in person.

He ran his thumb along the stack of passports, sensing which he might use for the next job. Then he replaced the panel, carefully arranging the jars just so, the way Madame liked them.

He selected three saucers, dividing the diced organs evenly. He fed the cats, re-arranging several of the bolder ones and a kitten, so each had its share.

On the counter, his glass of Beaujolais nouveau awaited.

He sat in his usual chair and settled in to the noise and the company of the woman and her cats. She raised her glass to greet his: *"À votre santé,"* always the beginning of their *fútbol* ritual.

He would be her eyes — for the pretty boys in their bright uniforms — and she would let him. She was his only contact with normalcy. But his mind kept circling back to Vienna, and he felt haunted by the dark-

SEVEN

Thirty minutes to cover fifteen miles between Dulles and safe house Stag, a faux-Colonial condo in the congested, crazy Tysons Corner. Ten minutes to splash water on her face, brush her teeth, run a comb through her hair, and rummage up a Band-Aid for her blistered heel. Another fifty-two minutes of mental and physical pacing. Until she finally opened the door to Chris Arvanitis, her direct boss at CPD.

At five-foot-eight, he stood barely taller than Vanessa, and he seemed to live in his silver-rimmed glasses and kept what was left of his receding hair cut in a military buzz. At first glance unprepossessing — at second glance, formidable. He pumped weights, belonged to Mensa, and his dark brown eyes could make you feel you'd been cornered by a tiger. He brushed past her with a black look, the fallout beginning.

She frowned, on her guard. "Where's

the DDO?"

"You're lucky I got here first." Chris pivoted so abruptly he pinned her in the corner with her back against the wall and they were eye-to-eye, his thick lashes magnified behind the lenses of his glasses. "What the hell, Vanessa?"

"Chris —"

"Why the hell did you ignore my order to abort?"

"Why the hell did you call me off?"

Chris shook his head sharply. "Don't you dare provoke me, not after all I've done for you, not after Prague. I covered your ass. Without me you'd be in fucking backwater Montevideo."

His face loomed so close she flinched. "You're right." She swallowed, her mouth gone suddenly dry. "Sorry."

"Goddamn it, Vanessa." His dark brows pulled together sharply, and his eyes still bored through her, but he lowered his voice and took a step back. "We had intel from MI6 that one of the Iranians at the conference might be a target."

"When did this come in? I wasn't read in —"

"I don't have to read you in. *If I give you a direct order, you follow it.* What the hell about that don't you understand?" He turned and strode into the living room, and she followed.

"You're absolutely right, Chris . . ." Her voice softened, the corners of her mouth pulling down. *God, she hated this feeling — like a contrite child.* He still had his back to her, but she did her best to reach for words he needed to hear her say. "Of course I need to obey orders."

Now she reached out physically, touching his sleeve just as he turned to face her. "But I got the intel, and, Chris, it's what we need to put nails into Operation Ghost Hunt, so we can get Bhoot, so at least hear me out."

"You're missing the point —"

"No, I get that I screwed up, I get that — but if I had obeyed your order, if I aborted the op, my asset would still be dead, and I wouldn't have shit — and this is big. It's what I've been waiting for."

His eyes narrowed to slits. *"You?"*

"It's what *we've* been waiting for," she corrected herself quickly. "Our team at CPD."

He stared at her now, intently, and she felt him take in her bruised cheek, the shadows beneath her eyes, her bare feet. His expression shifted among anger, exasperation, and open concern.

As she met his gaze, he turned away, rubbing the knuckles of one hand hard against his cheek, a familiar gesture of fatigue. He checked his watch. "The DDO should be here any minute."

"Okay, good. I made coffee. High-test," she said, deliberately pointing Chris in the direction of the small, sterile kitchen. When he followed her cue, she took her first deep breath since his arrival. Sleep-deprived and running on fumes, Vanessa could safely assume Chris was in a similar state — straight from an eighteen-plus-hour day at Headquarters, where he'd been dealing with the fallout from Austria. *Her* fallout.

Seconds later she opened the door to the Agency's Deputy Director of Operations, Phillip Hawkins. The DDO breezed past Vanessa with eyebrows raised. "Clearly what happened in Prague hasn't kept you out of trouble or improved your judgment."

Damn.

"At least you made it back in one piece." But he didn't make it sound like a plus. As he passed from foyer to living room, impeccable in his black silk tuxedo, he left behind the very expensive scent of Clive Christian 1872, his signature. Clearly she represented a bit of business to settle before he moved on to this night's benefit or gala.

Vanessa smoothed the rumpled suit supplied by Prague Station. She'd already lost the Band-Aid, and she'd given up on the ill-fitting pumps, relieved to be barefoot again. A hot shower would be her reward when she completed the debrief.

"There's coffee," she told the DDO, just as Chris appeared from the kitchen with a steaming mug.

Phillip Hawkins stayed standing, his sharp eyes on Chris, clearly waiting for the answer to an unasked question.

The thought shot through her wired brain: *Christ, was Chris supposed to take me off the op?*

She looked to Chris, unable to keep the shock and disappointment completely hidden. She read a warning on his face.

He stayed silent long enough that she broke a sweat. Then he took a tired breath. "Vanessa's prepared to debrief us on Vienna and the intel she got from her asset. I believe it's worth hearing her out."

"Her *dead* asset, you mean?" The DDO met Vanessa's eyes with his own icy blues. Long-standing rumors held that he had used those blues to seduce more than his share of women, assets, and political allies over the course of his thirty-year career. Now they stayed squarely on Vanessa, and he frowned sharply. Blowback from Vienna was a personal affront, a black mark on his agency and his ambitions.

But he sat, sinking into the best of the faded leather chairs, crossing his black-trousered legs and adjusting his left cuff — his gaze flicking obviously to his gold-and-silver Rolex. "Then let's do this thing."

She pulled up with a nod and forced herself to sit. "Right." But she held off just long enough for Chris to take the black Windsor chair next to the DDO.

Before the DDO could look at his Rolex again, Vanessa launched in, taking them through the sequence of relevant events as they had unfolded in Vienna.

"I ran a full three-hour SDR . . . meeting set for 1630 hours, but Tree/213 did not make that meeting . . . at 1725 hours I saw him walking rapidly toward me along the Hauptallee just as my sterile phone went off."

Refusing to hesitate, Vanessa looked directly at Chris. "At that point, I was less than ten meters from my asset. We made eye contact, and I made a judgment call to proceed with the meet. He immediately told me about a previously unknown secret underground facility in southeastern Iran. Sistan-Baluchestan Province."

The energy shifted palpably. Chris pulled

forward to the edge of his seat and skimmed one hand across the flat of his close-cropped hair. The DDO narrowed his eyes, and his nostrils flared. For the moment, she had their full attention.

"Tree/213 relayed that he'd been to the facility, and they have just started producing weapons-grade uranium. Also, according to my asset the facility has resurrected an earlier program using UD3, uranium deuteride, to test a neutron initiator, a component with no legitimate civilian uses."

"A trigger?" Chris pulled up sharply. "Was Tree/213 part of the earlier program?"

"Yes. And all of that is actionable intel — but he also had vital time-sensitive intel. The Sistan facility is prepping for a visit from a VIP, a non-Iranian, possibly a Westerner. The visit is scheduled for the thirtieth of this month."

"That's just two weeks," Chris said, his forehead sharply creased. "Did he give you a name?"

"Two weeks minus the day it took me to get back here," Vanessa said. She took a deep breath. "He believed the VIP is Bhoot, the ghost."

She did not have to remind either man that uncovering Bhoot's identity and unraveling his international arms-smuggling operation had been the focus of CPD's Operation Ghost Hunt for the past three years.

"What did your asset offer to confirm it was Bhoot?" The DDO asked the question, and Vanessa directed her answer to him.

"He didn't get the chance to tell me."

"Did he say who gave him this information?"

"No."

The DDO exchanged an uneasy look with Chris. "Did he overhear a conversation?" Chris prompted Vanessa. "Did he get his hands on an internal document?"

Frustrated, Vanessa shook her head. "I don't know. He said there were rumors raging and amped-up operations at the facility; they were running tests and drills in preparation for the thirtieth, and this was extremely unusual."

For a few seconds, no one spoke. Then Chris sat back in his chair. "If your asset was correct, then where the hell is the facility? Baluchestan Province covers about forty percent of Iran."

"He was killed before he had time to give me the geo-coordinates to memorize."

"That makes it a needle in a very big haystack." Frowning, the DDO crossed his arms over his heart. "They've managed to keep other facilities hidden."

"But they can't hide the procurement trail," Vanessa said tensely.

Chris nodded. "It explains the amping up of black-market shipments to Iran. It's been driving my team crazy, those of us working on Operation Ghost Hunt. We couldn't figure out where the hell those components were going. Like they were swallowed up in a black hole."

"Southeast Iran is a *massive* black hole," the DDO said. "Without coordinates, it could take months to confirm or disprove the existence of an underground facility."

"And we've only got two weeks if we believe this stuff about Bhoot," Chris said.

Vanessa pressed on. "I believe that Tree/213's wife has the geo-coordinates that he was going to give me. XYTree/214 is solid, extremely smart, and she will be on the move by now —"

She paused, just for a second, to see if Chris would jump in and state the obvious — the need to get the exfil operation going immediately.

But it was the DDO who said, "It's been more than twenty-four hours since the incident in Vienna. Tree/214 may already be in the hands of the Revolutionary Guard."

"She knows she's in extreme danger,"

Vanessa said quickly. "She has a six-year-old daughter. We have to go on faith that they're both safe for the moment. We need to get them out of Iran *now.*"

"She may be unwilling to deal with you, Vanessa," Chris said quietly. "Her husband was your asset. And she may blame you for his death."

Vanessa cleared her throat. "She may blame me, yes, but she's tough and she's smart, and she can't get out of Iran without our help. She'll play."

A low whine filled the room: the signal of a phone set on vibrate. The DDO stood, reaching into his pocket, and then he disappeared into the kitchen to take the call in private.

Vanessa pulled her chair toward Chris. He was still hunched forward intently. But now he fingered the blue-beaded amulet he always carried on his key ring, a gift from his *yia yia* in Greece. Vanessa knew it provided protection against the *matiasma,* the evil eye. He might be Phi Beta Kappa and a techno junkie, but he was superstitious as hell.

"There's something else you need to know," she said, diving in. "I got a look at the shooter as I was leaving the park."

Chris eyed her sharply. "Then go over the

file photos tomorrow, see if you find him. Tonight, focus on your summary cable."

Before she could respond, the DDO reappeared from the kitchen, clearly on his way to the door and his waiting armored SUV.

"I'll come into Headquarters tonight," she began, following him, "to be there when you move on contacting the Poles about the exfil—"

"We can contact the Poles without your assistance," the DDO said. "Chris can fill me in on the rest of your intel."

"But every hour my asset's family is out there on their own —"

Abruptly, Deputy Director Hawkins raised a hand to silence her. "Be at my office at 0900 hours sharp." At the door, he paused just long enough to lock on Vanessa with his eyes. "We have to consider the possibility that you've been compromised."

Chris placed something in her palm. She looked numbly down to see her Agency badge — Chris always held it when she was in the field. "Until we sort through this and take a look at what the hell actually happened, the DDO agrees with me that it's obviously not in anyone's interest to have you dealing with sensitive assets."

Her skin pricked with the heat of sudden

anger. "You need me on this, Chris. I may have just moved us years closer to catching Bhoot. You see how important it is not to cut me out now? We're close, I can feel it, we have to stop him —"

Chris wrapped his fingers around her wrist, his grip firm but not hard. It startled and confused Vanessa to read his expression — he was afraid for her. "Write up your summary and then get some sleep," he said wearily. "And change your clothes. We'll deal with all this tomorrow."

She almost blurted out the truth — *I can't sleep* —

But she didn't. Instead, she watched his back until he disappeared down the stairs of the second-story condominium, and then she began the three-hour job of composing a detailed summary cable for Operation Ghost Hunt's bigot list, the short list of those read in on the op and cleared to read traffic on it.

She clawed her way out of the nightmare sometime between one and two a.m. — the Kurdish boy and girl, bodies splayed out against hard earth; the dead kitten sprawled between them; the strange snow the color of straw falling all around, hot against Vanessa's skin, apple sweet on her tongue . . .

Awake, the minutes dragged on and the thin plaster walls of the condo seemed to slant in on her. She pulled a miniature of Maker's Mark from her toiletries bag, broke the seal, and finished it.

She sucked in a ragged, shallow breath, silently reminding herself — *It happened twenty-five years ago. You were a little child growing up halfway around the world when Saddam Hussein ordered the massacre in Halabja.*

But the recurring dream always felt like a premonition, as if it came from the future instead of the past.

When she could function, she sent a text message to her brother, Marshall, who was with the Marines in Afghanistan: Second Platoon, Alpha Company, 3rd Recon Battalion.

A code phrase they'd used between them since they were kids.

drop — eat dirt — and give me 50 private pierson!

Almost an hour later when she was walking out the door of the condo, she read his text reply:

love you baby sis. who'd you po now?

EIGHT

Pauk strode deliberately along the Quai Malaquais past the *Vélib* stand with its stable of gray bicycles, quickly skirting the Institut de France to the Quai de Conti, where he jogged through traffic to reach the river. Here, so close to the Pont des Arts, families and tourists filled the *quai,* but Pauk quickened his pace and they moved out of his path. A young woman glanced at him but quickly looked away. He slowed for a moment as he approached the busy steps of the old wooden footbridge. An unusually warm evening, and the mice had come out to play — picnicking students just back from August break, artists and street musicians, and the ubiquitous trolling *bateaux-mouches,* their loudspeakers blaring in German, Spanish, Mandarin for the tourists.

Fine, the crowd served his purpose, allowing him to remain invisible in light or shadow. Even as he climbed the steps, inhaling the hazy cloud of tobacco and dope, he slid his hands into his pockets, fingers feeling for a pulse from the disposable cell phone. It would take him seconds to reach the midpoint of the bridge, past the *bouquinistes* that were shuttered for the evening — before his time was up.

He walked quickly, despite the strollers and the stoned couples and the human statues. Always moving, always assessing — the unicyclist pedaling his way, circling now to juggle colored balls, and the small crowd gathering as if choreographed; the couple kissing in the shadows, both of them girls; and beyond, the Americans yelling at their feral brats.

He carried a book under one arm — *Et Si la Mort N'Existait Pas?* Madame Desmarais had pressed it into his hands when they first met two years ago.

Just past the unicyclist's audience, Pauk slowed again to press himself against the railing. A *bateau-mouche* nosed from beneath the bridge, a Swedish-speaking tour guide pointing out Notre Dame in the distance. Pauk lit a Gitane, sucked in pungent smoke, let the match drop to the Seine. As he exhaled he pulled the cell from his pocket almost before it began to vibrate with an incoming message.

He gazed intently at the small, bright screen and the face that filled it. Although the image was grainy, its poor quality did not distract him from his study of the features. He memorized the heavy jaw, the deep-set eyes, and thick, low brow.

His eyes flickered over the brief text: cyprus 0920.

A tiny roar rose from the crowd, and he glanced up just as the unicyclist caught a yellow ball in his mouth. The women still embraced, and the American brats clustered on the opposite side of the bridge from their parents.

Pauk took one last look at the screen before he powered it off. He pinched out the Gitane, exhaling bitter smoke. As he approached the American kids — three boys and a ragamuffin girl — they launched stones off the bridge. A parent yelled, "I'm warning you!" And Pauk peered over the railing to see if the children had done damage. No passing boats. It was easy enough to toss the phone into the dark waters of the Seine — and with it all traces of his next kill.

NINE

The target snapped into place forty yards in front of Vanessa. She slid the magazine into the Glock and felt it lock. Her stomach clenched, her arms pulled up, fingers of her right hand closing around the grip frame.

Was it only thirty-six hours ago that she annihilated targets with a toy gun while waiting for Arash in the Prater?

She exhaled slowly, pressing her feet into the concrete floor, adjusting her stance. The Glock belonged in her hands. The first firearm she'd ever fired was a .243 Winchester when she was ten and finally allowed on a hunting trip with her father and Marshall. She was at home here inside the shooting cage at the Agency firing range. How many times had she practiced this ritual? Fifty? A hundred? In the early hours of the morning, her only company was the invisible range master. It was all so familiar: the muting cradle of her earmuffs, the lingering smell of gunpowder, the faint glow from the call-indicator light.

Vanessa lowered the Glock and wiped the sweat from her hands.

Was she here to kill the impotence she'd felt in Vienna?

She knew how to deal with loss and pain and whatever else her life and the job demanded. She knew how to get on with it, to do what needed to be done. And yet here she stood, almost frozen.

She focused again on the Glock's front sight. She squeezed off the first round, the pistol jumping stupidly, the shot wild.

She shut her eyes and bit down on her lip. At first all she heard was the drum of her own heartbeat. She pushed the earmuffs back and caught the soft fall of footsteps and the light clang of metal as another shooter entered a cage.

She raised the Glock, returning her attention to the sights, even as she remained aware of the shadowy silhouette of the target beyond.

This time, Vanessa fired evenly and solidly, unloading the remaining rounds into the target's paper heart. When she pulled it from the line, all six holes overlapped almost perfectly.

Ten

For the third time in five minutes, Vanessa checked her watch: 0903. Another ninety minutes until the briefing with DDO Hawkins, and still no update from the Poles on Yassi and her daughter Zari. There should be something by now, she thought, staring uneasily at the desktop screen at Headquarters.

She scrolled quickly back through the latest cables from Operation Ghost Hunt's bigot list, skimming through content just to make sure she hadn't missed something. As she worked, another part of her remembered the frigid weekend in Berlin, the meetings with Yassi and Arash, when they'd gone over how it would all work, this business of spying.

"If something happens," Vanessa told them, avoiding the most horrifying words — *arrested, tortured, killed* — "then you will need to get to the Polish embassy."

For a moment, Vanessa avoided their eyes. "You will give them a code phrase — tell them 'We are friends of Ms. Dalton's, and we were told we could reach her here.' " Even now she remembered how her mouth had gone dry as she pushed the words out. She hated making promises when she could not control the outcome.

Now, to take her mind off Yassi and her daughter, Vanessa caught up with the intel feed from other agencies. She even checked open-source FBIS, Foreign Broadcast Intelligence Service cables — a kidnapping in Yemen, a bomb threat at the Frankfurt Airport, an Afghani soldier opening fire on his American allies.

As she read she drummed the desktop with the fingers of one hand. *Making noise.* Because CPD — a football field of gray carpet and cubicles located in the basement of the new Headquarters building — felt too quiet. Even for the early hour. A few keyboards clacking and coffeemakers bubbling, the soft drone of CNN and other news feeds, the constant stream of data from international intelligence links. Way too quiet . . .

Especially when you knew that in an hour the bullpen would be bustling with two hundred or so operations officers, reports officers, analysts, targeteers, military personnel, and assorted ABC-warfare experts, all of them tracking the illegal trade of biological, chemical, and nuclear weapons around the globe.

Vanessa craved that energy now, to match her own restless drive.

She flicked back her damp hair, and water droplets rained on the collection of darkly humorous cartoons and slogans tacked to the cubicle's walls. After forty minutes at the range, she'd quickly showered and dressed, grateful for the clean slacks and sweater from her locker. She'd searched out her "usual" temporary tour-of-duty cubicle, or TDY, found it unoccupied, sat, and kicked off her shoes.

Now she popped open a can of Red Bull and gulped the bitter-tasting liquid as she pulled up a file of grainy, flickering CCTV footage. Vienna Station (as conduit for anything from Austrian police, Interpol, or Europol) had come through on her blanket request for security video relevant to the assassination of XYTree/213. Footage routed to CPD analysts via secure link, copied to Vanessa. Pulled from closed-circuit security cameras in Prater, perimeter streets and intersections, and surrounding train, subway, and tram stations.

For now she skipped the footage from Vienna airport terminals — she'd lay odds the killer had crossed the border by car.

She chose two of the files from the Prater.

She took another sip of the Red Bull. Even viewed via split screen, on simultaneous loops, it would take two lifetimes to get through all the footage.

With a ping, a new cable landed in her in-box. Skimming, Vanessa wiped a drop of Red Bull off her chin. The pale officer from Vienna sending the security footage she'd requested from the Ringstrasse Hilton, the Iran delegation's hotel of choice.

Arash's killer was a professional. He hired a punk to create distraction and confusion, and perhaps to draw them into the open. He took the kill shot in a public place and then he walked away. How had he known where Arash would be? Best chance, he followed him on foot from the hotel to Prater.

But if I were you, Vanessa thought, closing her eyes to bring his image to consciousness, *my first choice would be the Hilton. I would case the delegation hotel very carefully. And I would do it before they arrived . . .*

She pulled up the flash file to begin its loop. Minutes evaporated.

"Hello," she murmured suddenly, staring intently at the screen.

ELEVEN

She tracked Zoe Liang across the bullpen to the conference room that also served as Operation Ghost Hunt's war room. Barely slowing, she entered to find the willowy, Asian CPD procurement analyst alone in the glow of screens and the constant hum of computers.

Slapping a photograph from CCTV footage on the table where Zoe was monitoring a stream of computer data, she said, "You were working with a tech guy —"

"I heard you were back," Zoe said without looking up.

"— and you were tinkering with facial-recognition markers —"

"I'm busy."

"Good to see you, too," Vanessa said. "I need to follow up before the lead goes cold."

"Fuck." Zoe spun around in the chair, nailing Vanessa with her deep-set black-brown eyes. "What's your problem this time? In a hurry to drive another asset underground or get him killed? Lately, your track record sucks."

Vanessa stared at Zoe, reminding herself this was the only analyst who hadn't given up on Jost Penders. Zoe still occasionally tracked his accounts in Prague for any sign of activity seven months after his disappearance.

"Maybe that's fair," Vanessa said slowly.

"It's fair." Zoe turned back to the computer screen, ignoring the photo Vanessa had pulled from CCTV. "Chris transferring you from Prague to Nicosia wasn't exactly a promotion."

Vanessa heard the triumph in Zoe Liang's surprisingly deep voice — the relationship between the two women had been prickly from day one at CPD. They were almost the same age, but they came from different worlds. Vanessa knew Zoe had been born in China, abandoned to an orphanage, and adopted by American parents when she was five years old. Raised in New Jersey, she'd graduated top of her class at Harvard, was a whiz at math and languages, and spoke fluent Mandarin, Cantonese, Spanish, Italian, and English — with or without a wicked Jersey accent. Zoe had made no secret of the fact she resented Vanessa's successes and her closeness with Chris. But now Vanessa had fallen from grace and, at last night's debrief, Chris had made clear she would work only with low-level assets.

She pushed the photo a few inches closer to Zoe. "Anything else you want to say while we're clearing the air?"

"Yeah. You're reckless and you take stupid risks."

"Think what you want of me. I don't need you to like me —"

"There's no danger of that," Zoe interjected sharply.

Vanessa shook her head, and then she laughed, surprising Zoe and herself. "Fine. You're sure as hell honest. And you're the smartest analyst in CPD. And I need your help to track down the man who killed my asset." Once again she found herself wondering if Bhoot had ordered the hit.

She turned toward the collection of photographs and maps tacked to the largest wall of the ops room. CPD's team had been working to identify Bhoot by tracking anyone remotely connected to his network. Vanessa had supplied a good number of the links — but the closest she'd come to a picture of Bhoot was a 1999 photograph of a mystery man meeting with Asad Z. Chaudhry, the Pakistani physicist. Before his "retirement" in 2001, Chaudhry had been tracked by the CIA and other intelligence agencies because of his successful efforts to provide weapons-grade nuclear expertise and equipment to rogue regimes such as Iraq, North Korea, Libya, Syria, and Iran. In the photo, taken in the Netherlands, Chaudhry was facing the camera while a younger man (probably early to mid-thirties, making him mid- to late forties today) with dark hair and an olive complexion avoided it. Only the left side of the younger man's cheek and head were visible, revealing his left earlobe decorated with a diamond stud.

The photograph had come to Vanessa through her asset Jost Penders, who had claimed the man meeting with Chaudhry was Bhoot.

When Vanessa turned back to Zoe, the analyst was watching her.

"Are you sure you're not trying to rewrite the truth about Prague while you're at it?" Zoe asked.

Vanessa crossed her arms in front of her chest, tipping her head in challenge. "What truth is that?"

"The truth being that you were never in control of your asset and he took advantage of you?"

"You really don't want to go there," Vanessa said, her tone deepening in warning.

Zoe shrugged grudgingly, but she picked up the photo. "From your Vienna footage? You think this is your hit man?"

"It came from the Hilton's security cams, inside an elevator," Vanessa said. The frame revealed a conservatively dressed man, slender, medium height, shoulders of his jacket padded, face hidden by the brim of his hat. He was reaching out to press an elevator button, and his gloved hands stood out, seeming too large for his body. "He knew he was on camera."

"Shitty contrast, but the fedora's classy," Zoe said, handing the photo back. "And one of how many zillion fedoras in Vienna?"

"Forget the hat," Vanessa said, pushing the photo almost under Zoe's nose. "Check out his left wrist, the exposed skin between his jacket cuff and his glove. See those marks?"

Zoe stared closely at what Vanessa had noticed when she slowed the footage down frame by frame. The analyst made a low, catlike noise in her throat. "Maybe . . ."

"It's something," Vanessa said, tapping her index finger against the photo. "The edge of a faded tattoo or one that's partly removed or a scar." She waited, eyes on Zoe, even as she marked the second hand jerking forward on the large wall clock. She contracted her toes, pressing carpet — realizing then that she'd crossed the bullpen barefoot.

"I can have it run through the NGI databases covering Europol and Interpol," Zoe said finally. "Your take is Eastern European?"

"Best guess. I have days and days of digital footage to go through . . ."

Zoe shrugged. "I'll see what I can do."

Vanessa nodded, but her attention returned to the dates, event markers, mug shots, and surveillance photos, most of which she had carefully organized into a timeline on the wall. Chris called it her "mosaic magnus." The steps had been agonizingly slow, but the CPD team was beginning to identify Bhoot's closest allies, a network of black-market suppliers, scientists, technicians, and terrorists from around the globe. If they could do that, they reasoned, they should finally be able to connect the dots to the ghost himself.

So just how close was this hit man to Bhoot?

TWELVE

On her way back to her cubicle, Vanessa found Chris at his desk.

Before she could open her mouth, he waved his hand and said, "We heard from the Poles. They've been contacted — *let me finish* — by someone who *knows* XYTree/ 214."

Vanessa nodded, instantly relieved that they had news, but also deflated. "Why hasn't she made contact herself? It's been thirty-six hours."

"Traveling with her child makes everything much more difficult; you know she's been hiding for both of their safety. The Revolutionary Guards are everywhere; she has to move slowly."

Vanessa frowned. "Do the Poles have any sense —"

Chris glanced at the set of world clocks displayed on his wall. "It's afternoon in Tehran — my guess is there's a conversation going on about how to move her at night."

Vanessa held her silence this time. There was nothing to say.

For a moment, she honed in on Chris. "You get any sleep at all?"

"At this point, it's best to stay awake."

"How's your son? I had a present for Dimitri, but I had to leave it when I couldn't go back to the hotel."

"Well, if you had aborted the mission as ordered —"

"You've already taken me off high-level asset assignments. Is there going to be more blowback around this?"

"Other than a million hits on YouTube?" He frowned. "Don't screw up again."

She bit the corner of her lip. "Anything new that hasn't come in already?"

"Not that I'm aware of, but maybe the DDO . . ." His voice trailed off.

She saw it then — the extra crease between his wide-set brown eyes, the taut lines around his mouth. He wasn't just exhausted and preoccupied, he was disappointed and pissed off. She didn't think this anger had to do with her.

"What's going on?"

For a moment it seemed he would engage with her the way he used to not so long ago

— over the occasional after-work cocktail at a non-spook bar on the U Street corridor. Midway through his second martini, the alcohol loosened his normal professional reserve and freed his Greek volatility to shine through, so that he ended up advising Vanessa on life and work issues, mentoring her through some rocky bureaucratic terrain.

But now he shook his head, waving her off. "It's getting late. We need to head upstairs for the briefing."

"Coming?" she asked, when he made no move to leave his office — and she realized how much she missed their usual connection.

"Just finishing up here. I'll meet you on the seventh."

"Sure." Vanessa stopped briefly at her cubicle to put on her shoes and grab her notes — but just as she was dodging out, she turned back to the monitor, caught for a moment in the hypnotic gray world of CCTV surveillance and rapidly moving images.

THIRTEEN

Yassi Farah stumbled from the white glare of the subway into Tehran's hazy neon shadows. Zari pressed close, her small, hot fingers clutching her mother's hand.

Yassi steadied herself even as people pushed past. The small bundle of vital possessions still hung knotted from her waist. She fixed the dark flowered scarf again over her daughter's braided hair, so it covered most of her small forehead. Tonight of all nights, they could not afford to stand out.

Almost two days ago — after receiving word from a neighbor who'd seen the news of Arash's death on his illegal satellite — they slipped away from their home near Old Shemiran Road to hide in their landlady's house. Waiting for the man who sat all day in the black car to leave.

When he finally drove off, Yassi urged her daughter from the house into the danger of the open streets. She prayed they would survive this journey across Tehran to the gates of the Polish embassy.

But eyes were everywhere.

Yassi pulled Zari forward now into the flow of pedestrians. At the corner she turned, leading them down a side street, slowing at a bakery window where soft sheet loaves of *sangak* and *barbari* bread and buttery turnovers filled the display.

"Mama." Zari tugged on her mother's hand. "I'm hungry."

Arash loved to bring home delicacies from the bakery, and he would fill a cloth satchel until it was a feat not to spill a loaf or a turnover.

Shuddering, Yassi almost yanked Zari past the window. She could not allow memory or grief to deaden her when she needed every sense to be alert.

For a moment she had to tell herself to breathe. In the crowds and darkness, could she possibly know if they were being followed?

Their American spy had talked them through the protocol, she trained them both, but that was three years ago, and Yassi knew she was rusty now, perhaps dangerously so . . .

Is that what happened to Arash? Had he been rusty and inadvertently careless?

Could the American have done anything to save him?

"Mami!"

Yassi half-lunged back into the flow of pedestrians, stumbling to avoid trampling Zari.

She'd almost collided with a very old man on crutches.

That's what she got for not keeping a pinpoint focus.

She touched her daughter's shoulder in apology.

A shrill, angry voice rose above the others: *Can you move?*

Yassi turned, this time actually colliding with something — a bulging sack. Cans and bottles clattered to the ground. A face emerged from beneath the sack, and round, dark eyes stared up at her — a filthy, ragged boy her daughter's age. The boy muttered, scolding as other pedestrians stepped around them.

Yassi stood frozen. She should be paying attention every instant! If she couldn't avoid knocking over a child, what else had she missed?

Move, old woman!

Yassi took a breath. The sack knocked against her knees, and she stared down as the boy hefted his impossible load.

Yassi felt Zari's hand tugging on her chador.

This boy was probably at least a year or two older than Zari but malnourished, a child of one of the city's southern neighborhoods who had migrated north to forge a living. Where the boy came from, Yassi would indeed qualify as an old woman. She had just turned thirty-five.

Voices of passersby merged into white noise.

If they were going to stay alive, she had to get them the last of the way to the Polish embassy.

FOURTEEN

A soft hiss as the elevator doors slid open to the seventh floor. Vanessa nodded at the fit, middle-aged woman waiting for her in the hall. Hildy B., the DDO's secretary, renowned for her brightly patterned dresses as well as her crack organizational skills.

"They're waiting for you," Hildy said crisply.

Prompting Vanessa to check her watch: 0903.

The CCTV footage . . .

Damn. She made a rule of arriving at least five minutes early to any meeting — but on this of all days, she had managed to run three minutes late.

The DDO was leaning casually against his executive desk, a flag from 9/11 framed on the wall behind him. "Glad you could join us."

A heavyset man, silver-haired, in a tailored slate suit filled one of two matching dark leather armchairs. Vanessa recognized Allen Jeffreys, Deputy National Security Adviser, an extremely conservative member of the former vice president's inner circle. At the moment, he was busy speaking quietly into one of the DDO's three office phones. It wasn't unheard of for him to be sitting in on an Agency debrief concerning Iran's nuclear facilities, but it was unusual.

Chris and the others were seated around the conference table, laptops humming, folders open. Chris said nothing, motioning for Vanessa to join them.

Vanessa dropped her file and notebook on the table in front of the only empty chair. Greeting her colleagues, she took stock: Zoe to Chris's immediate left; continuing clockwise, the ever-rumpled Sid, a fiftysomething almost-annuity guy; and then a thin, ferrety-looking man, one of a sprinkling of CPD specialists on WMDs: biological, chemical, nuclear, pick your poison. Harris. The Agency operated on a first-name basis, claiming a sense of egalitarianism (Vanessa found it bogus) as well as security issues (valid on the security point).

A striking, dark-eyed woman sat to Chris's right. Vanessa recognized her as an analyst/targeteer in WINPAC, in the DI, the Directorate of Intelligence.

"You two know each other?" Chris asked, gazing over his silver-framed glasses. "Vanessa, Layla — we've enticed Layla to make a move to CPD."

Vanessa remembered; Iranian American, smart, a hotshot, and on a steep upward professional trajectory the opposite of Vanessa's current free fall. CPD had no doubt poached her from the DI.

"Welcome, Layla," Vanessa said, as she opened her notebook.

"Thanks, Vanessa," Layla said, neatly. "Following up on your summary cable, and the intel from XYTree/213, I was just beginning to update everyone on Baluchestan Province." She clicked a laptop key, and Vanessa realized the Iran analyst had already begun a PowerPoint presentation. A series of satellite images filled a large, wall-mounted flat-screen monitor, one of three. As far as Vanessa could decipher, the images depicted open, desolate land crisscrossed by barely visible trails.

Allen Jeffreys cupped his palm over the phone long enough to say, "I remember talk a few months ago about a 'road to nowhere' near the border close to Afghanistan and Pakistan. Could that be the secret site we're trying to pinpoint?"

Another click and the images shifted —

doubling, then quadrupling.

"We are always tracking anything that might indicate traffic in unusual, remote locations," Layla said, her voice clear and distinct. "But, unfortunately, there are many, many possibilities in Baluchestan — as you can see."

Using the track pad, Layla changed the scene yet again, this time pulling back from the images, a vertigo sensation, as the world opened up to reveal the breathtaking scale of Iran's no-man's-land.

There was an audible intake of breath in the room. Even though they were all familiar with Iran's geography, the visual was undeniably effective.

It was Harris who asked the question on everyone's mind: "How the hell will we find it?"

"We won't," Vanessa answered. "Not without the geomarkers."

The door to the DDO's office opened, and Hildy B. stuck her head inside. "We've got a link with the UK."

And just then a second flat-screen flickered. A larger-than-life-sized image of a woman filled the screen, her mouth moving, and, after a few moments, her voice became audible. "Hello, Phillip."

The DDO smiled. "Alexandra, glad you

could join us."

Alexandra Hall, officially known as C, Director of Britain's MI5. A woman with a reputation as brilliant, ruthless, politically powerful, and lethal to terrorists. Vanessa and Hall had crossed paths briefly about a year earlier when Vanessa helped bring down two specialists in Bhoot's black-market procurement network.

This had turned into a morning filled with surprises.

Vanessa was struck again by the fact that public images failed to capture Hall's intensity. She studied her now, seeing a woman in her early fifties, still strikingly attractive, even dressed as she was, in a plain gray jacket, no jewelry, and without any visible makeup. But what struck Vanessa most acutely was Hall's piercingly intelligent gaze.

Allen Jeffreys spoke up now, his tone quite cool. "Madame Director."

"Mr. Jeffreys."

"Congratulations on your latest legislative victory. I would love to move a similar bill through our own congress, widening our powers to examine financial data —"

"We're not there yet," Hall replied tersely. "Just one step closer."

Addressing Hall, the DDO said, "Shall I introduce you around —"

"Not necessary." Without masking her impatience, Hall shook her head. "We've been getting your PowerPoint, and I know Chris. Go on, and I'll jump in with questions if I have them."

"I have a question," Jeffreys interjected sharply. "We're here to discuss a previously unknown, underground nuclear weapons facility located in southeastern Iran. If your intel is valid, if the Iranians are back in business on the UD3 project to develop a nuclear trigger, there is no question this indicates Iran has nuclear weapons capabilities." His lips compressed as he stared at the DDO. "This *is* what you have and what you believe, right?"

DDO Hawkins hesitated, and when he did begin to speak, he barely avoided stumbling over his words. "If the intel is valid — and that's a big if. But then, yes, Iran may be in possession of a nuclear weapon."

Jeffreys nodded. "What is the probability of success in militarily wiping out multiple facilities in Iran?"

Obviously taken aback, the DDO hesitated again, and almost immediately Hall spoke up on-screen. "Before we waste too much energy debating options, military or otherwise, let's see if this facility actually exists and is not the imaginative manipulations of an asset eager to please."

Vanessa recoiled internally — they could assume nothing until they had corroboration, and she had no desire to feed into Jeffreys's neocon redline arguments, but Arash had given his life to get intel out of Iran.

"He was my asset," she said sharply, "and he always delivered quality intel. And if his latest intel is accurate, we have a chance, a target date in two weeks, to capture Bhoot. But only if this operation becomes our team priority, twenty-four-seven, from now until September thirtieth."

Hall's eyebrows arched. "Thank you for the urgent reminder, Ms. —"

"Vanessa."

"That's right — Vanessa." Hall nodded. "Blond becomes you more than brunette. Phillip, if your case officer is correct and this intel is actionable, we are working within very tight time constraints. Two weeks to set up a *cooperative* operation to capture Bhoot." Hall's eyebrows rose beyond their natural arch. "What are the odds of getting these missing geo-coordinates in any reasonable time frame?"

Chris turned to Zoe. "What's your take?"

But before Zoe could respond, Vanessa interjected: "That makes it all the more vital to get Tree/214 out of Iran alive. Because then we will have the coordinates in a matter of hours."

"You can't be certain —" Zoe protested.

A shrill ring filled the room.

More than one person started.

The DDO answered his green secure phone. For less than thirty seconds he listened, then with a nod and a terse, "Thank you," hung up.

He addressed the group. "The Poles got word, Tree/214 is on the move. She's requesting safe passage from Iran, and when she's out, she will *only* talk to 'Ms. Dalton.'"

For a second there was dead silence. Then slowly, all eyes turned toward Vanessa.

Chris said, "How fast can you get on our plane to Incirlik, Turkey?"

Already pushing out of her chair, Vanessa grabbed her folder and moved toward the door.

FIFTEEN

Zari moaned sharply as the ancient Mercedes shuddered over something hard on the road. She clutched at her mother with the fierceness of a baby bird clutching to its nest.

"Eshgeh man," Yassi murmured, desperately trying to sooth her child as they lay pressed together inside the stifling blackness of the trunk. How long until they were free of Tehran? Could she keep Zari from panicking again before they were safe to leave this filthy, cramped prison?

She'd carried her daughter the last few meters across the street to the elaborate gates of the Polish embassy. What if the soldiers had refused to let them in? She barely managed to recite the code the American had given them so long ago.

A new cloud of fumes filled the trunk, and Yassi retched, barely holding back the sickness. She braced for the next wave of nausea, pushing her mind's eye to the turquoise-and-silver beaches of Kish Island last February, the foamy lick of sea around their sun-browned ankles . . .

She bit down hard on her lip — she couldn't allow these thoughts of her husband, *not now.* Her fingers found her belly and the bundle tied at her waist — for this, Arash had risked everything.

The Mercedes braked abruptly, and Yassi and Zari rolled hard against bare metal.

"Mama!" Zari hissed, fear making her small voice shrill.

"Hush." Yassi pressed her forefinger lightly to her daughter's lip, felt the quivering of fear and fatigue.

Voices so close!

Zari squirmed as her mother kept her grip.

One voice belonging to their driver —

Yassi barely breathed through fear. *Keep still, little one,* she silently prayed.

The other voice snapping out a sharp command — *a Sepah, a Guard?*

Yassi felt her body lighten to nothing, as if every bit of substance drained away.

A harsh barking noise —

Zari jerked in Yassi's arms.

Laughter! Their driver and the other man bantering! And now the driver saying something about getting into trouble . . . the wife waiting . . . and his father-in-law's car!

Yassi held her breath as if to still the tremors running through her child.

Finally, the car inched forward, settling into the blind see-saw motion. But now the trunk felt safe, and the blood began to flow through Yassi again. She even felt her daughter's little body ease a bit in her arms.

Only two things mattered — get Arash's message out of Iran and stay alive.

For the briefest instant, Yassi allowed herself to picture her husband's face.

Somehow we will make it without you — I will not let them take anything else from us.

Sixteen

Aboard the C-17 the hard plastic netting pinched Vanessa's spine, and, even with earplugs, the roar of the engines made her head ache. A familiar experience reaching back to the best of her childhood as an Air Force brat: trips to Europe, Greece, the Middle East; the journey to the new and unknown. But today she shifted restlessly in the nylon jump seat. Real seats were hard to come by, and she'd given hers to a harried mother who was traveling with three young children and an infant.

Not even two hours ago she'd watched the asphalt landing strip at Andrews Air Force Base disappear as the hulking Globemaster III military transport lurched airborne. She'd been told to hitch a ride, as the CIA Gulfstream was otherwise occupied. The flight to Turkey, a straight shot, would take approximately eleven hours. Once she hit the ground, she needed to be alert and ready to face Arash Farah's widow.

She'd taken Ambien, and still her eyes stayed wide open and her mind refused to shut down. How soon would Yassi and her daughter reach the border?

She had a good idea what they would endure — hours hidden in the trunk of a car until they were well outside Tehran; at least then they could ride *inside* the car, crossing the border if their fake papers held up to scrutiny, and then another day of driving rough roads through remote and barren sections of Turkey.

Vanessa blinked in the half-light of dawn. The few windows on the C-17 were portholes, but she could feel the plane begin its descent. She closed her eyes, letting her mind fill in the landscape — a patchwork of green and brown, myriad villages and towns scattered to the rolling arid hills, and the steep mountains in the distance.

A year ago she'd visited Turkey secretly with Khoury; the trip through small villages around Cappadocia had been a journey five hundred years back through time. The underground cities and "fairy" chimneys were magical, and so remote, there was almost no chance the forbidden lovers would encounter someone they knew. They picnicked and wandered through the village markets bargaining for trinkets, Vanessa thumbing through her dog-eared Turkish phrase book while Khoury, amused, refused to bail her out.

For those days, their lives together had been more than just a collection of stolen moments.

The C-17 touched down. Vanessa, a connoisseur of landings, judged it rough, fast, and well done. Navy pilots — used to the limited landing space on carriers — always put down hard.

A man stood waiting at the bottom of the stairs. As Vanessa stepped from shadow, blinking and slightly dazed, into full morning sun, she caught her first glance of his familiar, pushed-together features. Chuck Hamm, Chief of Station Ankara.

The COS nodded once. "See you're still packing light."

Six years ago at the Farm, Hamm, a smart, sober ops officer with a soft drawl and fifteen years' field experience, taught Vanessa to jump out of airplanes in the paramilitary course. He seemed to tolerate her, always pushing her to take it to the next level — even when they butted heads over her tendency to push the envelope and fly solo. Hamm was that rare breed of ops instructor who made Vanessa want to prove herself, and he quickly earned her respect; no surprise he'd risen to COS of such a serious posting.

"What's the latest?" she asked, following him to a black, four-wheel-drive Suburban.

"They crossed the border about two hours ago."

"Thank God." She tossed her small duffel in back and then claimed the passenger seat.

"It will take them another ten, maybe twelve, hours if they're lucky," the COS said brusquely.

Vanessa knew Hamm was fully briefed on Vienna and the exfil operation; the assassination of an asset and the extraction of his family from behind hostile borders didn't happen every day.

"What you need to remember," Hamm said, breaking into her thoughts, "we're a team at my station, and I keep a close eye on my people." He turned the key, and the Surburban's engine thrummed to life. "I'm in charge but can't protect you if I get any surprises."

He drove across base quickly, over dirt roads, past dusty shops, and finally past dormitories, where naked lightbulbs glowed faintly in daylight and Turkish palms offered slivers of shade.

He braked in front of 21B, a cinder-block prefab — one of about thirty — painted a color that was almost Pepto pink. Vanessa winced; nothing she'd lived in on any Air Force base growing up had been this disheartening.

Inside, the few bits of furniture were worn and the walls dirty white except where a brave occupant had painted the kitchen blue.

The COS crossed his arms. "Make yourself at home."

She took a quick inventory and found the cupboards mostly bare. "I'll need to get some basics," she said. "Food. Chocolate. Juice. Coffee. Tea and a teapot. Oh, and a good bottle of Bourbon."

"Sure," Hamm said, his slow drawl heavy now. "Why don't we throw in a Jacuzzi while we're at it?"

SEVENTEEN

Close to midnight, Vanessa turned the last corner, winding down her five-mile run. She pulled up short. A battered, dusty Mercedes sat parked in front of 21B; a disheveled, dark-haired man leaned against it, smoking a cigarette. Yassi had arrived sometime in the last forty minutes, during the one window Vanessa had taken to run off some of the nervous tension after a day of hurry-up-and-wait.

She crossed the last twenty meters to the house at a dead sprint and entered breathing hard, and doing her best to wipe the sweat from her face with the sleeve of her *IAB-Turkey* T-shirt.

The COS was waiting by the front door. "They just got here." He tipped his head, indicating the disheveled woman standing just inside the living room. Even at close range, Vanessa didn't immediately recognize Yassi Farah.

Then she did — an older, weary Yassi.

Vanessa shot the COS a pointed look. After hesitating, Hamm nodded. "If you need me, I'll be outside," he said, leaving the women alone with each other.

"I'm so glad you made it safely," Vanessa said, assessing even as she moved to greet Yassi. But she stopped when a wide-eyed child peeked out from behind Yassi's back. Vanessa knelt down. "You must be Zari."

The child didn't smile or respond, and she disappeared again, a tiny rabbit ducking to safety.

"She won't let go of me," Yassi said wearily.

And now the two women touched cheeks, but it was a greeting without warmth, without real emotion.

Vanessa found herself hoping to see a glimmer of outrage and defiance, the spark she'd seen often in Yassi's eyes. "You must be hungry, and I have —"

"I need a cup of very black tea with lots of honey," Yassi said.

"We have coffee, if you'd prefer it."

"Tea is better." Yassi pressed a hand to her belly.

"I just have to heat the water." Vanessa switched on the gas flame beneath the already filled kettle and then she gestured to the chairs around the kitchen table.

Yassi nodded but almost immediately shook her head. "The bathroom —" Her eyes widened, and she clapped her hand abruptly to her mouth.

Vanessa pointed, urging her toward the small hallway. "First door on the left." She barely finished the sentence as Yassi hurried inside, closing the door behind her.

Putting her concern on hold, Vanessa caught Zari gently, guiding the startled child toward the counter and a small blue case. "I have something just for you," she said, smiling encouragingly, handing her the case. "Shall I help you open it?"

Zari held the case tentatively, but her eyes had gone as round as black moons. *"Maman?"*

It was impossible to ignore the sounds from the bathroom; clearly, Yassi was very ill. Vanessa knelt toward the child. "She'll be fine, Zari, I promise." She hoped she was right.

She went to work, opening a package of tea biscuits and a bar of chocolate. "Do you like chocolate?" She knew Arash and Yassi had taught their daughter English — she was probably fluent — and Zari seemed to understand everything she said. And now, thankfully, the house was quiet again except for the faint sound of the tap running in the bathroom.

Zari nodded, but she turned her careful attention to opening the case. She took her time, examining the contents — a small, plush white tiger with glass-green eyes, a tiny silk mouse, a locket, and a small bag of jacks. All simple treasures discovered at Incirlik's Local Closet, a secondhand shop for nomadic military families.

"*Mamnoon,*" Zari said, ducking her head shyly as she clutched the mouse and the tiger. "Thank you very much."

"*Khahesh Mikonam.*" Vanessa stumbled over the Farsi phrase, and she rolled her eyes, mocking herself for Zari's benefit.

Zari smiled. Vanessa smiled, too. She held out an offering of chocolate.

"*Maman?*"

"*Man khoobam,* Mama's fine, my love, much better." Yassi crossed the kitchen, her face and hair damp where she'd splashed herself with water.

And, watching her, Vanessa noticed she moved with more of the fluidity and confidence she'd seen at their very first meeting, when Arash introduced them at the hotel in Berlin.

Yassi looked up, meeting Vanessa's eyes. Then she kissed the top of her daughter's head. "Chocolate?"

"Is that all right?" Vanessa asked slowly. "I should have asked you first . . ."

Her voice trailed off as she put the signs together — the light in Yassi's eyes, the intensity of her sickness. Yassi was pregnant.

For a moment she couldn't think of anything to say, and she was grateful for the shriek of the kettle covering the silence. She pulled it from the burner, filling the teapot to steep.

As Yassi took a seat at the table, her demeanor shifted. However exhausted she and her daughter were, however drained, Yassi was here to deliver Arash's message — and to negotiate for a new life.

"Zari will stay with me while we talk," Yassi said flatly. She patted the chair next to hers, and her daughter sat easily. Vanessa set down two mugs for the still-steeping tea, honey, and a mug with milk for Zari. Then she took her seat at the table with what was left of Arash's family.

As Vanessa poured steaming tea into their cups, adding honey to one, Yassi turned to her daughter. She hugged her, speaking to her softly, quickly in Farsi. She pressed the mouse into her daughter's arms, and Zari wrapped her arms around it.

Yassi met Vanessa's eyes. "I told her she is

going to hear some hard truths about her father's death. We can begin."

Vanessa tried a small sip of tea, but it scalded her tongue. She nudged the cup with her finger and pulled herself up in the chair. "Arash told me about the secret facility. He said he had geo-markers, but he didn't get the chance to tell me what they were."

Yassi nodded. "When he came back from his first visit, he was deeply frightened by what he saw. They had many more capabilities than he'd known about."

"Did he give you specifics, Yassi? It's vital that you tell me everything you remember."

Yassi lifted the mug but held it with pale fingers halfway to her lips. "He said they had figured out the trigger system for detonation — they were weaponizing."

"He told me that, too. Do you know who helped them?"

"There were many."

"We know your country has worked with Pakistani scientists and with the Russians. There have been meetings with North Korea and the Chinese."

Yassi set the mug down hard, spilling tea. "Then you know more than I do about those things." Her delicate features tightened in anger, and she glared at Vanessa.

"You can never understand what it is like living the way we lived. We were never sure if the Sepah were listening to us, we had to assume they were, but, when he could, Arash told me enough."

Her voice dropped to a harsh whisper. "He was frightened because he believed there was a new kind of alliance between the most powerful men in Iran, the Guardians, and a man who belongs to *no* country, who has expertise to sell, who can provide whatever you need to create whatever weapons you want —" Yassi broke off.

Vanessa's whole body went still. "This man with no country, do you know his name?"

"No. But Arash said he is not Iranian."

"Was he coming to visit the facility?"

"Maybe — Arash believed so, but I don't know."

"Yassi, think hard —"

"Arash did not tell me any more than that!"

Vanessa sank back in the chair, deflated.

"I'm sorry," Yassi said, working to regain control as she sipped her tea.

"What about the geo-markers?" Vanessa said slowly, almost holding her breath. "Do you know what they are?"

Yassi shook her head.

Vanessa's skin went cold. Arash had died and she'd come all this way to end up with nothing? They could not lose this one chance to capture Bhoot. She was so caught up in her churning thoughts, she barely heard Yassi.

"What did you say?" Vanessa whispered.

"I might have them."

She stared at Yassi. "You might have the markers?"

Yassi reached to her waist, carefully unknotting a bundle of dark blue silk that had been hidden beneath her cotton jacket.

Vanessa's pulse quickened. Had Yassi managed to smuggle out the location?

As Yassi carefully unrolled the silk, small items spilled onto the low table: coins, a key, a man's wedding ring, and a pack of Iranian-brand cigarettes.

"He kept his most valuable possessions inside a special box in a hiding place only known to us at our house," Yassi said.

Vanessa began to reach out, but Yassi brushed her hand away. She picked up the cigarettes, holding the pack in the palm of her hand. "I found these. But my husband did not smoke."

Vanessa waited now.

"Inside," Yassi said, using two fingers to press the pack so the opening widened.

"Empty the cigarettes and you will see there is writing inside. When I asked him, he said if anything happened I should get this to you."

Vanessa held out her own hand again, but Yassi pulled the cigarettes away. "I need you to swear you will get my husband's murderer!"

Vanessa pulled back, almost shocked by Yassi's intensity. An image flashed through her mind: the killer leaving the Prater in Vienna. "We're following leads —"

"I don't care about leads. You are Ms. Dalton —" Yassi looked at her, mocking, clearly aware the name had always been a lie. "Arash did this work for you. He gave his life because he cared for you . . . and he wanted to stop the madness . . ." Yassi took a shuddering breath. "You used my husband. And I think he was a little in love with you."

"That's not true, Yassi, I certainly didn't mean to —"

"Maybe you did not mean to . . . but I think it happened for him anyway." Yassi raised her palm. "It is your job to use people, to know their weakness and their strength. That is just how it is . . . so now, in return, I ask you for justice. The man who pulled the trigger in Vienna and whoever sent him — make them pay for what they did."

Vanessa swallowed hard. "I promise. I will do everything within my power to bring them to justice."

"I know people, too," Yassi said finally. "I may not like you, Ms. Dalton, but I believe you will do what you say. You will honor your word." She slid the pack of cigarettes across the table. "Look here, the seam is open."

Now Vanessa worked gently, spilling out the remaining cigarettes before easing the pack wide. Middle Eastern characters curled and dipped exotic and indecipherable, where Arash had carefully penned columns — fifteen columns filled with tiny, flowing script — along the cheap paper lining. A thin sticky line marked where he had re-glued the pack.

What is this?" The writing was softer than the Script of Nails Vanessa had seen on tombs in Turkey. Confused, her frustration rising to anger, she looked to Yassi. "It's not Farsi. Is it some form of ancient Persian or Arabic?" She shook her head sharply. "We need geo-coordinates or geo-markers to locate the facility."

"When Arash was at university, studying to be a nuclear engineer," Yassi said, speaking with some difficulty now. "He also studied the ancient languages, because in his heart, he was a poet. I can only give you this because I think this is what you are looking for."

"But what *is* it?" Vanessa repeated. In the brief silence she shrugged, pushing beyond her plummeting mood, the frustration and disappointment. Yassi wouldn't — couldn't — give her anything more. She forced herself to speak quietly, practically. "I checked with people in Washington, and your bank account is set. You have funds, a lot of money. Anything else you need now that I might be able to help you with? You can contact me . . ."

As she spoke, Vanessa slipped her cell phone from her pocket. The COS would send the cigarette package back to Headquarters via courier, where it would go to decryption analysts. Once she turned it over to the COS, Vanessa wouldn't get her hands on it again. She set to work, photographing every detail of the columns of characters.

Now she turned her attention to the other items on the table — the coins, the wedding ring that she guessed had belonged to Arash.

Vanessa gestured to the items. "We need to take these . . ."

"I know," Yassi said.

"I'll make sure they are returned. I'm so sorry, Yassi."

"You were with him when he died?" Yassi said. "Did he suffer?"

"No." Vanessa was grateful she could speak the truth. "It happened very quickly."

They were both standing now, and Yassi's eyes filled with a grief that made Vanessa ache. But something else, a sliver of light.

"Arash knew about the baby?"

"Yes, he knew."

Vanessa nodded, and she reached out to squeeze Zari's tiny hand. It felt as delicate as a bird. "I promise, when I have news, I will get word to you . . ."

Five hours later, at Ankara Esenboğga Airport, Vanessa boarded a Lufthansa flight headed to Cyprus. With luck, Yassi and Zari would have a few days to rest before they boarded a military transport that would take them to Frankfurt. They might spend weeks in Germany before they moved on to the United States and a new life. It was only the beginning of a journey that would demand incredible strength and resilience, especially with a new baby. She hoped they would find a way to begin again.

EIGHTEEN

The moon illuminated the midnight ferry sliding out of Taşucu's harbor, sailing south across the Mediterranean to the island of Cyprus.

Pauk sat alert behind the wheel of the beige Fiat 500. He fingered the ferry receipt — an open return for a standard car and driver. He'd almost been delayed a day in Taşucu by reports of a Turkish strike, then of a Greek strike — typical local bickering — but finally the long lines of vehicles were allowed to board the massive ferry. He should arrive in Kyrenia on Northern Cyprus before dawn, an unremarkable journey undertaken by a seemingly unremarkable man.

With the windows cracked, he caught the bite of gasoline from the trucks and buses along with the smoky scent of meze from the vendors. A jet rumbled overhead. Music and voices speaking mostly in Turkish drifted from the rows of cars around him. A baby's cry pierced the early morning, followed by a man's deep voice raised in quiet song and a woman's laughter shivering abruptly through darkness.

These sounds of life meant nothing to Pauk.

Two children ducked between the cars in front of him. A boy and girl, hide-and-seek. The girl hesitated for a moment to stare in the direction of the Fiat. Out of habit, Pauk slowed his breathing as he retreated internally, a way of "disappearing" that seemed to translate externally so that others paid him no attention.

When the boy called out, his voice teasing, the girl pivoted, darting after him.

Abruptly, the urge to escape the car's containment filled Pauk with restlessness.

But he had trained himself long ago to deal with silence and immobility. So now he tucked the brim of his soft hat lower on his forehead, covering eyes that remained open but sightless. He stared into darkness and settled into the semiconscious state he knew as sleep. He could gauge the passage of time with surprising accuracy, and the occasionally rough waves of the Mediterranean seemed to find their own rhythm. He could let his mind embrace the blackness — he

NINETEEN

Vanessa let herself in through the wrought-iron gate to her landlady's garden in Nicosia, where the air held the bittersweet scent of lemons. The widow always clucked over her tenant, *koukla mou,* my sweet little doll. In turn, Vanessa willingly called her landlady *yia yia,* grandmother. A night bird fluttered from *yia yia*'s fig tree as Vanessa strode barefoot, her duffel over her shoulder, through the patch of lush grass.

She jogged the exterior staircase to her second-floor apartment. After the flight back from Ankara, she was impatient to see if Headquarters had passed the code to NSA decryption division. If Arash was right, they had eleven days until Bhoot would be in Iran visiting a facility that could already be producing nuclear weapons. She had to believe it was possible to respond to the immensity of the threat.

As Vanessa slid her key into the dead bolt,

something warm brushed her ankle: Vasilias, *yia yia*'s huge gray cat. He darted into her apartment, racing a beeline to the kitchen, and she followed. She hit the TV remote and it brought up the voice of *MasterChef* UK's Gregg Wallace discussing caramelized frog legs with a contestant; the show, one of Vanessa's favorites, caught on Sky TV Cyprus via the four-meter dish on *yia yia*'s rooftop.

Still moving, Vanessa tossed down her duffel. She spilled cat kibble into a saucer and poured herself a generous shot of her favorite bourbon, pausing a moment to watch a sweet-faced, curly-haired wannabe apron winner dicing onions. As he tossed them into a sizzling pan, she carried the tumbler into her office. She took a glancing assessment of her personal calendar and new e-mail tally on her laptop, and then she logged on to her secure program.

She pulled up files from CCTV cams located on streets that ran between Iran's delegation hotel and the Prater. Vanessa had taught Arash about surveillance detection routes. Plan the predetermined stops and factor time and distance ratios. *If you spot someone at point A, and then you spot that same someone again when you are at point H, chances are very good that you are being followed.*

Vanessa knew the streets in that part of Vienna. She also knew something about Arash and his habits. He'd loved sweets, especially the Viennese specialty, the chocolate and marzipan Mozartkugeln, or Mozart balls. Even late and hurrying to Prater from the Hilton, he would lean on habit and choose a familiar route, perhaps the one that took him past the confectionary Furst. If she was right, he'd passed one of these cameras on his way. If she was lucky, the camera had caught an image of his assassin in careful pursuit.

She forwarded through the digital images until she reached the time/date stamp ninety minutes before Arash's death. She clicked play.

Forty minutes later, she paused the files. 1730 hours in D.C., and still no word from Chris confirming the handoff to NSA decryption.

Nothing from Zoe or her guy in Tech.

Did you find a match or not? she pinged Zoe via secure IM.

Reaching for the tumbler of bourbon, she saw a reflection distorted in the window. For a moment she didn't recognize the raw, wired woman with the tangled blond hair. She took a long drink, letting her gaze move irresistibly back to the flickering CCTV images.

0030 hours, Cyprus.

TWENTY

Vanessa started at the familiar burble, the Skype bubble bouncing in the corner of her screen. Her mother's face appeared in the icon prompt. *Shit.* Vanessa arranged her smile.

Her mother (one of only three people outside the Agency who knew where she really worked, the others being her brother and her college friend Marie) would see the dark lines around her eyes and the faded bruise on her cheek, and she would know that something hard had happened. Vanessa couldn't go there.

Her mother would also carefully avoid any mention of Vanessa's brother, Marshall, and the latest casualties in Afghanistan. Instead, she would fill the silence with talk of Vanessa's father, Colonel Jack Pierson, and the cancer and his death ten years ago, until she closed the one-sided conversation with the latest Agent Orange litigation and the new research on generational birth defects.

Vanessa's father's exposure to the chemical defoliant Agent Orange was a legacy of his Air Force service in Vietnam in his early twenties. Career military and deeply patriotic, he went on to serve three decades at other dangerous posts until he was diagnosed with a rare and aggressive cancer. When research linked the cancer to Agent Orange, he refused to blame the government. What was past was past. As for the future, he died without acknowledging that his two children might pass birth defects to their offspring.

Vanessa's mother would remind her daughter, "You really should talk to a doctor about getting tested —"

Not tonight. A quick guilty breath, the fortifying taste of aged whiskey, and Vanessa clicked ignore.

She let the endless looping flow of gray CCTV images draw her back in until a new prompt box popped up on her secure screen. Zoe Liang responding to her request for secure face time.

Vanessa remembered to push the tumbler of bourbon out of sight just before she linked.

Zoe's scowling face filled the box while, behind her, activity in CPD's ops room played out visibly and audibly. The teams were monitoring signal and satellite imagery for any sign of unusual activity in southern Iran. Analysts were scouring through open-source intel, while translators tracked chatter for references to Bhoot and any activity in his worldwide network. Operation Ghost Hunt was moving forward — without Vanessa. But she wasn't going to let any vulnerability or resentment show. So she scowled back at the analyst. "Good to see you, too."

Now Zoe smirked. "Heard you had a great time in Turkey and discovered the newest Dead Sea Scroll."

Right, from a pregnant widow who risked her family's life escaping Iran. "Glad it went to NSA and not to you."

"You really believe we're going to find coordinates?" Zoe let the unspoken implication linger — *while the rest of us are doing the real work*?

"No, I just get a kick out of wasting everybody's time and resources," Vanessa said, not quite controlling her anger. She took a quick breath. "But your relevant question should be: *Will they break it fast enough so we can use it to capture Bhoot?*"

"Hold on." Abruptly, Zoe turned her back to the screen cam to deal with a muted question from a female CST, or career service trainee, someone Vanessa didn't recognize. She tried to control her frustration until, a good minute later, Zoe turned to face the screen cam again. "I've got to get back to the grown-ups, but I wanted to let you know Tech got a lead on your hit man."

Letting the insult pass, Vanessa pulled up in her chair. "A match?"

"Remember, you owe me."

"My firstborn, right. What do you have?"

A click of keys, and Vanessa's screen filled with two images: the first, an enhanced and enlarged partial of the very faded tattoo on the hit man's wrist from the original Hilton security footage; the second, a striking image of a black wolf, framed with a full moon, and ringed by a distinctively ornate border.

"If we overlay the images like this," Zoe said, accomplishing it on-screen as she spoke, "we get an eighty-five percent match on the border, where the nine dots or marks run symmetrically."

Vanessa's temple throbbed, and she felt the shiver of her blood quickening.

"The official seal of the Chechen Republic of Ichkeria," Zoe said. "And apparently, during the Chechen Wars, one particularly hard-core faction of Chechen rebels liked the tat displayed on the wrist."

"So the shooter's not Russian, he's Chechen."

Twenty-One

The sharp slap of the jump rope against tile drew her back to the manic rhythm of childhood and the grueling military drills their dad had put Marshall and Vanessa through. At ten, she'd worshipped him, and she'd been irresistibly drawn to the challenge. By thirteen, she hated him but pushed herself anyway, refusing to lose. Now she got it — her father had driven them the way he drove himself and his recruits. He'd done it believing that it would instill much-needed discipline, and, perhaps, save lives.

At this moment for Vanessa it was merely a way to sweat out insomnia at 0330 hours and still keep her focus on the CCTV images to be sure she didn't miss him — the Chechen.

Over the past three hours since the news from Zoe, she'd isolated an image of Arash and an image of the biker, but still nothing more on her target, the assassin. Her eyes ached from strain.

"A ghost just like his boss," Vanessa murmured, breathing hard. But she was beginning to put together a few pieces: from her first glimpse of him in Vienna to the footage from the hotel, she guessed he was late twenties to mid-thirties, so born in the late 1970s to mid-1980s. And that meant he'd been a kid in the middle of the brutal fighting of the First Chechen War and barely out of his teens by the beginning of the Second Chechen War in 1999, when Islamic separatists invaded Dagestan and Russian troops entered Chechnya in response.

A logical place of first contact with foreign Islamic resistance fighters who joined the Chechen separatists.

"And a hell of a training ground for a sniper." She'd surprised herself by speaking aloud, and a throaty assent came from Vasilias, who was hunkered down on the kitchen counter, studying her with improbable golden eyes. On the now-muted TV next to the cat, a very tall, very thin woman topped a lustrous chocolate cake with whipped cream.

So maybe that's where the Chechen first met Bhoot, Vanessa thought, doubling her speed as she counted out her last fifty jumps. Had Bhoot supplied Chechen rebels?

Or was it possible he'd actually fought with the resistance in Chechnya like the legendary Saudi Emir Khattab, Ibn al-Khattab? If so, that gave her new places to look, old files to scour, to cover the First Chechen War in 1995 through Dagestan and the beginning of the long and bloody Second Chechen War in 1999.

She swung the rope toward her ankles and almost tripped as the new prompt box appeared on her secure screen.

Chris Arvanitis.

She slid into the chair and clicked to connect.

Just as Chris appeared full screen, Vasilias bounded onto her lap and off again, and Vanessa blurted out, "Shit."

"Catch you in the middle of something?" Chris asked, eyeing her curiously.

Suddenly she felt too aware of the sweat running down her face, her damp blond hair clipped haphazardly into a ponytail, and her raggedy T-shirt that read, *If zombies chase us, I'm tripping you!*

She met his gaze squarely. "Skipping rope with my landlady's cat. And you?" It was 2030 hours on the East Coast, but Chris looked as if he'd been up for days, his striking Greek features muddied by exhaustion.

"Why aren't you at home with your family?"

"Who skips rope at three-thirty in the morning?" Chris asked, sliding past her question.

"Now you're checking my bedtime?"

"NSA is on your code. They've verified that it's classical Persian, and they suspect that it's from a classical Persian text, but —"

"I could have told them that much," she said and groaned. "Jesus, have they tried testing for invisible ink? Seriously, they've got to think outside the box on this, and they have to do it fast!"

"They're going to pull in somebody from linguistics, a specialist in archaic Indo-European languages." His brows pulled together over bloodshot brown eyes. "We're gambling on this having a full payoff, but we can't be positive —"

"The geo-markers are there, Chris. I know they are." Vanessa spoke with an intensity that surprised even her.

He studied her silently for a moment, and she couldn't read him as clearly as she wanted. But then he nodded, his expression still thoughtful. "I may be crazy, but I'm counting on your instincts, Vanessa."

"I am, I'm right." But she felt a pang of

apprehension — not for herself, for Chris. Was there more going on than the usual and relentless pressures at work? An Agency career was hard on a marriage and a family.

For a few moments, neither of them spoke and the silence lengthened.

Until, finally, he said, "You did your part of the job when you turned over the intel from the wife."

"You telling me to let go of Bhoot?" she asked softly. "You know I can't do that."

He took a breath, releasing it with a sigh. "You don't have a choice, Vanessa."

She shrugged. "Go home."

"Go to bed," he countered.

After they disconnected, Vanessa sat staring blindly at the monitor. She had the nagging sense that Arash's code just needed the right eyes. She'd take reasonable odds the decrypt folks would break it — eventually. But would they do it quickly enough to get the op up and running to capture Bhoot if he showed in Iran? Operation Ghost Hunt was almost out of time.

As if she'd been startled out of a trance, she paused the CCTV footage, found the almost-empty glass of bourbon, and stood.

0400 hours. She stretched, rubbing bleary eyes. But just as she was going to call it a night, she dropped into her chair again and pressed play on the CCTV footage.

She was six minutes in when she found her Chechen.

She almost missed him, camouflaged as he was behind the fedora, sunglasses, and overcoat. The satchel over his shoulder. *I would have missed you — if you hadn't turned your face just enough to glance quickly at something in the window of an antiques shop. What are you looking at?*

She caught the best frame and froze it, staring at the stark angles of his bones, the thin, flat line of his mouth. But mostly he presented as eerily ordinary. There was nothing to make him stand out. And that made him perfect for his chosen profession.

She sent the file Priority to Zoe at Headquarters — so the Chechen's photograph could be added to the standard watch lists for Interpol and Europol.

She stood abruptly, needing to move. A shadow flashed past, and she turned to see Vasilias spring out her open window. *Damn cat.* But Vanessa followed his instinct, ascending the short, narrow staircase from terrace to rooftop. Vasilias had vanished. Had he jumped the few meters from one rooftop to the next?

Vanessa perched near the edge of the roof and stared out at the now fading lights of

Nicosia spilling into the distance.

She pictured the Chechen. *Where are you? Who are you hunting now?*

TWENTY-TWO

Just as day began to break, Pauk guided the Fiat over the ferry ramp and onto Cypriot soil. He'd studied satellite maps of Cyprus, had memorized the most efficient routes from Kyrenia, south across the island to Limassol and a new development of luxury condominiums, where he would begin to track his latest target.

Stuck behind commercial trucks, he followed the double lanes of debarking traffic from the harbor, where a Roman castle still stood sentry, into an old section of town.

Traffic was thinning, and he saw signs for the A1, the highway he would travel most of the way to Limassol, where the expat Russians lived. Since the 1974 Turkish invasion of Cyprus to counter long-standing hostilities with Greece, the island had been divided into the Turkish Republic of Northern Cyprus and the Greek-controlled Republic of Cyprus. Near Nicosia, he would pass through one of the divided island's border checkpoints.

His long fingers brushed the top of his EU passport in his shirt pocket, an excellent forgery. He would pick up the necessary white visa form at Turkish Cypriot passport control.

Each new assignment came with certain, calculated risks. It was never his job to question his mentor's vast business dealings or to understand each move he made. It was simply Pauk's job to make sure all obstacles were cleared in advance. A point of honor. A point of life or death.

TWENTY-THREE

Vanessa braked her gray convertible Renault directly in front of Café Kiji. Beyond the surrounding shops and restaurants, Larnaca Bay shivered metallic blue beneath late-afternoon sun.

After her almost sleepless night, she'd showered and dressed for a long day at her cover office in Nicosia. She was still at her desk at 1745 hours when a cable from Sid dinged her secure laptop.

HQS REQUESTS THAT PER PREVIOUS DISCUSSION WITH C/O VONN, C/O GROVES MAKE CONTACT WITH GZROBUST/258. ALTHOUGH R/258 HAS NOT YET PROVIDED INTELLIGENCE OF HIGH VALUE ON FINANCIAL DEALINGS AT HIS LOCATION, HE IS CLEARLY IN A POSITION TO DO SO, IF HANDLED AND MOTI-

VATED APPROPRIATELY. C/O VONN HAS MADE ARRANGE-MENTS WITH R/258 TO MEET C/O GROVES. R/258 WILL BE AT IDEN A TONIGHT–REPEAT TONIGHT–AT 2000 HRS.

She'd changed quickly, catching her hair up into a butterfly clip and applying a dash of makeup before slipping into a light mauve silk dress and black heels from her office emergency stash. And here she was — rushed but glad to be in action — about to meet her newest Russian asset.

Café Kiji offered valet parking. She dropped her keys in the young man's wait-ing palm.

Inside, Vanessa took in the manic scene. The large main dining room and bar, with its hum of electronic dance music and its neo-rococo designs, overflowed with the requisite diplomats, financiers, a generous sprinkling of air-kissing Eurotrash, and Mafia types from various corners of the globe. But no sign of her host Sergei Tara-sov, otherwise known as GZRobust/258.

She pressed her way toward the bar, mov-ing as quickly as possible. Even so, the Brit-ish ambassador managed to clutch her arm, then a handshake with the Cypriot Minister of Foreign Affairs, and on to an air-kiss exchange with the Iranian rug salesman she highly suspected was up to no good.

Small world, smaller island.

That was one of the reasons for the meeting — a casual public introduction to Sergei would help serve as an inoculation. Future meetings would be clandestine, but if someone happened to spot them together, there would be a logical explanation: Sergei Tarasov was a Russian banker, entrepreneur, investor, and as far as most of her world knew, Vanessa Pierson was Vice President International of Entheo Venture Capital, headquartered in Nicosia.

She stepped up to the long bar, stainless steel framing solid blue-tinted ice and a mirrored bank of vodkas lining the wall. Although a chilled shot of Reyka was sorely tempting after the long day, she needed to keep a clear head. "Soda with a twist," she told the bartender, scanning faces as she waited.

With no sign of Sergei anywhere in the main room, she took a sip of her soda and gauged the distance to the enclosed beach terrace: another fifteen meters of meet-and-greet. She turned sideways to ease through a huddle of Mafia types who were staring up at a huge and ornately framed copy of

Ingres's *Grande Odalisque* hanging on the pink plaster wall. Two musclemen with bulges under their jackets stood conspicuously at the terrace entrance. No doubt several others kept watch on the beach.

Affluent Russians often employed a cadre of bodyguards, and Sergei Tarasov had reason to be vigilant. His uncle had been gunned down on a Moscow street in early 2010, a hit ordered by a Russian Mob boss involved in the trafficking of black-market nukes who was intent on laundering money through the Tarasov family bank, Troika.

Evgeni Tarasov's murder had been the key to turning Sergei, Vice President of Troika Bank, who had a wife and two children to protect. Sid's initial report to CPD read: "GZRobust/258 is highly motivated to cooperate." But almost four years had passed since Sergei's recruitment, and he'd proved a disappointing asset. All of Sid's meetings with him had yielded only dribs and drabs, barely enough for the CIA to rationalize keeping the banker on their books. Vanessa held no illusions about this low-level asset handoff. But Sid had decades of field experience as a NOC, and he'd recruited and run dozens of assets. He was also smart. If he believed Sergei was holding high-value financial intel . . .

She needed Sergei to deliver — accounts, front companies, and, if possible, the names of the men behind them; men who financed the black-market proliferation networks that CPD was tracking under Operation Ghost Hunt. She also had the feeling her future at the Agency depended on a big win. So tonight, as Vanessa took over as his handler, she would see for herself what they had in Sergei.

Smiling coolly at yet another well-armed muscleman, Vanessa set her empty glass on top of a faux-Greek pillar and stepped through the terrace doors onto the enclosed slate patio. A cluster of partygoers stood taking in the view as the sun dipped like a huge copper spoon into the shimmering harbor. A deep voice rose above the general hum, English with a heavy Muscovite accent.

Sure enough, he's holding court.

She turned; he had his back to her. From pictures in his file, she recognized his broad shoulders, squat body, balding head. Sergei could pass for a boxer off his training. He shifted, and she saw him in profile, his blunt features and the shadow of beard. Huge Russian hands cuffed air, and the group laughed at a punch line Vanessa missed.

His arm was draped around a tall, slender

young woman dressed skimpily in Russian haute chic: a strapless pink mini, a pink fur bolero jacket, and beaded-crochet headdress. She looked young enough to be his daughter. Sergei pulled her close and tight — from Vanessa's vantage point, aggressively so. The girl pushed free, her face blanched, her smile taut. *A lover's spat?*

Hovering behind Sergei was a massively bulky guy with a cleft chin, wearing a tight black tee and gray jacket with conspicuous bulges. He had to be his personal bodyguard, the must-have accessory for a Russian businessman. In addition to Sergei's group, perhaps a dozen other people occupied the enclosed patio, but most were making their way down an ornate marble staircase to what appeared to be a newly renovated basement club.

Vanessa kept Sergei in her periphery. She made sure to stand in his sight line, giving him the chance to figure out who she was. It didn't take him long.

His eyes narrowed, and his body tensed. With a glance at his watch, he turned to his young companion, leaning close to whisper in her ear. He held up five fingers. Pouting, she shot him a scathing look with her kohl-rimmed eyes, almost shoving her drink into his hand. She then led several of her clubby friends back into the crowded restaurant, leaving Sergei alone with his bodyguard.

Vanessa's cue to move.

"Pozdravlyayu!" She could speak basic Russian but not well, so she eased into her carefully memorized Russian spiel, *Congratulations on your restaurant. I'm Vanessa Pierson, and I have a venture capital firm in Nicosia —*

"Speak English," he snapped, with a dismissive flick of his hand.

She pulled up sharply. "Fine. English then, *Gospodin* Tarasov."

Sergei waved off his bodyguard with a scowl. The man retreated.

"You know the work of Yiapanis?" Sergei asked brusquely, leading Vanessa to the spiral staircase, which was guarded by a slender bronze statue, a nude in the style of Modigliani.

"She's lovely," she said, intentionally admiring the sculpture.

"And very expensive," he snapped, his tone petulant.

With a quick, modulating breath, Vanessa returned her attention to Sergei. He slid his sunglasses off, revealing reddened eyes, more than a hint of Russian melancholy — and an emotion somewhere between vexation and exasperation. "I'm so glad you could be bothered to show up," he growled under his breath.

Barely controlling her own impatience, Vanessa said, "It's a pleasure to finally meet you." And in a lower voice, "Let's not make a scene. I'm here, and you're the one who missed the last few meetings with your former contact."

"Our friend told me you were beautiful and young," Sergei said, drinking too quickly from his glass as he began to descend the staircase.

Vanessa followed in spite of her misgivings. When they reached the basement, Sergei's waiting bodyguard lifted the thick red sash anchored between stanchions that served as gateway for his boss and Vanessa. The room was large, low-lit, and leaning toward bordello décor. It was also equipped with another full bar, as well as several billiard and poker tables, all new and apparently professional-grade.

Sergei shooed away a hovering waitress, then said, "But I didn't realize they were handing me off to a baby . . . *devka.*" He glared at Vanessa as he delivered the verbal slap.

So that was it? He hated that he'd been passed to a young handler, especially a woman?

But she believed there was more. According to Sid, the Russian mogul had recently been acting as balky as a spooked horse. Even as she watched, the skin around his eyes contracted and his lower lip pulled taut. Sergei was afraid.

As if he'd read her thoughts, he frowned at his now empty glass. "I see the news, the assassinations, and I hear things in my business, so I'm looking out for myself and my family, because you people obviously cannot keep me safe."

"Did something happen, Sergei? Were you threatened?" Vanessa spoke under her breath, keeping her smile in place even as a tremor ran the length of her body.

He pushed his face toward hers. "I am Russian" — as though those three words explained everything.

"I know you love your family and your homeland," Vanessa said, speaking urgently. "Don't forget we have the same objectives — we both love our countries, and that's why we're working together."

Past Sergei's shoulder, the girlfriend was returning with her coterie. Vanessa's private window with the Russian was closing quickly.

"Here comes your friend," she warned.

"Anya is not my friend —"

"She's your *daughter,*" Vanessa finished in a quick, low voice — just now registering it. Sergei had nineteen-year-old twins, a boy and girl. Both had fallen prey to the wilder hedonistic pleasures of Moscow.

Spitting out his words in a low growl so she felt the heat, smelled the vodka and bitterness on his breath, he said: "I take care of my own — what you pay is shit money to me. I haven't risked everything I have for shit. I do it for my family, for my country, to stop the Mafia from destroying Russia."

Before she could respond, he snapped out a quick command in Russian to his bodyguard. Olaf — but she didn't catch anything else.

With a heavy grunt, Olaf stalked toward them, and Vanessa braced herself for the hard bounce.

Olaf pulled a cue stick off a rack. He hefted it the way a batter preps a bat.

Vanessa waited, her eyes on the huge man's every move.

Olaf inhaled loudly, and then he righted the cue stick and held it out to Vanessa like a knight's staff.

"You play?" Sergei asked.

Vanessa shrugged. "A little."

When she still ignored the cue stick, Sergei growled, "Come on, *devka,* let's see who is better at this game, you or me?"

She met Sergei's eyes and saw their darkness. Only then did she accept the cue stick, and, with it, his coded challenge. "Sure . . ." She thought her voice sounded almost normal. "Stakes?"

"A friendly game," Sergei said slowly. His smile, lips only, reminded Vanessa of a hungry python she'd met years ago in Brazil. "If you lose, you owe me nothing, a beer, a drink." He waved his hand to indicate the bottles behind the bar.

"If I *win*?"

He pushed out his lower lip and nudged air with his chin. "You won't."

"But if I do," she insisted.

He lowered his voice so only she could hear. "Then I will give you what you want."

Behind Sergei, his bored, rebellious daughter, Anya, stared through Vanessa for a moment while her friends talked and laughed and nibbled on bar garnishes.

Where was Sergei's son? Vanessa wondered, sensing that the Russian and his daughter were both disturbed by Valentin's absence.

Sergei held out his hand, cupping a euro fifty-cent piece. He eyed her impatiently.

She reached into her small evening bag and retrieved a shiny Turkish lira. "More reliable than a euro," she said, smiling coolly. Sergei's bodyguard caught the coin when she tossed it his way.

"Your call, *devka*," Sergei said, not bothering to soften his tone.

"Heads."

The bodyguard gazed down at the coin, and then he spoke too quickly in Russian for Vanessa to catch the words.

"Your break," Sergei said, smirking. He racked the balls, arranging them properly, and gave the triangle a snap.

As Vanessa chalked the cue point and turned her attention to the table, a cocktail glass brimming with clear liquid appeared almost out of nowhere.

The waitress holding the drink nodded toward Sergei. "On him."

"Jewel of Russia," Sergei said, crossing his arms across his broad chest. "In Russia, vodka is water." She accepted the drink and took a taste — finding it cold and dangerously smooth. She looked for a place to set it down.

"You don't like?" called a female voice from the bar.

Vanessa looked over to see a sulking Anya, kohl eyeliner beginning to run. She guessed the edgy but wilting teenager was coming down from something — cocaine or ecstasy?

"I like," she said, swallowing half the shot, breathing in the velvety taste before she set it on the closest empty pool table. *And I need to keep a clear head.*

She took more than a few moments to study the lineup — long enough that Sergei began to fidget. *Good.*

Then she stretched across the table cushion consciously revealing a little cleavage — once again taking her time — to make the break shot. As a young teen, in Air Force rec facilities, she'd witnessed countless games between Marshall and anybody he could con into losing a few bucks. With his easy looks and charm, he was a born pool shark. Every once in a while, her cocky brother had relented and played Vanessa — and she had learned the hard way to keep up with him — by losing. Until she finally won. Not often, but sometimes.

Three balls bounced soundly off cushions while the fourth, her six ball, found its way into the pocket. But on her next shot the ball missed the pocket and jumped the cushion. Vanessa let her shoulders sink, and she shook her head, faking a half-giggle. "Oops."

Now the Russian stepped up to the table with his well-used cue stick. He barely gave Vanessa a look — just leaned in and began the play. Two stripes, then three, and in a matter of minutes, he cleared the stripes and pocketed the eight ball. "I win," he said.

"One more?" Vanessa prompted, still pretending to be flustered.

Sergei grunted, but he waited while she racked the balls, and then he made the break shot. He called solids again, and he'd pocketed five when he lined up for a shot that would demand shooting past the eight ball. He took his time, surveying possible angles. And when she thought he was on the verge, Vanessa leaned forward to whisper two terse and pointed questions in his ear. Striking where she gauged he was most vulnerable.

His ball went wide and the eight ball fell into the pocket. A foul.

He glared at her, visibly enraged. Olaf closed in, but Sergei regained control. He took a drink of his vodka, and Vanessa joined him, taking another sip from hers. Now it was her turn.

She took her shot, neatly pocketing two stripes and opening the table. And then, methodically and with obvious ease, she sank every stripe and followed up by sinking the eight ball.

Sergei downed his drink.

Vanessa walked slowly over to the Russian

banker. She pushed the cue stick into his free hand. Their eyes met, and she held his dark gaze. For an instant his lips flicked up at the corners, then just as quickly his lips turned down into his customary scowl. But Vanessa held her smile and she let it reach her eyes.

She leaned close to his ear and simply said, "Make the next meeting."

As she wound her way back through the throng upstairs, a new song started, the beat louder, vibrating, and she picked up her pace, striding toward the exit. She couldn't wait to escape through the gilded doors.

She passed more security, tipped the valet, and slid behind the wheel of her Renault. After the encounter with Sergei, she had to shake off the adrenaline. He'd made her play games. Fine. She'd played him, whispering questions: *Where's Valentin tonight? How do you plan to keep your twins alive?*

For a moment she felt hollow — duty done. Then something faint and obsessive surged inside her. Even though Chris had punished her, she was still in the game.

She kicked off her heels and touched her bare foot to the accelerator. Then she sucked in a breath, easing back her energy. She had at least two hours of driving before she reached her home in Nicosia — this was not a time to push the limits.

Aware of headlights in her rearview mirror, she merged with the traffic just as full darkness blanketed the island. She was definitely on edge. Had she picked up some of Sergei's fear?

TWENTY-FOUR

Pauk couldn't quite believe his eyes when the woman from Vienna strutted out of the private party at the Russian's trendy beach restaurant. He'd been watching from the street, and somehow he'd missed her entrance but not her exit. It didn't matter that she was blond this time, because he recognized the fluid and athletic way she moved. He'd studied her on the You-Tube video again and again.

But he wasn't expecting to see her, especially not there.

So now his plan had changed. Instead of following the Russian to see if he could take his kill shot tonight, he made an instant decision to track the mysterious woman wherever she was headed.

Because he knew absolutely: She was bad luck.

Pauk kept his Fiat 500 at a good distance from her convertible so he wouldn't spook her. As soon as her Renault eased into the merging lane for the A1, he moved to exit, too, but maintaining the space, not pushing.

And so he followed, staying well back for now.

Vanessa turned off the A1 ten kilometers outside Larnaca. Two cars almost immediately followed, and she slowed so they both passed her by — a Citroen and a Fiat. She executed a series of sharp turns on surface streets until, after about fifteen minutes, she headed north again, but this time using the old road to Nicosia. The old road wasn't well maintained, but traffic was light and that made it easier to know if she had unwelcome company. With the top down and leaving behind the infrequent highway lights, she had the sensation of burrowing through a velvety darkness.

As soon as he'd exited the A1, Pauk was forced to pass her Renault — now she'd marked his Fiat. Cursing, he followed surface streets. She'd pulled the same detection move he often used, and unless he switched vehicles, he had to let her go. He couldn't risk trying to pick up her trail again — too much chance she'd make his Fiat.

He cut back toward the A1, resigned but still angry. As he pulled up at a side-street stop sign, a sleek gray Renault convertible raced through the intersection. Hers.

As Vanessa gained on a slow truck, she pulled right into the oncoming lane and passed easily. Since leaving Larnaca, she'd traveled without incident for thirty minutes, and her hands had steadied on the wheel. She leaned into the winding descent on the lonely road, the Mediterranean at her back, Troodos Mountains ahead. For an instant she closed her eyes and replayed Sergei's reaction to her questions — fury, deep fear, and a flash of relief. He was arrogant, and he would be a challenging asset, but she had the feeling he might prove valuable. She blinked open to the arid, stubbled landscape racing past. Cool air whipped at her hair. Her bare foot nudged the pedal, and the engine surged.

The road wasn't well lit, so she found herself braking abruptly behind a van with only one faint red taillight. She pulled out to pass and noticed a new vehicle — light-colored — now passing the truck in her wake. She couldn't identify the vehicle model, not yet, but when it stayed behind the barely lit van for another eight kilometers, she began to relax again. Except she realized that the van was going slow. And the light-colored car had passed the truck with ease. Why would it stay back now?

She accelerated, driving up hard on the rear of another truck. She pulled out to the right to pass but swerved back into the left lane as two oncoming cars raced by. She tried again, and this time had plenty of open road on which to pass.

She tracked the distant light-colored car in her rearview mirror as it pulled out and passed the slow van. She tensed, and her heartbeat kicked up. Cyprus had recently suffered a rash of car hijackings and highway robberies, courtesy of local criminals and gangs. No way she planned to become the latest victim.

She had another thirty kilometers until she reached the outskirts of Nicosia. From there she'd only be minutes from the soldiers manning the border crossing if she needed them. But it was thirty kilometers of remote road, rough in some stretches, very dark in others, no houses, no farms.

She felt herself settling deeper in the seat, hunkering down for the rest of the drive.

Her Renault had played point car for several minutes, and now the truck behind her turned onto a side road and there was no other vehicle between hers and the light-colored car. At which point the driver switched on his high beams — an obviously hostile move — so Vanessa had to squint into her rear-and sideview mirrors.

Now the driver closed the distance until the other car remained approximately seventy meters behind her Renault whether she accelerated to 125 kph or slowed to 85 kph.

Tracking her, playing with her, psyching her out?

Twice in one goddamn night. She thought she'd left the games behind with Sergei.

Earlier she'd welcomed the night air and the clarity it delivered. But now the ceaseless rush of night air shook loose images, some of the worst from the past weeks.

A dark heat filled the pit of her stomach, rising through her until she tasted her own rage — for a few wild seconds, the dangerous emotion fueled her before she regained control.

After several minutes, she caught the lights and shape of a battered VW just ahead and felt a fleeting rush of relief as she sped past at 150 kph. She checked her mirror, blinking through the glare as her pursuer passed the VW, too, matching her moves and her speed.

Maybe twenty kilometers, ten to fifteen

minutes, now until she reached the outskirts of Nicosia. No traffic from either direction except the two of them and the fading VW in their wake. Was he going to make a move? Did he have a partner waiting somewhere just ahead? Did he want a fight? She could give him one. She ran through her memory of the last stretch of road ahead, frustrated by her inability to recall specific details.

Until she passed a landmark — a long-ago-abandoned truck — and she remembered the old bypass road. Efforts to repair and widen the highway had been abandoned at some point. But the road still existed and ran parallel with the highway for roughly ten kilometers. She was coming up on the turnoff.

She pressed down hard again on the accelerator and at the same time cut the Renault's lights.

Almost instantly she panicked at the abrupt onslaught of darkness and the sensation of speeding into a black vortex. But she breathed through the cold sweat, kept the wheel steady, and felt the first swell of the highway as it passed over a series of rises and dips.

Her eyes adjusted just enough to the dark to catch a visual of the undulating highway ahead, and she counted — one rise, one dip . . . and two . . . and three . . . and four.

At the lowest point of the fourth dip she cut left, the Renault swerving off the road to pass between metal guard posts, so close she thought she heard one steel post scrape her paint. But she was on the old bypass road, sheltered half the time by long-abandoned mounds of road construction debris, the gravel road finally straightening more or less to run on a parallel trajectory with the highway. Now she tracked the other car and she could finally identify it as a Fiat 500. It alternately sped up and braked as the driver tried to figure out where she'd gone. *How the hell was a Fiat 500 keeping up with her Renault? He might have an advantage on a curvy mountain road, but not here on the flat.* She turned the wheel sharply but couldn't avoid some road debris so the Renault jerked and slid while Vanessa weighed her next move.

Brake hard and wait and pray he didn't spot her waiting?

Keep moving but let him get ahead?

Catch as much speed as she could, so she'd cut him off as she merged back onto the main road — then run flat out for the last ten kilometers before civilization?

Just then he cut his headlights.

Both of them traveling on parallel roads

in darkness.

And instinct told her he'd spotted her. So it was door number three.

She pushed the accelerator all the way down, fishtailing for the next fifty meters before she regained control.

He was accelerating, too, and gaining. She wouldn't be able to go much faster.

She crested a rise, where the roads converged, positive at that moment she would slam into his Fiat. But her tires hit asphalt just a few meters ahead of him, so her car barely clipped his.

The Renault lurched, and so did the Fiat as it swerved off the road. The world spun wildly until Vanessa slammed against the driver's-side door as her tires got traction one more time.

She sped up again, not sure if she was headed south or north, but then the Fiat's headlights filled her rearview mirror and she switched the Renault's lights back on.

The glow of Nicosia warmed the sky in the distance, so she felt safety ahead and she was ready to accelerate into the last stretch. But then the Renault's headlights illuminated a pale wave flowing across the highway — a herd of animals? Vanessa cut the wheel, and now the Renault spun 180 degrees before it stuttered ten meters to a halt. Dust and tiny specks of straw swirled around her. She was facing the stopped Fiat, fifty or so meters between them filled with the blinding beams of their headlamps. Seconds passed, and she was aware of her own ragged breath and the Renault's engine ticking as she squinted into the glare.

She hadn't stalled out the Renault. It would drive. But where? Should she make a U-turn and race the last stretch to Nicosia? She didn't know if the road had cleared behind her, and she wanted the Fiat's driver to make the first move.

What the hell was he waiting for? Was he going to try to drag her from the car? Or try to shoot her?

If he tried anything, she'd do her best to run him down.

But after what seemed like an eternity, the Fiat began moving slowly. Backing away. Then into a U-turn, too far away for her to see the plates. And then the Fiat disappeared into darkness. At first Vanessa didn't move — couldn't move —

What the hell was that about? A long, elaborate game of chicken? Did the idea of the border crossing scare him off? What if he wasn't a local and there was something she'd missed?

But then into the new silence rose an irritable bleating, and a high-pitched whistle filled the air. Vanessa unclipped her seat belt and managed to turn gingerly in the driver's seat to see the source of the noise.

Shit. She'd almost slammed into a herd of bearded goats. She blinked as the herder stepped into view. She went a little rubbery in her limbs. Adrenaline aftermath. She raised her hand. *Hello, sorry —* "Signommi." He stared at her for a moment before hoisting his staff in return. As he shambled across the road, his whistled call rose shrilly over the pallid sea of animals, one indecipherable from the other. Her father's voice echoed sharply inside her from childhood: *Stay present, stay alive.*

Ninety minutes after he left the woman from the video, Pauk sat in the idling Fiat outside airport parking in Larnaca. Undecided. She couldn't have missed the fact that the car chasing her was a light-colored Fiat 500. But there were hundreds of cars similar to his on Cyprus. He'd thought about ditching the Fiat and stealing a car from the long-term parking area. But that created new problems — in case the car was reported stolen before he left the island tomorrow. He could rent a car under his current identity, because his cover was solid.

But rental cars could not be driven from the Greek side of the island to the Turkish side. So in the end, he decided to keep his Fiat. He was taking a risk, but it was small — and he was attached to his vehicle and its customizations, which he'd personally overseen.

As he began the drive back to Limassol and the "borrowed" condo that provided an unobscured view of the Russian's penthouse, he replayed the chase toward Nicosia.

He'd already notified his mentor of the woman's reappearance and sent a text of the Renault's license plate. Not that he believed that would lead back to her. He now assumed the plate was registered to a front company. She'd handled the Renault like a professional. And when she'd faced him off in her car, for once, he'd been uncertain how to proceed, what moves to make, whether to eliminate her or let her go. He hated the sense of no ground beneath his feet, as if he stood on a precipice, one foot out over thin air.

TWENTY-FIVE

After last night's strange chase across the middle of Cyprus, Vanessa had arrived at her apartment in Nicosia safe but troubled. She'd shrugged off the fear, but she still felt spooked by the oddness of it all. She'd planned to watch the early news on the local station, alert for any reports of carjackings or highway robberies, but her plans were preempted thirty minutes ago.

At 0530, she'd been surprised by a secvid, or secure-video request, from Hawkins's secretary, Hildy. "Sorry about the crazy hour, but we've set up a conference for thirty minutes from now — the DDO's weekly update with Alexandra Hall, and she's got a plane to catch. Chris will be joining in today." Vanessa was about to ask what any of this had to do with her when Hildy added, "Oh, by the way, Director Hall asked specifically that you be on the call as well."

Vanessa's immediate internal reaction:

dread. Who the hell had she pissed off now?

But she'd pushed away the paranoia — because that's what it was.

Now she ran a brush quickly through her thick, still slightly tangled blond hair. It had grown several inches past her shoulders, and she was overdue for a trim. She set the brush down and pushed her hair behind her ears. She pulled one side free again — and then the other. The light layer of sunscreen and a dusting of bronze powder had helped liven up her skin tone, and she dug through her makeup bag to find her favorite lip gloss. She didn't let her gaze linger on the mirror, just another quick check to make sure her smile worked and her blue eyes looked clear (thanks to Visine) beneath the strong brown eyebrows she'd inherited from her father. *She would do.*

She was settling in front of her laptop screen just as the sec-vid conference call came through.

Vanessa found herself staring at a dimple in the DDO's chin before he took a step back and said, "Good morning, Vanessa. Glad you could make it today."

"Good morning, sir."

She saw Chris running his fingers through his hair and tightening his slightly lopsided tie. He turned toward her, and she anticipated his cursory greeting. But his eyes narrowed behind his silver-framed glasses. "You look like — are you okay?"

"Of course," she said, hearing the edge in her voice.

"Good," he said.

His tone was now so cool that she inhaled painfully through the tight knot behind her third rib, near her heart. "Early for me, a late night for you," she said, keeping her tone neutral.

And then she heard Hildy's voice acknowledging a new incoming connection, followed by Alexandra Hall's throaty and disembodied alto, asking, "Good morning, gentlemen. Are we all here?"

"We are, Alexandra," DDO Hawkins said, nodding tightly. And Vanessa noted the characteristic way he pulled himself up, opening his chest, his alpha stance.

Chris said, "Madame Director, it's always a pleasure." Vanessa had a clear view of Hall's face filling a screen inset.

"Chris," Hall said, cocking her head slightly. "I'm not sure that's true, but we have more important points to cover." Hall's focus moved to Vanessa, or, more accurately, Vanessa's image on a monitor. "I'm genuinely pleased that you are working on Operation Ghost Hunt. I haven't forgotten your useful contribution to Operation Ulysses last year. Those two South Africans took us a step closer to Bhoot, and both gentlemen will be guests of the Queen for several years to come."

"Thank you," Vanessa said, trying to cover her surprise — and the bit of awe she felt at being singled out so favorably. From the corner of her eye, she saw the DDO's expression and determined his reaction to be something between general pride that one of his had been praised by Hall and specific irritation that it happened to be Vanessa.

Chris showed no reaction, maintaining his distance.

Vanessa held her silence for a few minutes while the DDO and Hall covered issues Vanessa could follow only very generally. Several times Chris was asked to contribute his two cents.

The topic shifted abruptly when Hall said, "Phillip, bring me up to date on Operation Ghost Hunt — we're picking up some vibrations that our mutual friend may be in Iran next week. And I want to hear from your case officer on this, because she's spent the most time of anyone in your operation tracking Bhoot. Vanessa?"

"Ma-Madame Director?"

"Although your results have varied, you've been spot-on several times when predicting Bhoot's next steps. Do *you* believe he would risk visiting a facility in Iran?"

In the pin-drop silence following the question, Vanessa tried to ignore a ribbon of sweat trailing slowly along her ribs. Her mind raced through the possibilities, a lightning search for definitive threads, but she pushed aside the craving for absolute evidence and took the leap. "Yes, he'll risk it — but only because he's escalated his involvement. This isn't just any other facility or any rogue nation that he's supplied with black-market nuclear components. As far as we know, up to now he's kept his business dealings impersonal — *brutal,* yes — but almost antiseptic, in contrast to his narcissistic predecessor, Asad Chaudhry. Chaudhry had a God complex, and a religious justification, openly proclaiming he would ultimately bring justice to the world by arming all Islamic nations with nuclear weapons." Vanessa took a quick breath. "Bhoot's mission is different — his reach, his money, his actions, his power — it's been driven by his need to dominate. Bhoot will risk a tour because he's changing his MO, he's evolving — because he is claiming ownership in this new venture."

If anything, the silence deepened in the wake of Vanessa's prediction. But only for a few weighty seconds — until Hall broke the tension by nodding brusquely. "So now the big question remains: *Where the hell in Iran is he going to show?*" Hall looked pointedly at DDO Hawkins. "What's happening on the geo-codes? Your case officer flew to Turkey to get them. Do we have the locations? Are they decoded?"

DDO Hawkins raised one eyebrow in Chris's direction, and Chris cleared his throat before he said, "NSA is still working on it — and they're close . . ."

Vanessa knew what he was leaving out — their Farsi expert had major surgery last week, it hadn't gone well, and he would be on medical leave for at least the remainder of the month. She also knew they would never ask the Brits for help — that would qualify as complete humiliation.

"This matter is urgent," Hall snapped. "If yours can't break it, show it to our people."

Chris looked startled. "I'm sure NSA will have news any minute —"

"Then let's get someone else," the DDO sputtered. "I'm getting all kinds of pressure from Jeffreys and his posse over at the White House about moving things into place. Not to mention the Pentagon. And damn it, we're not even close to finding the damn needle in the haystack. Chris?"

"I'm on it," Chris said through gritted teeth.

"I want to hear from your officer," Alexandra Hall interjected.

"Madame Director?" Vanessa said, pulling up sharply.

"The code came from your asset — you're the one who knew him, who knew how he thought."

Vanessa nodded slowly.

"Are we waiting for someone who can decipher a complex algorithm?" Hall asked, sharply. "Or is this something else . . ."

This time Vanessa didn't hesitate. "My asset was a nuclear engineer, quite brilliant, and capable of a complex algorithm. But my best bet, it's something else — very much mired in Persian cultural references — something much simpler, if you just know *how* to look."

Twenty-Six

Church bells rang out suddenly over the *imam*'s invocation to Asr, Islam's afternoon prayer, shrill songs echoing over the pyramids of Giza. Taking in the view of city and sand and ancient pyramids from the open terrace of her hotel room, Vanessa stabbed out her Dunhill in an ashtray.

Following the conference with Alexandra Hall, DDO Hawkins, and Chris, it had taken only minutes before she realized she'd already made a decision to seek Khoury's help. Two hours later, after an abbreviated text-message exchange to confirm he'd be there, she boarded EgyptAir's ninety-minute non-stop flight to Cairo. She felt more than a twinge of anxiety that she had not reported her travel to anyone in chain of command — so this rendezvous was completely under the radar. The additional undercurrent of guilt centered on Chris and the fact she still hadn't managed to tell him the truth about her relationship with Khoury.

She'd made it to the hotel in time for a hot shower to ease at least some of the tension from her shoulders. She'd dressed simply, in a sleeveless silk tee and a pair of loose silk pajama trousers. Her small travel clock, set to Cairo time, showed 1630 hours.

How long would Khoury keep her waiting?

It felt like it had been forever since their last illicit rendezvous — a long weekend on a Tunisian beach two months ago. And before that, late last spring, they'd managed almost a full week of rock climbing in the National Park of Paklenica in Croatia. A relationship built on brief, intense getaways — tough under the best circumstances. And so much had changed. These days, she and Khoury were more like strangers than lovers. She couldn't name the latest book on his night table. And she knew that when she asked for his help, she would be crossing into new and dangerous territory. Until now, their affair had remained separate from the rest of their lives and work.

She couldn't shake the profound sense of unease that remained since their brief meeting in D.C. Something about his behavior dug at her, something unidentified — at the same time she craved him, ached for him.

It would be so much easier just to make it about sex. Why couldn't it be that simple? She paced the room, stepping again out onto the terrace, where the endless cacophony of Cairo's traffic — car horns and radios — clamored up from the hectic boulevard. And just beyond, looming like an extravagant mirage, the pyramids shimmering through Cairo's desert haze.

But it had never been simple for them. Khoury saw behind the surface of her; he saw behind her mask. From the first, somehow he knew how to penetrate the fortress of emotional defenses she had built over a lifetime. Every shield she used to keep others at a distance. Khoury understood her in ways she sometimes didn't understand herself. He was like her father that way — except he didn't use his insight to command.

She lit another Dunhill, exhaling smoke into Cairo's smoggy air, hoping the nicotine would calm her. She worried the single strand of simple wooden beads on her left wrist, a gift from Khoury when they were in Tunisia. A minute later, she stubbed out the cigarette and ordered a bottle of wine from room service. When it was delivered, she left it on ice for Khoury's arrival. With a stab of frustration, she pictured the single sheet of paper with Arash's flowing Pahlavi script. The decryption experts should have broken it by now.

She stood in front of the room's safe for almost a minute before she unlocked it and removed the sealed envelope containing a copy of the single sheet of code. She slipped the unopened envelope inside the paperback of *Madame Bovary* that she left on the writing desk.

The suite closed in around her, the air still and warm, so she took refuge a third time on the terrace, forcing herself to sit, sipping mineral water. A new layer of sound, traditional Egyptian wedding music, floated up from the lower level of the hotel, adding to the general din. For a few minutes she turned questions in her mind. And then she surrendered to the chaos that was Cairo, watching as the sun began to dip low behind the Sphinx and the Great Pyramid.

Two sharp raps at her door, and her stomach pitched.

A glance through the security peephole, a click of the lock, and then Khoury was inside the room. He looked exhausted, bruised beneath the eyes. She reached out to touch his face gently, resting her palm against the roughness of his beard. In return, he traced the angles of her cheek.

Let his fingers skim to the well of her throat. Slid his hand lightly around the base of her neck. Very carefully, he touched his lips to her forehead.

She took one step, pressing her body against his so she could feel him respond instantly. She tipped her head back, her mouth meeting his lips, tasting cigarettes and mint. He lifted her off the ground, carrying her toward the bedroom, making it only as far as the plush rug. So much they needed to say —

She heard him whisper, *"Habibti."* My love.

After that, no thoughts at all.

TWENTY-SEVEN

Whispers summoned Vanessa back to the world. She opened her eyes. Khoury smiled down at her. He rested on one elbow, his skin two shades darker than hers.

"Hey, sleepyhead," he said softly. "Let's go see the pyramids."

"Later," she moaned. She yawned and stretched, her fists punching feather-filled pillows. "How did we make it to the bed?"

"You don't remember?" Khoury teased gently. He reached for something on the bedside table: the bottle of wine. He drank freely from the already open bottle, and then he offered it to her. She shook her head, eyeing him seriously. Was he more than a little drunk? Although a non-devout Muslim, Khoury rarely drank, and she was about to ask if he was okay when she heard the low vibration of a cell phone.

Khoury reached for his where he'd left it on the table. As he read the incoming message, his frown cut a deep crease across his forehead.

"Bad news?" she asked softly.

He met her gaze, and for an instant she saw a dark glint of emotion, but then it was gone.

"Hey, Khoury . . ." She shifted, turning her body toward his. She could read him well enough to know he had wanted to say something. She also knew she couldn't push him if he wasn't ready to confide. She pressed her index finger against his breast-bone, his heart. "What's wrong?"

He almost answered, but then he pulled back and rolled, and Vanessa ended up on top. "Hey, beautiful, stop worrying," he whispered, stroking the hollow of her throat.

She inhaled sharply at his touch. "David —"

"Nothing's wrong, I promise," he said, brushing his fingers lightly across her breasts.

She leaned over him, eyes fierce, voice hoarse. "So, has your mother fixed you up with any nice Lebanese girls lately?"

"Yes."

"Really."

"Really. One of them is a belly dancer when she's not curing heart disease."

"I'll show you a belly dance . . ."

TWENTY-EIGHT

"Habibti," he whispered again, tracing his finger along her ribs, an erotic touch that quickly turned ticklish.

"Hey," Vanessa said, laughing, "that's not fair." She rolled over and off the bed, feeling his eyes on her as she made her way across the suite, following the trail of clothes they'd left behind only an hour ago. She pulled on her T-shirt, then picked up his boxers and tossed them casually back to him over her head.

"Let's get out of here," he said.

"We need to talk." She took a quick breath, her voice fading as she turned toward him.

He shook his head, swinging up to sitting, donning his shorts. "Talk can wait, *the pyramids . . .*"

He grabbed the bottle of wine and walked past her onto the terrace. She followed to stand by his side. It was full darkness now,

and the illuminated perimeter of the pyramids glowed eerily beyond the bright city
lights. Still, the noise never stopped: the
endless honk and rumble of traffic and the
voices, laughter, and music rising up from
the sparkling hotel pools and surrounding
gardens.

She eased the bottle of wine from his
hand, setting it down on the table. Then she
pressed her palm gently to Khoury's back.
He was still bare above the waist, and his
dark olive skin radiated warmth. "David . . ."

"Talk can wait," he repeated, still staring
out across the desert. He pulled a cigarette
from the pack she'd left on the table and lit
up. Exhaling smoke, he deepened his voice
melodramatically: "Here on the plateau of
Giza stands one of the world's mightiest
wonders. No traveler, soldier, emperor, or
poet has trod on these sands without gasp-
ing in awe —"

"Just so you know," Vanessa said, taking a
quick hit on his cigarette while it stayed
between his fingers, "I saw the same light
show when I was ten."

"Then you know the curtain of night is
about to rise," Khoury said, reaching for
her.

She kissed him, happy and even a little

relieved they felt easy again. Their rhythms matched. She leaned back just enough so she could see the gleam of white when he smiled. And she knew that was her cue. She kissed him again, lightly. Then she held up one finger, leaving him on the balcony as she walked to the bedroom. She picked up her copy of *Madame Bovary* from the small writing desk, slipping the envelope from inside the cover.

She turned to walk back to Khoury, but he had followed her and now stood just inside the bedroom doorway. She pressed the envelope into his hands.

"What's this?" he asked, his voice wary, his eyes reading her face.

"Open it," she said, suddenly apprehensive. She knew her timing wasn't always good . . . and that had created problems at work and with men. But she pressed on. "Just take a look, please, David."

Still he stared at her. "Vanessa . . ."

"I need your help. My dead asset sent this to us through his wife."

His expression hardened. "Let me get this straight, you're handing me top-secret intel that came from your Iranian asset?"

Her mouth had gone dry. "It's vital or I would never ask."

He shook his head, and she hated what

she saw on his face: the disbelief and disappointment. But she pushed on: "NSA isn't making any headway. They're just saying that it's Middle Persian, but we already knew that. And our Farsi expert had emergency surgery . . . I'm positive these are the geo-markers my asset promised me, but he's embedded them in some kind of code."

"Jesus, Vanessa." He tried to press the envelope into her hands, but she backed away.

"We can't afford to waste time while decryption flounders around. You'd do the same, David."

"You're asking me to go outside the bounds of an active operation? Christ. You know what this means —"

"Just take a look."

"No." He dropped the envelope, unopened, on the writing desk. "Do you even care about me? About us? Or is this just about what you can get out of me?"

She stood frozen in place. She knew she was right to ask for his help — she needed his help. But she heard the echo of her own voice, how ruthless she'd sounded.

"I'm sorry, you're right, forget it." She shook her head, a sharp heat flooding through her body. It was hard to meet his eyes. "Let's just get out of here."

At first he said nothing. But after a long moment, eyes cutting away, he shrugged. "I can't. They need me back at the embassy. That was the message I just got."

Was he lying to her? She thought so. He was gathering his shirt and socks. As he walked toward the bathroom, she called to him. "Khoury? You wanted to tell me something earlier. What was it?"

Without turning, he said, "It doesn't matter now, it can wait."

As he closed the bathroom door halfway, Vanessa sat heavily on the edge of the bed. They had moved from strangers to lovers to strangers again. The whole emotional energy of the day had left her weary.

He stepped out of the bathroom, fully dressed, a few beads of water still on his skin and hair where he'd dampened it. She saw the bone-deep exhaustion again, and she felt a pang of fear as she moved toward him. But she stopped when he reached for the envelope containing Arash's code. For a moment Khoury held it between them, and then he slipped it into his pocket. She knew enough not to say a word.

He kissed her coolly on the cheek and then walked out of her hotel room.

TWENTY-NINE

Vanessa returned the prospectus to its folder and set it on her desk. She'd arrived back in Cyprus midday from Cairo, and the trip had left her with a short day and little ability to concentrate on venture-cap deals. For the last ten minutes she'd read the same paragraph a half-dozen times and still couldn't accurately quote the numbers. Her thoughts kept turning obsessively to the memory of Khoury as he walked out of her hotel room.

Now she had five minutes to exit her sixth-floor office if she planned to maintain security and also keep her clandestine meeting with Sergei Tarasov at a safe house in Limassol. She couldn't use her personal vehicle to get to a secret meeting, so an inside officer had a "company" VW waiting for her on the street. She already had the keys, but she needed at least ninety minutes to carry out a surveillance-detection routine.

She couldn't wait to take a good look at

Sergei's financial spreadsheets.

But even as she stood, easing her cotton jacket from the chrome coat hanger, a sharp trill from the red desk phone jarred her back to earth, and she grabbed the handset. "This is Vanessa Pierson."

"Tag! Hallo —"

She pegged the voice on the phone immediately: the German lawyer representing a hot biotech startup in Munich. "*Guten Tag,* Werner. You caught me on my way out the door."

Good at her day job, Vanessa usually enjoyed the intricacies of venture capital, from seed funding to working capital to mezzanine and bridge financing.

Not today — Werner loved the sound of his own voice too much.

Sergei would be gearing up for their meeting and she was taking no chances, unpredictable as he was . . .

With the handset wedged between chin and shoulder, she slid her keys into her bag and grabbed her iPad. "Yes, looking forward to lunch on Wednesday." Already on the move — "I'll e-mail you with time and place" — she almost collided with Michelle, her receptionist, who now stood in the doorway waving her arms, miming that Vanessa had another caller.

Won't give his name, Michelle mouthed. *Very rude!*

"*Perfekt,* Werner. See you in a week." Vanessa clicked off before the lawyer could launch into a lengthy response.

She raised her eyebrows at Michelle. "Yes?"

Now Michelle spoke rapidly, in theatrically hushed tones. "He insists on speaking to you, refuses to give his name or number, and" — she sucked in a quick breath — "he sounds very *Russian.*"

Shit, Sergei. Vanessa produced a practiced smile. "Thank you, Michelle. Put him through. I'll handle it."

She closed the door.

It wouldn't be the first time an asset did something dumb or foolish. After all the trouble to be clandestine, he was calling her on an open line.

"I cannot meet you today," he pronounced before she even finished saying hello. "Something doesn't feel right."

"I'm leaving the office now," she said. "Call me in five on my other line."

Sergei had the contact number for a disposable cell to be used in emergencies.

"*Nyet, nyet, nyet* — tomorrow. I call you."

Then he was gone, and Vanessa replaced the phone in its cradle with exaggerated care. Had something happened, or was Sergei acting paranoid? For a moment she stared at nothing, with the sharp sense she'd just witnessed a cat dangling from a ledge by its claws ten stories up.

Fuck.

THIRTY

With the Dragunov resting snugly on his shoulder in firing position, Pauk frowned as he adjusted the Leopold Mark IV scope to a magnification of 6×. He had stretched himself long and belly-down on the room's heavy dining table. Could he make a clean head shot from this angle? He was beginning to feel at home in the sparsely furnished third-floor condominium across from the Russian's Limassol penthouse. The development was so new the brokers had strung little white, blue, and red triangle-shaped flags across the cul-de-sac. Russian colors, Pauk noted, because wealthy Russians living or vacationing on Cyprus loved this area of the island in particular. Until the latest crisis, they'd loved the banks, too. The flags flapped lazily in the breezes — at about six knots, Pauk gauged — coming from the southwest this afternoon.

Even seen from a distance of five hundred

meters, the bodyguard stank of steroids. The Dragunov's scope caught so much detail Pauk could see the fine red rash peppering the bodyguard's massive, pumped-up body. The kind of child-man who grew bored as soon as no one was looking at him.

But now the bodyguard sucked in his belly, puffing up, and Pauk knew before he had a visual that the Russian boss had entered the room. For a brief time, the two men filled Pauk's sight, and he focused on his target's wide forehead as it danced in and out of view behind the bodyguard. He reminded Pauk of the red-faced Russian commanders at the checkpoints around Urus-Martan and Tangy-Chu, strutting and grinning like vicious dogs. But this Russian still had a few moves. *Cagey,* Madame Desmarais might say. He did not stay long in one place, he kept the bodyguard close by, and, in general, he shied away from glass.

No problem. Pauk was good at lying in wait.

THIRTY-ONE

"We need a team on R/258." Vanessa tipped her head toward the monitor, where Chris Arvanitis stared back, mouth pursed, brows raised, forehead creased in obvious exasperation. Roughly six thousand miles between them, and she could almost smell the stale coffee in his mug, thanks to Headquarters' secure version of FaceTime. He was in his office, door open, and she sensed the energy and bustle of activity surrounding Chris and CPD. She was sticking it out on Cyprus, doing her best to protect her erratic, possibly paranoid Russian asset. She was the one who should be overseeing the options for capturing Bhoot — she had the best shot at predicting his movements, his behavior once he realized he was cornered —

"Come on, Vanessa, you know you've got it."

"He's tipping out of control, sounding

paranoid, and probably has good reason to be."

"Are you telling me you can't handle him?"

Damn. Was that condescension in Chris's voice? "*No* — that's not what I'm saying."

"Good." Chris glanced at his watch, frowning. "Listen, I've got an ops meeting in five. So hear me on this: The closest surveillance team is in Beirut for two more days. So the answer is *yes* — in forty-eight hours."

"That may be too late." Vanessa gnawed the corner of her lip, unable to shake the sense that something bad was on the way. "I'm talking about now."

Chris raised both eyebrows. "Who do you want to call, Batman?"

Thirty-Two

Her thoughts chaotic, Vanessa paced the length of her apartment a half-dozen times, growling at Vasilias each time she passed the kitchen counter where her landlady's fat cat sprawled, eyeing her dubiously. On *MasterChef,* a sweating man in a purple chef's hat inched a tall, pouffe-shaped soufflé from a gleaming silver oven — smiling in triumph until it collapsed. The audience gasped, but Vanessa barely noticed, stabbing her cigarette out in her one and only ashtray — a very small brass dish bought from a vendor in a village on Rhodes; a gift from Khoury.

Which brought to the front of her mind again, still no word from him.

Finally, she stopped trying to deflect the various waves of agitation and frustration, and she retrieved the sketch pad from the drawer of the small drafting table by her office window. She opened the pad to the last page, where she had hidden two charcoal sketches. As she pulled out the pages, Tunisian sand dusted her bare thighs.

The first was a sketch of Khoury when she'd caught him unaware on the beach: leaning back on his right arm, a cigarette in his left hand, hair tousled from salt water, his profile barely visible as he stared out to the horizon.

She'd sketched the second when she found him sleeping in their bed on their last afternoon. As she studied the drawing, she traced her index finger very lightly along the charcoal lines. Her stomach clutched at the worry and fatigue she saw so clearly on his face. How had she missed it then? And what had he wanted to tell her in Cairo?

For minutes she sat with the pad and sketches lying in her lap. These were the only drawings she had of Khoury, and maybe she needed them to reassure her that their relationship was real. It went against protocol to keep personal photographs, although she had a few snapshots locked inside her small safe along with her personal firearm, a FN Five-Seven pistol, her passports, and other irreplaceable documents. Vanessa Pierson's cover identity rarely touched her other lives. But her relationship with David Khoury crossed that boundary, and that made it dangerous.

THIRTY-THREE

The children's bodies blocked her path through the narrow streets of the Kurdish village; at first she thought the kitten was dead, too, but then she saw its eyes were open and it seemed to be watching her expectantly. She reached out, wanting to take the tiny animal into her arms, but someone whispered to her — "Go back to sleep, don't dream of this" — and just then she heard the sound of footsteps and she was on her hands and knees. When she turned, she saw a faceless soldier in the distance. *Help them,* she called out. *Please help them!*

A siren sounded shrilly, but they were coming too late to help.

Vanessa lost the images as a ping from her computer made her bolt from the urgent nightmare up to consciousness.

Groaning, she dragged herself from the chair where she must have fallen asleep.

Dark outside. No sense of time.

She leaned toward the monitor, clicking accept.

"About time," Sid said, as his creased and crinkled face filled the screen.

Vanessa pulled herself straight, skimming strands of loose hair back from her face. The clock on her monitor showed 3:48 — she'd slept only minutes.

Sid stared back at her over the top of an oddly small pair of reading glasses kept around his neck by a lanyard; deep purple circles pooled beneath his bloodshot eyes. Close to sixty, with an oddly luxurious head of Cary Grant hair, it was easy to get that he'd lived hard, traveled wide, and seen it all and then some.

But for a moment Vanessa worried that he wouldn't live to make retirement.

"You don't look so hot yourself," he cracked blandly, reading her too well. "Maybe it's time for that spa vacation."

"Thanks for the tip." She played along, curious and ready for an update on Operation Ghost Hunt, but also wary. Why was he reaching out when almost everyone else at Headquarters had no problem ignoring her? Was he on a fishing expedition? If so, fishing for . . . ?

"My last ex-wife went on and on about

the Silver Door or the Copper Door," Sid said, breaking into her thoughts.

"Think that's the Golden Door, and I'll book it ASAP," she said. "But first, what's the word on the SAD team?" SAD — the Agency's Special Activities Division — had been the first U.S. personnel unit into Afghanistan after 9/11; they'd gone in on horseback. "Are they ready to move as soon as we get the geo-coordinates?" Her speech accelerated as she began asking about the mission, and she was startled when Sid tapped a small yellow notepad against his monitor.

He said, "Forget the op and SAD for the moment. I've been curious about your shooter . . ." He paused to drink something from a coffee cup.

Not coffee, Vanessa was quite certain.

"So I cashed in a couple of chits that I had to use up before their expiration date. I fed the database what we had: MO, sniper, partial tattoo, Chechnya, et cetera." He drank again, this time spilling almost clear liquid down his chin.

She pushed her face close to the screen. "Is this bus going somewhere?"

He looked at her, his Groucho eyebrows twitching. "Smile, darlin', I'm about to make you sing."

"Screw you," she said, but she grinned back at him. Jesus, she had to admit at the moment she was grateful that somebody, *anybody,* seemed happy to see her, even an old-timer like Sid.

"Europol has an open file, could be your shooter, your Chechen, and if it is, they can connect him to at least three other hits."

Vanessa's pulse kicked up, and suddenly Sid didn't seem like such an old-timer.

He pushed his reading glasses up on his nose, glancing at what she guessed were his notes. "Spring 2011. The murder of a Spanish prosecutor who was going after two smugglers involved in black nukes probably linked to guess who?"

"Bhoot," Vanessa murmured, "I remember that one . . ."

"Well, you might. The unfortunate prosecutor was shot in the open — outside the Gaudi in Barcelona. The date on this one is interesting: April first."

Vanessa's mouth turned down. "April Fools' Day . . ."

"April first, and as you probably know, Vanessa, April 1, 1939, also happens to mark the end of the Spanish Civil War." Sid pinched the bridge of his nose, and his glasses slid even lower so he looked like a mad professor. "Then, two months later,

June third, they're pretty sure he was in Moscow at the same time an engineer working at Sverdlovsk-forty-five was assassinated in front of his residence, I'm tracking down various ballistics reports — but for two of these, the round was the 7.62×54R — the *R* standing for Russian — 168-grain, hollow-point boat tail. The Russian-made Dragunov, a lethal, very effective sniper rifle, uses this bullet." Sid's mouth pulled wide. "The utter casualness after each kill impresses me as absolutely chilling. And — *get this* — apparently some kids actually saw the shooter *walking* away. He matches the basic description for your Chechen, except one of the kids said he had huge canines . . ."

But Vanessa didn't register Sid's attempt at punctuated levity — Sverdlovsk-45 was one of Russia's major nuclear weapons assembly/disassembly facilities. "Any theory why the engineer was a target?"

"Seems he was selling stolen components as a sideline. And it looks like he might've been snitching to the Brits for more pocket change, although our cousins won't confirm or deny."

"You said at least *three* hits," Vanessa prompted.

"Hold your horses . . . eighteen October,

2012. Dutch officer in MIVD investigating black-market procurement, and he was killed on the grounds of the Van Gogh Museum, Amsterdam. If he's your Chechen, he took one kill shot, mid-range, and then he walked out cool as a cucumber. He's good. Precise. Enjoys his work."

Vanessa sat still, absorbing the wealth of new information. Sid had provided surprisingly detailed intel from another agency. And Europol was just as territorial as any other law enforcement and intelligence agency. She still felt grateful to Sid — but she definitely still felt wary. Call her paranoid . . .

Sensing his rising curiosity, she nodded. "Thanks for this," she said softly.

Sid rubbed his temples, his eyes meeting hers, weirdly enlarged by the lenses. "Listen, Vanessa, Europol would love to pin no less than a *dozen* other hits on this shooter, if they could track him down. Definitely not someone you want on your trail."

THIRTY-FOUR

Pauk settled back in the recliner as Lyon kicked off against Marseille on the condo owner's massive flat-screen. From here, in the most recessed corner of the living room, he could still see the Russian's penthouse clearly, and for the past three hours things had become very quiet.

He sipped a can of mineral water through the first half of the game and the movement and the energy on-screen soothed him. He'd had word from his mentor — one more day to finish up this job and get off the island. There would be another job very soon.

Pauk never questioned how his mentor knew so much — information came cheap, and everyone had his price. But he also knew, this time, they were working against the clock.

Pauk would be busy for the next ten days, but then he would take time off. He could afford to vacation anywhere in the world.

But he would probably spend his time with Madame Desmarais and *les chats,* enjoying *fútbol.* He found her company surprisingly tolerable.

He pictured his mentor's last text: this time leave no loose ends.

THIRTY-FIVE

Vanessa sprawled on her back on the weathered metal chaise longue on the rooftop patio, the dark heavens spilling out above Nicosia. At this liminal time between deep night and dawn, the neighborhood was mostly quiet. Even so, as minutes passed, night sounds rose up from the streets: tinny strands of music; a voice echoing, then gone; the faint rumble of an engine; the strangled songs of feral tomcats.

She closed her eyes, kept them closed, letting the darkness blanket her mind.

Gradually the shapes began to appear: oceans and seas and continents — filled in with the imagined stroke of brush, water, and pigment. Next came the mountain ranges, vast lakes, primary rivers; and finally the countries and major cities. Just as they did when she was a child, a military kid tagging after her big brother, tacking world maps to the prefab walls of her latest bedroom. And when she was tall enough, she tacked the maps over her bed, so she could lie back and stare up at the world.

Friends made, friends left. Teachers. Rivals. Boyfriends. Mentors.

But these days, her world, her life, was marked by terrorist activities and black-market weapons-procurement networks — names, players, events, locations, intel, operations — all etched to memory.

Mentally she added the latest pins:

Her Iranian asset murdered in Vienna.

A Spanish arms dealer murdered in Barcelona.

A dead Russian engineer suspected of spying for the Brits.

A Dutch intelligence officer assassinated in Amsterdam.

Whether or not her Chechen shooter was the ghost's minion — and she was more and more certain he was — he was killing off players in the world of procurement.

Suggesting Bhoot's reach was very wide indeed.

Vanessa pulled herself to sitting, and she wrapped her arms around herself, suddenly chilled. One more day and she'd have the protection team on Sergei.

THIRTY-SIX

The muted, disembodied voice announced the imminent boarding of Lufthansa's flight 2227 nonstop from Paris to Cairo as David Khoury set a crisp twenty-euro banknote on the kiosk counter.

He felt the intensity of the clerk's gaze and met it. Very young, very pretty. North African, he guessed — with a discreet faux-diamond piercing one dark brow.

She smiled as she slid the red pack of Gauloises across the glass. *"Vous avez des beaux yeux."*

Pocketing the cigarettes, Khoury smiled back. He shrugged, feigning bemusement.

With deliberate slowness, she counted out his change. Her slender hands made him think of Vanessa in Cairo — the heat and fierceness of her fingers against his bare skin. A memory defined by sharply perceptive desire and grief.

He held his palm open, but the clerk kept

him waiting. *"Vous partez déjà?"* Did he really have to leave now?

He'd spent the past twenty-four hours in Paris, traveling as Canadian businessman Michael Aubuchon, tracking down a skittish French-Lebanese asset who traveled frequently to South Lebanon's border district — the front line for the next war between Hezbollah and Israel. A war Khoury and many others believed would come soon.

"Vous devez rester à Paris . . ." She placed her hands on her hips, her eyes brightly innocent.

The second announcement of the Lufthansa flight's imminent departure sounded smoothly above the general hum of Terminal One. Khoury slid his hand into the pocket of his gray slacks, encountering the edge of his boarding ticket — and with it, a realization.

With an effort, he refocused on the girl. His look of regret was real but not meant for her. He couldn't shake the image of Vanessa, her blue eyes turned almost black as she asked for his help. Eyes like faceted stones: from one angle, tough enough to cut glass; from another angle, fragile. She had a depth of vulnerability she couldn't admit to herself.

He found his voice, "*La prochaine fois.* I'm sorry, there is somewhere I have to be."

He stepped out of the kiosk, turning toward his gate, walking quickly now, with deliberate strides. The line of passengers inched forward, snaking toward the jet bridge. The flight would depart on time, and Khoury would make his first meeting at the embassy in Cairo.

But only if he actually boarded.

As he reached the gate, he hoisted his carry-on bag higher on his shoulder and kept walking. He would help Vanessa — and no doubt buy himself more trouble in the process. But the thought crossed his mind: Could he actually be in any more trouble than the shit that was already falling on him at Headquarters? So, *what the hell,* why not push back a bit and help out his lover, too? Which created a new problem: what excuse to give the Station when he didn't return on his expected flight? Station management would be apoplectic if he simply failed to show on his scheduled flight.

He needed to buy himself twenty-four hours . . .

A ferocious case of twenty-four-hour flu?

He moved quickly away from the gate toward the escalator and the RER, the commuter train that would take him to Gare du

Nord and the Chunnel. With luck he would make London in less than three hours and Oxford in four.

A racy red Alpha darted past Khoury's rented Mini Cooper on the M40 motorway, eighty kilometers of roadway from London to Oxford. On another day, he might feel very frustrated that he was stuck in his Mini, carrying out a thorough SDR. But today, his thoughts kept circling back to Vanessa and the risk she'd asked him to take. If her asset hadn't been murdered in front of her, Khoury wouldn't be headed to Oxford — Vanessa never would have crossed that line; he was sure of that. He pictured the flowing curves of the Middle Persian script of code covering the page now tucked into a paperback copy of *Bitter Lemons of Cyprus* by Lawrence Durrell. En route from Egypt to France and now England, he'd stored the paper in his shoe — between sole and insole — until he moved it thirty minutes ago in the privacy of the rental car. Middle Persian or Pahlavi, yes, and probably related to some archaic verse. But that was as far as Khoury could take it, so he was on his way to Oxford to meet with a man he thought might have an answer.

His eyes cut to his rearview mirror, tracking vehicles. These days, he couldn't shake the constant sense that he was being watched.

THIRTY-SEVEN

Inside the small, dark lecture hall, Professor Shahrokh Mokri's deep voice seemed to dance with the consonants and vowels of New Persian as he read from the poet Rumi's *Masnavi-I Ma'navi.*

Khoury stood listening intently, watching from the back of the hall. Closing his eyes for a moment, he let Mokri and Rumi lead him to memories of childhood visits to Lebanon and hours at the beaches outside Beirut. The Mokris and Fadi and Sabah Khoury met while teaching in London in the 1980s. Neighbors in faculty housing, they remained friends, and, in 2000, when Mokri's wife died, Khoury's parents offered Mokri safe haven in their Boston area home. But Khoury hadn't seen Mokri in at least three years, and he was startled by the obvious changes — too thin, his tall frame hunched at the shoulders.

Mokri's star had risen on both academic

and literary horizons. When it came to speaking honestly about Iran, Mokri's beloved homeland, he was as vocal with his criticism as with his praise. His outspokenness had earned him formidable enemies. Khoury knew about the death threats, the chatter on extremist websites, falling just shy of a full-out fatwa.

Khoury gritted his teeth at the thought of asking Mokri for help. A flash of anger surfaced — at Vanessa for putting him at risk, yes, but also at himself for extending the danger on her behalf. He didn't like that he was pulling a trusted family friend into his CIA world.

The rising lights along with the rustle and hum of conversations in myriad languages drew Khoury back. With a bit of amazement, he watched the students gathering their books and papers — Indian, Chinese, African, female — not the old-boys' club at all. A good handful of them clustered around their professor, waiting for their chance to ask questions.

Khoury stood while exiting students streamed past him. Only one or two showed any curiosity at his presence, the rest caught up in their lives and their conversations. A line floated past him from the lips of a young Asian woman: "Rumi *is* and *always will be* the iconic Persian poet."

Mokri talked patiently with the students, never glancing up from the front of the hall. Teaching was an honorable profession — but Mokri's brilliance was wasted on these students, Khoury thought.

Finally, the last of the students were clearing out. Mokri gathered up his briefcase, and Khoury readied himself to intercept his old acquaintance.

A young Indian man chose Khoury's aisle to exit the hall. As he passed Khoury, he glanced up briefly, handing him a folded paper.

Khoury's eyebrows rose slightly. But then he turned and followed the boy out, opening the single page in dappled sunlight: *30 minutes, north bank, Folly Bridge.*

THIRTY-EIGHT

Khoury arrived first, highly alert, his affect belied by the casual way he pushed his hands into the pockets of his jacket and slouched a bit beneath a dark brown baseball cap and behind aviator sunglasses.

In February and May, this stretch of the River Thames, known as the Isis, would be filled with college rowing crews competing in the two annual regattas. Now the boathouses were fairly quiet, and strollers and joggers on both the north and south bank seemed to have agreed on a somewhat lazy pace. Khoury paid particular attention to a very British-looking mum pushing a pram in his direction and a bird watcher on the opposite bank. Both he and Mokri were potential targets for surveillance.

Restless after thirty-five minutes, Khoury felt a rush of relief when Mokri emerged from between the elms lining a narrow side trail. The men did not greet each other.

Instead, Mokri turned away from the bridge, following the path upriver, his gait slow enough to allow Khoury to catch up with ease.

They continued, side by side, Khoury watchful and sensing Mokri's constant vigilance. No sign of the bird watcher or the mum or anyone else particularly suspicious. But Khoury startled when a large bird took flight from its nest at the edge of the Isis.

As it disappeared in flight over the trees, Mokri spoke softly. "How are your mother and father? Sadeeqy Fadi? And Sabah?"

"They are well. They speak of you often. *Salam Agha-ye Mokri.*" Khoury pressed his palms together, offering the Farsi saying of hospitality, *"Ghadamet rooyeh cheshm."*

"Khayli mamnoon." Mokri smiled. "Your mother still receives grants and support for her elegant poetry?"

"Yes. She just received word that she has been nominated for the Witter Bynner Fellowships." Khoury knew that Mokri admired his mother a great deal. In fact, although the scholar would never admit to himself such improper feelings, Khoury believed the professor had always been a little bit in love with Sabah.

"I dream often of her *kibbet batata.*" Mokri's eyes twinkled and, for a moment, he looked much as Khoury remembered him from so many years ago. "And her baklava . . ."

"She makes her *kibbet batata* often on Fridays. A wise day to visit."

"It is good to see you, Dawood," Mokri said, calling Khoury by his Arabic given name. "But you do not look happy."

"I need to ask for your help."

"And this is the source of your unhappiness?" Mokri's graying eyebrows arched quizzically.

Khoury met his gaze intently. "This is not official. It's a favor."

"I am always happy to return a favor. I am eternally indebted to your family."

"It is a very dangerous favor I am asking, *Agha-ye Mokri.*" Khoury's eyes flicked over the runner approaching on their side of the river: worn running shoes, sweatpants, All Souls T-shirt. As the man passed, Khoury could hear the clean, strong rhythm of his breathing. "I know about the death threats. I know you are in a very sensitive position, a guest in England . . ."

Mokri veered slowly toward a bench sheltered beneath the limbs of a weeping willow. He sat, and Khoury joined him. A man on the south bank was leash-walking a nervous, gangling spaniel, both of them tangled together at the moment.

"That will never stop me from helping dear friends," Mokri said.

Khoury felt another twinge of anger as he placed the paperback copy of *Bitter Lemons of Cyprus* between them on the bench. Mokri looked straight ahead, not even glancing at the book's cover. "A few years back, if I remember correctly, there was a special young woman. Are you still seeing her?"

Khoury frowned, hesitating too long. Remembering suddenly how his mother had often teased the professor about his sixth sense. "Yes," he said finally. "We see each other when we can."

Mokri, in his silence, seemed to understand more than he should.

Khoury's eyes followed the man and the dog as they moved out of sight.

"So what are you leaving me?" Mokri asked finally.

"An inscription. Middle or classical Persian."

"From?"

Khoury smiled ruefully, shrugging his shoulders. "I thought you might be able to help answer that question."

"A puzzle, then," Mokri said. "I do enjoy puzzles." He smiled, and his face transformed for that instant, back to a better time. "You remember your lessons well, young Dawood."

Khoury trapped his lower lip between his teeth. He owned a certain fatalism about the risk he was taking on — a fatalism he'd come to believe might be part of the DNA of all Middle Eastern people. But honor made it impossible to put Mokri at risk without sufficient warning. "If anyone were to find out about this — if it gets into the wrong hands —"

"I've learned my lessons, too, Dawood, and I understand the risks," Mokri said, turning his face away. "Give me one day at least." Mokri's voice was almost inaudible now. "Where can I safely reach you?"

"A number, page one hundred seventy-seven." Khoury stood, pushing his hands deep into his pockets. Just before he turned to walk away, he said, "Be careful, my friend."

"*Enshallah.*" Mokri's smile made Khoury ache.

THIRTY-NINE

On the south bank, Harring, walking his wife's cocker spaniel pup, stubbed out his cigarette with care. Rita, his seven-year-old daughter, would bite his head off if she knew he smoked. But much worse would be littering!

At least Churchill had gotten over his puppy diarrhea. Harring was sick of taking jabs from his fellow spooks at Thames House.

He raised his tiny camera again, zooming in to photograph both men a final time. Identifying the professor was no problem. He had a massive archive on the old man — just two weeks ago there had been a flurry of new death threats against Great Britain's honored Iranian guest.

But the other, younger man — Middle Eastern, early thirties, tall, slender; Harring had jotted the descriptors in his notebook. Still, all his shots had more hat, shades, and

214

five-o'clock shadows than anything helpful. But one shot had been halfway decent — the younger man just beginning to walk away and the book he'd left behind on the bench. In his line of work, Harring had quickly learned, a book is never just a book.

Late that afternoon, Harring ran the photograph through the surveillance database and discovered the match — the man photographed with Mokri was David Khoury, Lebanese American, a credited third secretary at the U.S. embassy in Cairo. He was also suspected CIA.

Within an hour, Harring had discovered that Mokri and Khoury had crossed paths before, in Beirut and in Boston, where Mokri stayed as a guest of Khoury's parents. So they had multiple, mundane connections. But why was Mokri meeting with suspected CIA now?

And they *did* pass a book.

And the body language was just a bit off . . .

Adding up to enough so he flagged the file and made certain his Director-General — Alexandra Hall — had it on her desk.

FORTY

Grateful for the baseball hat shading her face from Nicosia's strong midday sun, Vanessa jogged in place at a street corner until a car cleared the intersection. Only minutes into her half-hour run, she was already dripping with sweat. The car passed, and she launched into her run again, setting her sights on the top of the next hill, accessed by a narrow street in an old residential neighborhood. As she matched her breath with the rhythm of her feet hitting flagstone, she picked out small details from the private homes, each butting up against the next so they seemed to form one solid wall of pastel rainbows. It was a lovely street on one of her favorite running routes — a route she didn't repeat often. But today she couldn't find the usual pleasure, because her mind was caught up with Sergei and the sense that he would call very soon. How crazy would he be today?

■ ■ ■ ■

A crash, a woman's cry. Sergei froze inside his study. Only for an instant, and then he dropped his cell phone onto the desk, yanked the drawer open, gripped his loaded Makarov, finger on the trigger.

"*Vse ponyatno,* boss —"

At the all-clear from Olaf, his bodyguard, Sergei peered out into the living area of his penthouse. The maid, a tiny woman in a pink uniform, stared dolefully at shattered crystal now covering the marble floor, all that remained of the Swarovski vase she'd demolished. A melancholy Olaf stood just a few feet from the maid.

Sergei eyed him sharply. Then, with a controlled breath, he shut the door. Olaf was trustworthy but sometimes a bit dull. Still, Sergei couldn't imagine replacing him, so Olaf would be on board, along with his daughter and several of her school friends, when Sergei sailed his yacht out of Cyprus later that day. Sergei's gut snarled that it was time — time to get off the island, time to lay low and protect his family.

He stared down at the pistol. It felt cool and satisfying in his grip. He pushed it into the black leather document bag, a gift from his wife, Zoya, purchased at Harrods. A Raf somebody, she'd said, as if that explained all. Knowing Zoya, she'd spent at least five hundred pounds on it, maybe a thousand. She wasn't a bad wife, just boring. But she heard things, kept her ears open, and spoiled the twins, Anya and Valentin. Their son's latest fiasco, a Moscow Yauza street-racing disaster. The Porsche 911 Turbo transformed into twisted metal and abandoned while Valentin limped away to his favorite after-hours club.

It was Zoya who warned Sergei to take extra precautions because she had a bad feeling — *Remember what happened to Litvinenko.*

And Sergei did, all too clearly. The poor bastard was poisoned with radiation.

For an instant, the black heat churned in his belly. How he hated the men who bought and sold Russia, men who would kill their own mothers.

"Rossiya-Matushka," Sergei muttered.

He strode to the wall behind the desk and carefully lifted a small Kandinsky canvas from the wall. He ran his thick fingers quickly over the previously hidden digital pad inset in the wall. A soft click, and he opened the customized safe. He slid out one of five mahogany trays, removing only a thumb drive. He concealed it inside the zipper compartment of Zoya's bag. Already, the bag was heavy from the Makarov.

A package that should make the hungry American spy very happy.

He closed the safe, entered the locking code, and repositioned the small abstract oil painting so that it was perfectly framed. For several seconds, Sergei let his eyes, his soul, dive into Wassily's image: a dark galaxy where richly colored "planets" orbited the vastness of space, a balance that confounded him with its delicate chaos.

Pauk pulled himself to attention in his seat behind the steering wheel of the Fiat. The Russian was on the move. Minutes before, the muscle-bound bodyguard had appeared on the deck of the penthouse, just as he had done twice yesterday, strutting around with his holstered Sig. Revealing his boss's routines. Might as well post a neon sign: *We're going somewhere in the Mercedes!*

Pauk glanced at his watch at the same time he turned the key in the Fiat's ignition. A throaty rumble as it sparked to life. He'd parked one street over from the penthouse, on a slight rise, where he had a clear visual horizon.

The heavy garage door began its slow rise.

219

Pauk watched now through the scope. Sure enough, out rolled the black armored Mercedes SUV. From the quality of the ride, the tension on the shocks, Pauk had gauged it fortified with two extra tons of metal, ranking it close to NIJ-IV standards. It would provide some protection against armor-piercing bullets.

Windows darkly tinted, the driver not even a shadow behind the wheel, the Mercedes cruised out of the cul-de-sac. He sensed his target in the backseat, directly behind the driver. Pauk shifted the idling Fiat into gear, following, staying parallel to the other vehicle. He kept the windows open just a few fingers' widths, the air-conditioning off, to maintain connection with his target. The hot, dry air outside held still, unmoved by even light breezes.

As the Fiat dogged the Mercedes north through the city, Pauk maintained a comfortable distance between his vehicle and the Russian's. They were heading for the now-familiar A1, a straight sixty-kilometer shot to Nicosia. If the Russian planned to drive beyond Nicosia, they would pass through the Metehan border checkpoint, crossing from the Republic of Cyprus to the TRNC, or Turkish Republic of Northern Cyprus.

Sure enough, forty-five minutes later, Pauk caught his first glimpse of the metal canopy of Metehan up ahead. And the beginning of the line of vehicles, bicycles, and pedestrians.

Yesterday, the Russian had arranged to depart the island on his fifty-one-meter yacht, the *Anastasiya.* Pauk had witnessed every tedious minute. It didn't take high-tech gear to get most information — a simple phone call to the Limassol Marina, inquiring about a berth to accommodate a fifty-five-meter yacht. "Berths of that size are limited of course," the woman had told him, "but you're in luck, one opens up tomorrow."

Pauk slowed the Fiat to join the checkpoint queue.

The Russian imagined this to be his last day on the island. *Actually,* Pauk thought, without any particular emotion, *it will be your last day in this life,* Barany, *old goat.*

FORTY-ONE

Vanessa broke stride, tugging the vibrating burn phone from the pocket of her sports capris. *Sergei.* Breathing hard from her run, she stared down at the screen: *New text message.*

Her body tensed. What would he throw at her now? She brushed the sleeve of her sweatshirt across her forehead, licking salt from her lips. She rubbed one hand against her hip, feeling the keys to the VW. Even her fingers were sweating.

She nudged the screen prompt impatiently with her thumb, scanning the message:

queens window 1315

Damn!
She hit reply.

hold off!

Even as she pressed send, she began jogging in the direction of her apartment. She would cut back to pick up the Station's VW — but only after she retrieved her Five-Seven pistol from the lockbox in her office. She didn't believe for a moment that Sergei would comply with her orders to hold off. After all that had happened, she wasn't meeting with a reckless asset without carrying protection. *She would deal with the fallout if she had to, but after Vienna, she wasn't taking any chances.*

Pauk grunted softly as the Russian's Mercedes followed the roundabout, accelerating onto the highway. He checked his iPad's GPS, and Google Earth opened automatically, recognizing his location. As he drove, he identified upcoming exits on the map. The closest, an access road, led into the mountains through a Turkish military base, and, beyond that, it reached a dead end at a landmark: Saint Hilarion, Crusader castle.

Within fifteen minutes of receiving Sergei's message, Vanessa nodded casually at the checkpoint guard as he handed back her passport. Acutely aware of the pistol tucked under her seat, she rolled forward onto Turkish-controlled land, revving internally, grateful for the relatively short line of cars.

Sweat dripped down her ribs beneath her T-shirt, but she ignored it. On the most uneventful day, border control was frustrating, but today it was torture.

When she'd first arrived on Cyprus, a friend showing her the ropes had summed it up: "The Turks and the Greeks hate each other, but they've gotten used to all this."

Another two minutes and Vanessa guided the VW onto the highway, speeding north toward Saint Hilarion and the Queen's Window. She hated that Sergei had cut himself off, disregarding instructions, calling shots on his own. At least he'd picked a fairly remote location, a famous Crusader castle on the island's Turkish side. She'd been to the tourist landmark almost ten years ago while visiting Cyprus on her honeymoon with her ex-husband, Jonah. A short-lived, ill-considered marriage in response to the emotional turmoil following her father's death.

Normally, her ops tradecraft would have been spotless — driving a rental car, following SDR, and meeting in a contained environment. She could usually at least control these aspects of the clandestine meeting, if not the asset himself. Well, this time she'd managed to salvage one out of three. Unfortunately, there was no time for SDR, and

Sergei had chosen the environment. The highway rose toward the stark, jagged Five Finger Mountains to the north.

Damn it, Sergei, if you let me do my job, I might be able to keep you safe.

Pauk could see nothing beyond the slow, belching bus, but so far, there had been no possible exits from the highway. So unless the Russian's Mercedes had suddenly turned into a spaceship, he was still just ahead of Pauk.

Behind the Fiat, a line of vehicles stretched several miles on the congested highway. A flagman wearing an orange hazard vest waved the cars onward.

As if there was anywhere else to go, Pauk thought, nosing his Fiat toward the cloud of bus exhaust.

"B'lyad!" Olaf punched the leather steering wheel with the heel of his hand, honking at the crawling line of vehicles ahead.

Sergei, in the passenger seat, snorted. Here he was in his $500,000 Mercedes, stuck behind an ancient truck filled with sheep! *Such was life,* he thought, shaking his head sadly. *Come prepared with the latest S600 Guard and God sticks you behind barnyard animals.*

He was glad to soon be rid of the burden of working with the Americans, at least for a while. For years now he'd kept a sharp eye on currency transfers through his bank, paying special attention to accounts exhibiting suspicious patterns.

There were rumors of a very powerful and ruthless man who ruled over the international arms black market, and Sergei knew his American spy and her CIA wanted to get their hands on him.

Well, I, Sergei Tarasov, might be handing the devka *just what she wants so desperately.*

Sergei glanced at the black bag near his feet. He'd been in banking long enough to see when clients were trying to hide something, and he knew the American forensic accountants and investigators who tracked daily transactions worldwide through SWIFT — well they would be able to follow the trail into places he could not.

There are always more thieves — catch one and another takes his place. But at least I can do my part to bring down one.

Vanessa kept her eye on the continuous line of traffic snaking uphill in the distance. She could just make out the point where vehicles were beginning to break away and pick up speed. As far as she could gauge, she had another eight to ten minutes before the logjam eased. She also knew she would reach the access road to Saint Hilarion at just about the same time. She could try to make up time, but the road — twisty, narrow, and rough — traversed a Turkish military base. Not the place to attract unwelcome attention.

FORTY-TWO

Glowering so intently at the cloud of black diesel smoke enveloping the Mercedes, Olaf almost missed the turnoff. But Sergei yelled to him that he should turn, and, at the last minute, Olaf managed to cut hard onto the smaller, rougher access road. For the next kilometer, the Mercedes shuddered across ruts and washboard gravel, the road rising, twisting, and narrowing.

After they'd traveled most of three kilometers, Sergei saw the large black-and-white signs designating the beginning of a no-stopping zone. Here, trucks and jeeps from a Turkish military convoy haphazardly lined the road. Near a makeshift village of scattered cottages, Turkish soldiers in camouflage, packing weapons, clustered in small groups, smoking cigarettes or just kicking dirt. Judging from their bored, stupid expressions, it was an exercise. This time they are only playacting at war and terror,

Sergei thought.

He glanced down again at the black bag. Perhaps it would have been wise to hide it in the security compartment of the Mercedes. Too late to second-guess himself.

A sharp report sliced the morning stillness. Then another. Then continuous — the unmistakable din of gunfire. Sergei's heart stammered, reacting as if he'd been caught on a street in Moscow ducking a burst of semiautomatic fire. That's how it had been back in the 1990s, when so many died. Even now, knowing the gunfire was almost certainly the product of a military drill, instinct screamed at him to have Olaf speed off the road and take cover. With trembling hands he reached for the pack of cigarettes tucked into the Mercedes's ashtray. Hopefully those stupid *sukas* were aiming *away* from the road!

A dusty beige Fiat raced past, and Sergei pushed up his chin in an ugly gesture. "*B'lyad!* What's your hurry? Eventually we all end up in the same place!"

Pauk passed a landmark sign, and he slowed the Fiat on the approach to the castle. From this distance, it reminded him of the castle at Disneyland Paris.

So the Russian was meeting someone,

because he certainly wasn't sightseeing.

And Pauk was arriving just minutes ahead of his target. No way to select the best location for a kill shot. He would just have to improvise.

Was the Russian's associate here already? No way to know.

Pauk counted sixteen tourist vehicles parked along the road and at the dead end near the visitors' center. He nosed the Fiat around the curve and braked facing the direction he'd just traveled.

Get in, get the job done, get out.

He opened his door to the stutter of gunfire echoing from the surrounding mountains. A few tourists stopped and craned their necks or peered around anxiously. But most visitors, like Pauk, ignored the noise.

Outside the car, he hitched his satchel easily over one shoulder. No one would guess he was packing the disassembled body of his customized Dragunov sniper rifle along with the Mark IV scope and the suppressor. The hollow-point rounds fit in a special ankle holster he had designed for efficiency and easy concealment. In twenty seconds he could assemble or disassemble his weapon — in the dark, in frigid temperatures, in drenching rain. He glanced back to the road, scanning for a first view of the Russian's black SUV.

Walking briskly for about fifteen meters, Pauk stopped to quickly study the tourist map posted outside the visitors' center. It revealed the layout of the thousand-year-old castle: ramparts, restored buildings, and ruins. A primary trail led up the mountain to the middle and upper wards, barracks, chapel, and the royal apartments. A secondary trail cut through a tunnel, offering an alternate, longer route. There were other tributaries. A tower marked the distant apex of the mountain.

Where was the Russian heading? He wore his fat like a wintering bear. Certainly not to the tower at the top.

A group of old women in hiking boots walked ahead of Pauk. They carried cases and easels. *Artists,* he thought, knowing that his sharply opinionated landlady, Madame Desmarais, would add *"Amateurs!"* He tugged his green cap low over his face, joining, and soon passing, the group. He would find a place to watch and wait, and then he would track the Russian.

Almost without any conscious effort, his mind had already factored wind speed and direction, egress — and soon it would add the effect of distance and visibility. Calculations he would check on the Mark IV's MILDOT reticle in order to choose the most efficient point for the shot.

He glanced down the trail toward the parking area. Ah, yes, the Russian had brought his old-dog bodyguard, and they were both headed toward the same trail where Pauk now walked.

Sergei gazed up the craggy slope at the ruins of the castle and sighed. Olaf strode ahead on the trail, but already Sergei needed to stop to catch his breath. Sweat trickled between his shoulder blades. Where had Sergei the Strong gone? He would have to get back to his training again — those eight-mile runs in the morning before the heat. Yes, when this was over . . .

He'd been puzzled at first by the handful of people scattered among the rocks and tough vegetation. Then he realized they must be artists, painting this formidable landscape. He would like to try his hand at painting the castle someday, when he could finally leave his family business to younger, stronger men.

He'd chosen to meet the American at the Queen's Window because, on an off day like this, he reasoned traffic would be light, hikers would be lazy. But it was too far up the mountain. It had seemed much closer when he'd brought his son here three years ago.

There were some who might condemn Sergei as a traitor. But those same men had sold Russia for scrap, and now they were dividing up the spoils among themselves. He dug his hand into the bag, his fingers grazing the cool, smooth body of the Makarov. At least they would never call Sergei Tarasov a coward.

Forty-Three

At 1321 — already six minutes behind Sergei's abruptly appointed meeting time — Vanessa accelerated the VW along the final approach to the castle and the foreboding sight of upthrust granite and the ancient stone fortress sheltered within and among the rugged scarps.

She slowed as she entered the parking area far below Saint Hilarion's highest tower — passing a beige Fiat 500 that could have been the car driven by her pursuer on the old highway. But then she noticed a second Fiat, this one yellow and white, and she reminded herself just what a common make and model it was, especially on the island.

She pulled the VW parallel to a battered Peugeot, braked, and then backed neatly into one of the few parking spaces left in the lot — already sliding her FN Five-Seven from beneath her seat. This time, she wasn't taking any chances.

Where the hell is your SUV, Sergei?

She secured the pistol in her waistband and stepped out into full sun, heat rising off the pavement in waves. Tugged the brim of her navy blue baseball hat over her sunglasses, scanning the parking area and the surrounding hillsides. No sign of Sergei outside the restored gatehouse, the only entrance between otherwise impenetrable Byzantine walls.

No Sergei anywhere in sight.

Was it fitting that he'd chosen a Crusader redoubt, a last stronghold for the armies of the faithful as they prepared to invade the Holy Land and rid it of infidels?

She walked quickly toward the gatehouse, sucking in a breath as she passed Sergei's black Mercedes obscured between a touring van and a bright green BMW with bicycles mounted on the roof. As far as she could discern through the tinted windows, his vehicle was empty.

A light, warm breeze scuffed across the rocky outcropping where Pauk lay prone with his rifle behind a knobby pine. From his vantage point, roughly four hundred meters off the trail, and six hundred meters from the large, ornate window opening, he had a view of the main trail leading to the royal apartments. He'd watched the Russian bodyguard take point for a good half-kilometer while his boss huffed his way among ruins. When the bodyguard reached the royal gallery — several minutes ahead of his boss — he quickly scouted the various apartments before returning to the main gallery, clearly keeping a watchful eye.

Making it easy for Pauk to choose his hide.

When the Russian had finally reached the royal gallery, he headed straight for the ornate Queen's Window — and Pauk almost pulled off a shot. Was the Russian stupid enough to choose the most open spot in these ruins for a clandestine meeting?

But the Russian's luck held this once — saved by the half-dozen painting students passing through with their easels. And when the Russian found no one waiting, he scurried back through the apartments to peer down the mountain and the trails, presumably looking for his associate.

But now the artists were gone and the Russian had turned around again, and he was on his way back to the Queen's Window. His bodyguard, taking cover with his pistol tucked ready inside his jacket, alternately tracked his boss and scrutinized the surrounding ruins and hills, his gaze crawling over Pauk more than once.

Pauk's long fingers moved unerringly along the scope of the Dragunov. A wasp hovered, darting toward his face. He remained oblivious even as a snake as long as his rifle slithered within arm's reach.

The Russian disappeared into one of the common rooms surrounding the gallery. Fifty paces until he reached the window and appeared within its carved frames. Pauk anticipated the moment the Russian would peek out at the view of the distant Mediterranean, a rippling sheet of blue — an irresistible vista.

Through the precision scope, he saw the Russian's shadow before he saw him. Saw his fist pressing possessively against the black leather bag he carried. Saw the Makarov in his other hand.

He eased the scope upward until he had a bead between the Russian's eyes.

Energy coursed through Pauk, just grazing the tips of his fingers onto the trigger at the same instant the Russian tripped and stumbled out of sight.

FORTY-FOUR

A distant volley of shots broke the hot stillness of the day, and Vanessa winced internally.

Part of the exercise she'd seen on her way through the Turkish military zone?

She stepped onto pavement, hesitating in front of a prominent sign displaying a map of accessible trails leading up and through the sprawling castle ruins — including the 732-meter summit and Prince John Tower. She remembered that the Queen's Window was located in the middle ward, in the large gallery near the royal apartments. Although there were several spurs, a main trail crisscrossed the grounds, ruins, and restored sections, eventually traversing the high, formidable walls erected in the twelfth century.

She stared up at the stone fortress; against the hard cobalt sky, the ramparts seemed to grow organically from the harsh, rocky hillside. She took a moment to grind the soles of her running shoes against granite to shed grime and then passed under the shadow of the parapets onto castle grounds. She moved quickly, but not so quickly that she would alarm the smattering of midweek visitors. The pistol pressed uncomfortably against her ribs.

She picked up the pace, jogging lightly past the stables where crusading soldiers had garrisoned with their horses in the lower ward. She scanned the visible portion of the trail ahead: a group of college-age students, two elderly women setting up easels near a second gatehouse, and a heavy-set man busily filming his sunburned wife or girlfriend. Vanessa had to cross another hundred meters of steepening grade before she'd reach the first buildings of the middle ward.

Pauk stretched long in his hide, viewing through the scope the ruins of what had once been royal apartments, fingers itchy. He had his target and the bodyguard to deal with now, and whomever else they were meeting. Of course, more tourists would amble up the path soon. He grunted, a rare expression of his impatience. Time to finish the job.

And fate cooperated. The Russian lumbered toward the window. Pauk inhaled, then paused his breath and squeezed his finger gently . . .

This time the Russian did not trip. The bullet hit him between the eyes, and he fell back against the blood-spattered stone pillar. The panicked bodyguard fired off a wild shot, and it went so wide, so high, Pauk didn't even blink. He watched as the dead Russian — who had somehow remained eerily upright — crumpled to earth.

Echoing off rock, the ruler-slap report of a rifle split the air and Vanessa flinched.

Long-range suppressed semiautomatic?

And now she lengthened her stride so she was running hard uphill, passing the students, one of whom was pointing excitedly across the canyon to a military convoy truck. But Vanessa was positive that wasn't the origin of the shot.

As she approached the arched, shadowy entrance to the church she heard another shot — pistol this time. She stumbled on rough stones, almost tumbling down the half-dozen steps to the lower level. She managed to brace herself, but not before her ankle twisted and she sucked in a painful breath.

More shots sounded, pistol again, three

quick, tight explosions coming from nearby.

She took a tentative step, and her ankle held her weight so she pushed her pace again, sucking in surprisingly dank, moldy air; the only sunlight was reaching thin fingers through crevices into the subterranean passage. She was confused by the mazelike ruins, but she thought she remembered this passage would lead to a stairway entrance up to the royal apartments.

She turned a corner, almost colliding with three young tourists, murmuring quick apologies in Greek and Turkish as she left them behind.

She heard voices, but the passage opened now and split, and she couldn't remember which way led to the gallery and the window. But she dodged right instinctually and found herself between another tunnel-like passage and stone steps leading upward toward light. And suddenly she had her bearings — the gallery with the Queen's Window was at the top.

She slowed, stopping at the third step to keep her head out of sight. Feeling the butt of the FN Five-Seven, she waited for more shots. Almost a minute passed with nothing.

Vanessa crawled to the top step, pressed close to the granite wall. Quickly, she peeked over the landing stone. She couldn't see anything but the clear frame of the Queen's Window. She inched higher and saw a sleeve and the edge of a jacket. A body slumped over against the stone floor. Male, facedown, dark hair matted with blood.

Oh, God.

FORTY-FIVE

A flash of motion caught her eye, and she recoiled back against stone. A second man, Sergei's huge, muscled bodyguard, hunkered behind the thick wall framing the Queen's Window. He was nosing his Sig to take his next shot. Apparently, his target was hiding somewhere in the low outcrop beyond the window.

Pistol in hand, Vanessa eyed the thick column to the right of the stairwell. It would provide her with protection from a sniper's bullet and from Sergei's bodyguard — she had no way of knowing if Olaf was dangerous or not.

She took a breath and scrambled from the stair, across open stone flooring to the column. Now she was only a few meters from the body. No sign of life, the puddle of blood around him no reassurance. The dark muzzle of a gun almost hidden beneath his right sleeve.

While she crouched, Sergei's bodyguard turned to stare at her, wild-eyed. For a twitchy instant she thought he was going to shoot her — but then recognition flickered across his gray, dirt-stained face just as she saw the blood darkening his black shirtsleeve where he'd been hit. Vanessa raised her palms, gesturing no-threat. A volley of shots rang out — she and the bodyguard both recoiled — but it was distant fire, AK-47s, the Turks.

Vanessa breathed again only after Olaf returned his focus to the harsh, rocky landscape, searching for the sniper. She stretched flat to reach the body. Avoiding the blood, she pulled the Makarov from between his fingers. His skin and the pistol both still warm. She straightened him enough to verify — Sergei Tarasov, with a single bullet hole punched between his eyes.

She flashed on the image of a faded tattoo — and a dark wave of rage almost knocked her flat.

It was her father's voice, his internalized command — *stay aware, stay alive, do your job* — that brought her back. She unclenched her fists and went to work — hefting her pistol, rechecking the cartridge, and then snapping it fully loaded back into place.

The sniper was out there right now, but why? Why was he still hanging around, still shooting after he'd eliminated his target? Unless he wasn't positive he'd killed Sergei. Or unless he had orders to kill the body-guard, too — eliminate witnesses — and get whatever Sergei carried.

She rifled through Sergei's pockets, left his keys and change, grabbed his wallet and passport, stuffed them into the pocket of her running jersey. Better if the Turkish authorities couldn't identify him quickly.

She saw the edge of a black leather bag caught under Sergei's right arm. She tugged it free, searching hurriedly through the contents.

"Nyet!" The Russian hissed at her. "No, *nyet!*" His eyes burned through her, but he stayed where he was. And she ignored him, sliding her fingers along the inside of the leather compartment. She found the flash drive, shoved that into a small key pocket inside the waistband of her pants. She'd take his burn phone and his BlackBerry, too.

"Nyet, nyet!"

She whispered back harshly, *"Da,* Olaf, *da, da."*

But that didn't convince Olaf she wasn't stealing. He reached out to stop her from taking what she needed, but she jerked away. He grabbed for her again, but any more argument was cut short by the crack of a long-range rifle, the invisible slice of a bullet racing past, and the sound of the shot ricocheting off stone. Swearing freely in multiple languages, Olaf swung around, returning fire wildly.

Voices echoed up the mountain, a man calling out to someone in alarm. They wouldn't be alone for long — either tourists would stumble on them or Turkish soldiers would be storming the castle as soon as they figured out this gunfight wasn't part of their mock-war.

Vanessa shoved Sergei's Makarov across the rough floor toward Olaf — he needed all the rounds he could get. She was already crawling away from Sergei's body, heading for an opening beyond the window, a seam where the walls had eroded to expose the craggy hillside beyond.

She stared out through the seam, her FN Five-Seven solid in her grip. Sweat ran from her forehead, stinging her eyes. She tried to spot the sniper's hide, but no sudden movements, no flash or glare, gave away his position.

But she could feel him still out there — she could feel the Chechen.

Another volley of shots rang out from the next hillside, and her finger twitched against the pistol's trigger. From across a canyon, a single blast echoed loud as a cannon, followed by a second and then a third — part of the military drill. Each blast so powerful it made her eardrums vibrate.

But it wasn't just the Chechen who concerned her — she had to consider Olaf completely unpredictable, but given that they were both being fired at, she had to assume that for the moment they were on the same side. And then there were the Turks and the certainty of an international debacle if she didn't get away clean. With Sergei's intel. As her mind raced, she crawled steadily toward the edge of the gallery. Crouched to launch herself across an open space, she heard the distinctive whack of the rifle and a loud grunt from Olaf. She jerked around in time to see the impact push him back. Spitting expletives in Russian — he clamped his left hand over his right shoulder. He was hit but still alive.

And this time, through an open frame in the ruins, Vanessa had seen the flash of sun against metal on the hillside — an outcropping marked by a scrub oak. Six hundred meters away, give or take. Way out of range for her pistol or Olaf's to be effective.

She froze for a second, knowing she had the flash drive with Sergei's intel safely tucked inside her pocket — the only reason she'd come here. If she left now, while the bodyguard still had bullets left, she could probably make it down the hill to her car.

She wasn't a soldier, and she wasn't special ops. But that didn't matter right now, because she knew she'd already made her decision when she heard the first sniper shot.

He'd killed two of her assets — maybe dozens of other targets. She was going after the Chechen.

She had one chance to get around behind him, upwind, uphill, with at most a hundred meters between them — close enough to take her shot. She hissed to Olaf, caught his attention, and communicated her intentions with hand signals. Grimacing in pain, he managed to nod. He'd switched pistols, and now he wielded Sergei's Makarov. When Vanessa counted off with her fingers, he fired a wild round toward the rocks. She launched herself low across the clearing.

FORTY-SIX

For the next forty meters, she had cover as she ran through the ruins of the barracks. She scared the hell out of a young couple as she darted past, the Five-Seven in hand, pressed hot to her belly under the hem of her running jersey.

Another twenty-five meters and she reached the base of the fortress walls. On top ran a trail about eight meters wide, where sentries had stood guard a thousand years ago. Once she made it to the top, she would be high enough to get a good bead on the Chechen with her pistol. Just then she heard the bark of Olaf's pistol — keeping the Chechen busy.

She took the restored staircase, and she was breathing hard by the time she reached the rampart. She crouched, turning slowly, getting her bearings. From here, the Queen's Window was just southeast of her — and the Chechen's hide was due west.

She ran half-hunched along the crest of the rampart walls until she estimated she was about fifty meters beyond the Chechen — a distance shot easily accomplished with her Five-Seven. She could still see the Queen's Window, but from the outside now, and she thought she caught the dark stain of Olaf's shadow.

She took a moment to catch her breath and steady herself, and then she raised up on her haunches to see over the rough edge of the wall. She'd aced firearms at the Farm, but it was the endless hunting trips with her father and her brother that had truly honed her skill with guns. But she'd never hunted a human until now.

Should she be overwhelmed by the immensity of her decision to go after him? Instead, she felt oddly light and totally focused, almost machinelike. No emotions. She had a job to do.

And now she had taken the high ground over the Chechen. She settled in, almost completely sheltered behind the thick wall of the rampart. She stared out toward the outcropping where she gauged she'd seen the flash. She blinked sweat from her eyes and slowed her breathing. Gripping the Five-Seven in both hands, the fleshy part of her index finger on the trigger, biceps pressed against stone for stability.

She found the lonely pine tree, crept her finger back against the trigger, and sighted a target a few paces beyond the visibly gnarled roots. Was she looking at the tree's shadow?

Not unless it could move.

She had the Chechen.

Just then she heard the shot, saw the flash from the hide as he took another shot at Olaf. Her sights aimed at the top of the Chechen's head to allow for bullet drop — her best guess of how he'd positioned himself — she fired, ready for the pistol's jump.

Shit. Without taking her eyes from her target, she brought the Five-Seven carefully back down. Had she hit him? She couldn't tell. But just as she fired again, she caught the ripple of motion when he rolled.

She felt his eyes scanning for her before she heard the tight, echoing crack of his shot.

She dropped fast, hitting rock so hard pain knifed through her left bicep.

She inched up again, desperate not to lose him now, always sighting with the Five-Seven. For a few seconds nothing. Then she caught a blur of motion about ten meters below the hide. He was on the move down the hill, roughly sixty meters from her.

She tracked him with the Five-Seven, aiming at his head, taking her last shot.

Her pistol jumped. He stumbled, going down on one knee — for that instant, she prayed he was dead.

But he lumbered up and kept moving, unsteady on both feet, disappearing behind rock.

She thought she'd hit him, but she couldn't be certain, and now he was gone. The bitter taste of disappointment filled her mouth — she should have killed the motherfucker; this had been her chance.

He won. She lost.

Now her body was flooded with new purpose. She had to get out of there. Turkish soldiers were probably already on their way up. If they arrested her, she was fucked. She was a NOC — no government, not even her own, would protect her. She had to get Sergei's intel back to Headquarters.

She pushed her pistol inside her waistband. Her left arm ached like hell, and for the first time she realized she'd been hit — blood stained the sleeve of her jersey. She pulled her cap low on her forehead and peeled off her jersey, wrapping it tightly, painfully around the wound. As far as she could tell her T-shirt was clean, no blood.

No time to do more until she was in the VW and out of there.

She stood shakily, close to passing out, but she didn't. She could walk. She could try to look almost normal. She began the journey back, light-headed, picking up her pace as much as she dared. When she started down the stairs, she almost blacked out again. But voices and shouting inspired her to stay conscious and get the hell away from the castle.

Luck was with her, because she quickly joined a group of artists hurrying down the trail toward the parking lot. She matched their pace. They passed four soldiers on their way up, but no one tried to stop them. Several members began to give her curious looks as they navigated the last descending stretch of trail. Grateful for the dark blue fabric, she pressed her good arm over the wound, biting back the flash of searing pain. And she pushed herself to move ahead, cutting away from the artists as soon as she exited at the gatehouse.

No sign of the Chechen, so he had to be moving at least as fast as she could.

Her pulse jumped when she saw blood droplets on concrete. She passed three more soldiers but only one even glanced her way, and not one of them had noticed the blood.

But she saw more, a slivery trail that disappeared abruptly across the asphalt. She felt the rush of triumph at the thought she'd at least wounded him. She wanted him to bleed to death.

She was about ten meters from her car when she registered Sergei's Mercedes. A wave of vertigo threatened to knock her flat. She couldn't afford to acknowledge the horrible fact of his death, not now. She had to keep going. But for a moment she faltered, abruptly dizzy. Was she going to be sick? *Pull it fucking together! Keep moving.*

She needed only sixty seconds to reach the VW and make her exit.

FORTY-SEVEN

Vanessa stared almost blindly down at the collection of Sergei Tarasov's possessions spread out on the marble floor. Late-afternoon sun cooked the air in her apartment, but she shivered. Raw energy kept her circling around the flash drive and her own weapon at her feet. Images kept intruding — Arash lying dead in Vienna, and now Sergei with a bullet between his eyes. Her thoughts kept diving to dark places and then resurfacing — how had this happened, and what could she have done to stop it?

Two assets dead — assassinated while she was meeting with them.

More and more, she felt the horrible certainty that Jost Penders was dead, too.

Was it all some terrible coincidence? It couldn't be.

Did that make her responsible for their deaths?

Yes, somehow — *but in what way?* Had

her assets been targeted specifically? If so, her security was breached — she was burned. Meaning someone knew who she was behind her cover identity. But she was sure she hadn't been followed in Vienna. The Chechen had followed Arash. He was the target.

And Sergei and the Chechen had beaten her to the castle — so the Chechen had followed Sergei that time as well. Was someone inside the Agency a traitor, a mole? Did Bhoot have access to top-secret intel? Did he know the identities of her assets?

But she couldn't put the pieces together — so it was useless and destructive to keep trying. She couldn't afford to freeze internally, overwhelmed by questions and her sense of guilt.

Thirty minutes ago, she'd locked the door to her apartment, but now she checked it again before she stripped out of her filthy clothes to step slowly, painfully into the shower. Her injured arm burned under the force of the hot water, but the punishing sting almost felt good. And she would live. At least two of her assets and a bodyguard murdered, and she would live.

She reluctantly left the warm, cleansing shower knowing she had work ahead of her. She focused on simple tasks. She rigged a butterfly closure and bandaged her arm where his bullet had grazed her biceps. It still hurt like hell, but the bleeding had slowed. She pulled on clean sweatpants and a loose cotton shirt. She swallowed three Excedrin and found herself staring at the small container of prescription pills she'd left hidden in the back corner of her vanity. She picked up the bottle, released the cap, and tapped two into the palm of one hand. They would ease the horrible anxiety. They would also dull her mind and slow her down.

She returned the pills to the bottle.

Her thoughts slid back to Prague and Jost Penders, and she moved numbly to her desk and composed a cable to Prague Station:

C/O GROVES REQUESTS STATUS UPDATE ON POLICE INVESTIGATION INTO DISAPPEARANCE OF FORMER ASSET SWGRAVITY/32 (G/32). ACCORDING TO REF DATED SIX MONTHS AGO, THERE WERE NO CLUES OR NEWS INTO G/32'S ABRUPT AND PUZZLING BREAK IN COMMUNICATION WITH C/O OR STATION. PER PREVIOUS DISCUSSIONS, THERE DOES NOT APPEAR TO BE EVI-

DENCE OF FOUL PLAY, BUT STA-
TION EFFORTS HAVE NOT
SHOWN ANY INDICATION THAT
G/32 IS ALIVE. APPRECIATE STA-
TION SHARING WITH GROVES
LATEST THINKING INTO G/32'S
FATE.

She sent the routine cable to avoid attract-
ing interest, and she used code routing
words — "slugs" — to minimize visibility
even more. She wanted to keep the inquiry
under the radar.

Next she sent a flash cable — eyes only —
to Chris Arvanitis, giving the barest facts:
two dead, including her asset, intel acquired,
shots fired, officer safe.

She wasn't going to mention she'd packed
her personal pistol or that she'd exchanged
gunfire with the shooter. Sergei's dead
bodyguard could take credit for wounding
the Chechen.

A ping on her secure laptop announced
an incoming message:

HQS, CHIEF OPS: MESSAGE RE-
CEIVED. STANDING BY FOR
MORE DETAILS.

She dreaded the next, much more detailed

cable she needed to send, but at least she'd bought herself an hour — to review Sergei's intel, to download a copy of his flash drive.

What she was doing, conducting her own investigation of Sergei's files, was completely against protocol, but that fact was irrelevant now. She'd already stepped so far over the line of Agency policy and procedures, she was dangling in space. And there might be a mole in CPD, feeding intel to Bhoot. The thought made her sick, but she couldn't ignore the possibility. Bhoot might have access to the most top-secret information.

Her watch showed 1725 hours. She tried and failed to light a cigarette. Three matches later, she inhaled, craving the dark rush of chemicals. As she exhaled, she lifted the shot glass she'd filled with cask-strength Bourbon, the strongest on her shelf. She downed it, bracing as the searing heat hit her belly.

A second pull on the Dunhill, sucking smoke deep into her lungs. She would give herself until 1830 hours — 1130 in Washington. At which point she would sit down and compose the longer, more detailed cable: *Immediate Precedence.*

By then, the story would be news: Turkish authorities would have discovered the bodies of two men at an historic landmark in

Northern Cyprus. Vanessa had BBC news muted on the TV and CyBC Radio 1 streaming at low volume, creating soft background fill. The format alternated news, features, and music, all catering to Greek listeners *in* Greek. And (as Khoury had liked to point out in better days) she spoke just enough *Ellinika* to get into trouble.

So far, nothing about a fatal shootout at a historic site on Cyprus.

The Turks had the bodies, but odds were they didn't have identities.

Sergei Tarasov was a wealthy Russian financier, but, except for the occasional gala, he'd maintained a relatively low profile.

Vanessa glanced at his wallet and passport, both placed next to the burn phone. She'd already been through the wallet, finding currency, credit cards, and an EU driver's license. His visa was folded inside his passport. Tech would go through his phone and his personal BlackBerry. She'd set aside the small, laminated color photograph Sergei carried with him: a family portrait. She couldn't bear to look at it now, even as she pictured Anya at her father's side in Café Kiji just nights ago. For now she'd try to block those images out of her mind.

Her laptop pinged, signaling the flash-drive files had successfully been transferred. She sat down at her desk to begin the job of reviewing.

Sergei had scanned his original documents, spreadsheets for what appeared to be at least three accounts. He'd made sharp and legible handwritten notes and questions in the margins — what she guessed were anomalies and facts worth tracking. And, possibly, the names of companies? Unfortunately for Vanessa, they were in Russian, a language she could barely speak and certainly couldn't read.

It made her crazy to stare at them without being able to comprehend what they meant. If only she'd pushed herself beyond studying basic Russian.

The Greek radio announcer let her know she was running out of her allotted time as the local news came on. She stopped breathing when she heard the word *ptoma* — corpse.

She unmuted the BBC televised broadcast and within minutes heard that *"the bodies of two unidentified men were discovered at a tourist site in Northern Cyprus. Turkish authorities are not releasing details, but anyone with information should come forward . . ."*

She would have to send the full cable to Headquarters in the next few minutes.

Vanessa hurriedly sent off copies of Sergei's files via secure link to Headquarters, to Lee, an extremely clever, extremely geeky forensic analyst who'd forever had a crush on her. A whiz at translation programs, Lee also had an old-fashioned advantage; his mother had been granted asylum from Russia by the United States, and her American-born son spoke fluent Russian. She followed up the scan with a call — on an unsecure line — and a casual phone message: "Hey, Lee, it's Vanessa. Something's in your mailbox — can you be sure to get a reply to my request ASAP?" She was going behind Chris's back again. But given Sergei's assassination, and the fact that Vanessa's actions would be scrutinized and investigated and she would be cut out of the official loop at least temporarily, she had to cover as many bases as possible through back channels.

1848 hours. She couldn't put off the second cable any longer.

Three minutes after she sent it, she had a reply:

HQS APPRECIATES C/O GROVES' DETAILED DESCRIPTION AND PROMPT AFTER-ACTIONS RE G/258. HQS MONITORING OPEN SOURCE NEWS FOR ANY INFOR-

MATION ON THE DEATH AS THE INVESTIGATION UNFOLDS. C/O GROVES SHOULD RETURN TO HQS FOR IMMEDIATE DEBRIEF. PERMISSION GRANTED TO HAND CARRY R/258 DOCUMENTS IN CONCEALED COMPARTMENT OF TRAVEL BAG. HQS OFFICER WITH APPROPRIATE CREDENTIALS WILL BE AVAILABLE AT ARRIVAL CUSTOMS IF NEEDED TO ENSURE THERE ARE NO PROBLEMS EN-TERING U.S. PROVIDE FLIGHT INFORMATION SOONEST. RE-GARDS.

She caught a glimpse of her reflection in the small piece of antique mirror she'd hung on the wall, a treasure from Crete. Jesus, she looked like hell. Her bad arm ached. She pictured the small droplets of the blood trail she'd followed down the castle trail. The Chechen had managed to move quickly — God, she hoped she'd really fucked him up.

FORTY-EIGHT

Pauk studied the wound on the outer edge of his right thigh. Her bullet had passed cleanly through, but the missing chunk of flesh was the size and shape of a bite out of a piece of bread. The bruised tissue immediately surrounding the cavity was shading dark red to blue-black. Nonlethal, but extremely nasty and very painful. As soon as he could, he would need reconstructive surgery.

It had been seventeen years since he'd been touched by a bullet — back then, a Russian soldier's round had smashed through his fourth rib.

But now this woman had broken his lucky streak.

He poured a slow stream of amylphenol into the wound, swearing silently, working to breathe again after the intensity of the pain.

He'd finally put it together — where he'd

seen her before Vienna.

Her athletic stride on the hill to the castle and one gesture had given it away — the way she twisted the strand of hair before she pushed it behind her ears. Blond hair this time, but the gesture was unmistakable to Pauk.

One other time he'd seen that exact gesture — in Prague, the redheaded woman who clutched the Dutch artist's arm, laughing as they entered his apartment building.

He should have killed them both when he had the chance.

Later, after the woman left, the double-crossing Dutchman headed out to the underground club frequented by the German known simply as Hans. Hans was a close associate of Pauk's mentor. Apparently, Hans had been seduced by the Dutchman's beauty before he realized his lover was a traitor.

So when the Dutchman hopped clubs to score his next high, Pauk killed him.

How strange that this same woman had shown up at three of his assignments. Why? For an instant he heard Madame Desmarais reading the Tarot in her nasal French drone. She liked to say, "Your fate awaits you."

Who did the woman work for? The Americans? Brits? Israelis? Or someone else outside official channels?

But the most interesting question of all for Pauk: Had his mentor known she would be at all three sites?

If yes, why hadn't he told Pauk specifically to kill her?

FORTY-NINE

Light cascaded in soft ripples along the
muted hallway of the Four Seasons hotel in
New York City. When possible, Vanessa
preferred to travel through the busier entry
port at JFK to avoid direct connections to
Dulles for security reasons.

She stopped at the door to 314, a room
she and Khoury had never used before. She
took a moment to gather herself, to breathe
through the pall that had seemed to sur-
round her since the horror at the castle.
There was so much she wanted to share
with Khoury — Sergei's murder, the intel
she was hand-delivering to Headquarters,
and the fact she'd been summoned. There
was the almost intolerable anticipation that
Khoury had brought her the meaning behind Arash's code.

And the regret she felt from Cairo, the
way she used him, the way they left each
other. She could make it up to him now.

She used the key card and let herself inside. "Khoury?"

No lights were on, but the curtains were wide and Manhattan's twenty-four-hour glow illuminated an embroidered, snowy white hotel bathrobe laid out carefully on the king-size bed. Two glasses and an open bottle of wine graced the table, arranged around a single burning candle. She expected to hear Khoury speak her name. She thought she'd turn and see him wrapped in the other robe, walking toward her.

Instead, there was only the immediate silence and the soft scrim of city noises outside.

Where are you, Khoury?

Vanessa set her travel bag on the edge of the bed. The bathroom door was closed, but there was no light escaping from the seams; it was empty when she checked. She found one spare pillow in the closet.

Her injured arm was aching and her energy threatening to dissipate completely, but she told herself he'd stepped out for a minute. It was possible he'd gone to the bar for a drink. But it wasn't like him to disappear when he knew she was coming.

She switched on one lamp and then another. The warm yellow light lifted her spirits slightly. She checked her phone just in case. No messages.

She'd sent him a text when her flight was delayed in Cyprus. No reply. Sent a second text when she was thirty minutes from the hotel and that time the reply came almost instantly: everything you need here waiting.

Had he been delayed? Had she just missed him? Sometimes she hated what passed for communication in the twenty-first century.

Someone, Khoury or a waiter, had opened the wine, but the bottle appeared otherwise untouched. She looked again at the single robe arranged so carefully. Was she imagining the faint and lingering scent of Dior's Eau Sauvage, Khoury's aftershave?

Across the avenue, lights shivered from office windows where a handful of lawyers or insurance brokers or bank auditors stayed late. Vanessa stopped for a moment, her eyes on them but her mind circling obsessively.

She scooped up the cork, brought it to her face, and then set it down again lightly. She poured out half a glass. When she swirled the wine around the bowl, it gleamed a deep, bruised purple. She sipped. A 2005 Rauzan-Ségla from the district of Margaux. A favorite. But tonight it left a faintly bitter aftertaste on her tongue.

Carrying her wineglass, she crossed over to the bed and sat on the edge. She gazed around the room: light earth tones pared with simple, elegant designs meant to soothe and relax. But the emptiness was palpable.

This was not her David Khoury. The Khoury she knew always came through.

A thought, reluctant to coalesce, nudged her consciousness — *I changed the game and our relationship when I asked him to cross the line.* But just then she heard the click of the electronic key. She tensed, turning as he entered the room.

Already, moving toward him, she felt a rush of relief and excitement that he'd shown up, even as she warily marked that his gray suit looked slept in and he hadn't shaved for several days.

"I was beginning to think I'd missed you," she said softly.

"I needed a drink," Khoury said, brushing past her. "Decided to wait in the bar." He splashed wine into the remaining goblet and downed half of it before he finally looked her in the eye. "I heard several versions of your shootout." His voice sounded cold, and he'd slurred his words just slightly.

She inhaled sharply, stepping back. "You know I couldn't risk more contact until we saw each other here."

"Of course I *know.*" He set the glass down

so hard she winced, thinking the stem might crack. "We abide by the same rules, don't we, Vanessa? Live by the same code."

"You're drunk," she said, setting her own glass on the bedside table.

"And you're alive — after you tried to get yourself killed on Cyprus."

"David . . ." She heard the desperation in her voice when she said his name.

He heard it, too, and he softened and his eyes took on sadness, but only for an instant, before the emotional wall went up again. "Aren't you dying to ask if I came through for you?"

She held her silence for seconds before she answered with the truth. "Yes, I want to know," she said simply, moving toward him again. "That's who I am, and you know that. You used to love that I don't give up, I keep pushing —"

"I don't have to like it, Vanessa, not when it's me you're pushing." He shook his head, and then, as if at a loss, he reached into his shirt pocket and absently pulled out a crumpled pack of Dunhills, fumbling for a cigarette.

She reached him — he didn't step away — taking the pack gently from his hands. "We're in a U.S. hotel room, Khoury." As her fingers closed around paper and cellophane, she met his eyes. "What's going on, what's wrong? You're not yourself. You're not okay, so don't try to tell me you're fine." She saw she'd surprised him with her questioning, and she tried to close the emotional distance between them with words. "I know I should have asked before, in Cairo. I should have pushed. I'm so sorry I didn't. But I'm asking now. I want to help. If you'll tell me, I'm listening."

For a few seconds he seemed thrown, his almond-shaped eyes narrowing with uncertainty. He looked past her, toward the window. When he met her eyes again, he'd shut down.

"There's nothing to tell. Not now. It's something I have to handle on my own." He shook his head sharply, backing away. "Let's kill the suspense. I did what you asked, and a friend of mine came through for you. A simple job if you're a scholar who studies archaic Persian manuscripts and speaks fluent Farsi. The Persian Book of Kings, the Shahnameh, specifically the Khaleghi-Motlagh edition, that's your code bible."

He might have been talking to a stranger now, Vanessa thought, watching him closely.

He said, "The verses come from the heroic tales of Simorgh, a bird so huge she darkens the sky with her wings, and the human child she raised, Zal" — he closed his eyes for barely an instant — "I remember the stories from my childhood." He opened his eyes again, shrugging off the memory. "It's all in here." He dug into his pocket, producing a flash drive. He held it out on his palm, and then, before she reached for it, he tossed it toward the bed. It landed on the pristine spread next to the robe. "That's the bottom line with you. I should know by now."

"But this isn't you —"

"Really?" His body stiffened. "What do you know about me? We see each other every few months if we're lucky. Are you sure you can even trust me?"

She flinched. "Why would you ask that, David? Of course I trust you."

He swung around, walking quickly to the door, setting his hand on the knob. "I don't want to hear from you, Vanessa. Not until I can sort things out. Do us both a favor and don't contact me again."

The door slammed in his wake.

Vanessa stood speechless.

You came through, Khoury, but you were wrong. Everything I needed wasn't here waiting.

She pictured another hotel room, Cairo, the moment when he almost opened up to her. Instead of staying with him, inviting his confidence, she had let the moment pass.

She walked slowly to the bed to retrieve the flash drive.

After six years, there was still a lot they didn't know about each other. But even as the thought raced through her mind, she felt the insubstantial weight of the tiny drive in her palm.

What did you give us, Arash?

She needed to know.

She picked up her bag and walked to the door without looking back. On the way out, she snapped the light off.

FIFTY

At 0630 hours the door to Chris's office stood open, and Vanessa barely slowed to deliver a cursory knock as she walked in, pulling it shut.

From behind his laptop, Chris looked up over his glasses — frowning, sleep-deprived, badly in need of a shave — a man who appeared older than his thirty-eight years. Once, a few years ago when they were working past midnight, he'd confided in Vanessa how much he hungered to be back in the field, how much he missed it. Anything but surprising, given the present atmosphere — frequent shifts in management, congressional probes, even the best of the best hunkering down defensively. But he was stuck at Headquarters for a few more years in order to take care of his aging parents.

"I heard you just got back," he said, his gaze narrowing intently as she stood facing him.

"I hand-delivered my asset's phone and BlackBerry to Tech, and the files to Lee in financial analysis, and I think some of the data will turn out to be pivotal for Operation Ghost Hunt."

Chris nodded but he looked distracted, almost as if he hadn't heard her, and Vanessa pulled up internally.

He said, "Cyprus turned into a hell of a mess."

"Bad, yeah." She was walking a very thin line — Cyprus *was* a mess, and Chris didn't know the half of it. She couldn't shrug off the gravity of her emotions, but she didn't want to give Chris time to dig into her, so she kept going. "But right now I've got something else." She set the palm of one hand deliberately on his desktop. With her other hand she pushed a thin manila folder across to him. Now she let the glimmer of exhilaration she experienced override her exhaustion.

He marked the moment with a kind of wired stillness before he nudged himself away from his computer and opened the folder. It contained fifteen pages: a copy of Arash Farah's original text of 105 characters of archaic Persian. Most important, the last four pages displayed columns of the Persian characters and corresponding columns of numbers.

While he riffled slowly through them, Vanessa waited — now using the rev of internal excitement to drown out a deeper sense of apprehension. She stood almost still while he tracked through the documents for most of a minute.

Finally, Chris set down the pages, inhaling audibly. "Where did you get these?"

"I know," Vanessa said quickly, ahead of him. "It's what we're looking for. My asset's original page from the cigarette pack had fragments of verses copied from — I'm sorry I'm going to butcher these names — the Khaleghi-Motlagh edition of the Shahnameh, the Persian Book of Kings, which was written sometime in the tenth century. Anyway, the thing is, Arash didn't use a code, he used a *cipher.* So the characters correspond to numbers and the first few lines present the key. With these pages to go on, the code guys should be able to figure it out very quickly."

Chris's dark eyebrows pulled together and he punctuated his words: "How did you get it, Vanessa? Don't try to case-officer me."

An old saying that meant *cut the bullshit already* — her pulse spiked and sudden heat pricked her skin, but she didn't skip a beat. "We need the guys at Fort Meade to verify coordinates, and they should have done it yesterday, Chris. We're five days away from D-day on Operation Ghost Hunt." She jutted her chin toward the pages on his desk. "Is this what we need to pinpoint the location of the facility and get Bhoot? That's what matters now."

"But if you want me to cover your ass, I need to know how far out you're hanging on this one."

She swallowed slowly. "David Khoury."

"Jesus, Vanessa. Damn." He shook his head, stepping abruptly back.

"But look at what we got."

"You're acting like a goddamn cowboy — I can't begin to list your sins, but, Christ, you've shared classified intel with someone outside this op, and you did it without authority. What the hell does David know about Operation Ghost Hunt?"

"*Nothing.* I told him he had to fly blind when I asked for his help." She shook her head. "He was the logical choice, a linguist, and with his contacts, it made sense. And look, the results are *good.*"

Chris eyed her sharply, his expression direct, his words matter-of-fact. "If there is something more to this, then you need to tell me *now.*"

She tried to swallow, but her throat had

gone suddenly, painfully dry. "There is nothing more to this, Chris, believe me." But the lie made her feel sick to her stomach.

"That better be the whole story," he said slowly. "Because if there's more, a relationship . . . trust me, Vanessa, then you're out where I can't help you."

For a moment she thought she would confess the truth — how clean it would feel not to carry the lie any longer. But the next moment brought realization — if she did confess, this would become about her failures instead of being about Operation Ghost Hunt and bringing down Bhoot. She would let go of Khoury, she told herself quickly, silently. She was strong enough. She would do what was ultimately best for both of them and end the relationship, and Chris never had to know anything about it. She took a quick breath and, hating to do it, forced out one more lie. "I swear, Chris, I've told you all there is to know."

His eyes stayed on her, his silent question almost tangible. Finally, he said, "All I need to know and all there is. I hope they are the same."

"You know me, Chris, we have history, go with me on this," she said softly. "This cost my asset his life."

He made her wait longer than she wanted before he slid the pages back into the manila folder. "I'll get it to the right analysts."

She nodded once, careful to mask both her relief and her disquiet. As she turned to leave, she puffed out a quick breath. Her fingers closed around the doorknob, almost clear —

"Vanessa."

Khoury — she couldn't afford to go there again, not now. She pushed the door open before she turned again to face Chris.

He held up the folder. "You think this is your card back in? You went outside channels, screwed up royally, and, ultimately, they'll count that as another strike against you."

"How do *you* count it, Chris?"

For a moment, her hope spiked.

But as the seconds ticked by, his silence was answer enough.

She took him in for a moment, seeing a man who was both familiar and a stranger. She'd counted Chris and Khoury as the two men who mattered most in her life next to her father and her brother. Men she trusted absolutely. *They had her back.* But now she found herself wondering if she'd let them both down badly. She found it difficult to meet Chris's eyes.

"One more thing before you go, Vanessa."
Chris set the folder on the desk, pulled off
his glasses, and massaged the painful pink
imprints left by the nose pads. "You need to
stop at OMD. Dr. Wright."

One of the Agency's shrinks — shit.

"Can't it wait until we hear back —"

Chris shut her down. "Take care of it now.
You're not doing anything else until OMD's
done with you."

FIFTY-ONE

In the muted glow of the tastefully appointed office in the medical division, Dr. Peyton Wright's glass-green eyes drilled into Vanessa. "You must know there is concern about your immediate ability to function effectively and safely as a case officer."

It took all Vanessa's willpower to stay seated in the soft, padded leather chair, but she knew enough not to interrupt the Agency psychologist's opening statement. There would be nothing diplomatic or therapeutic about this evaluation. Dr. Wright had an agenda, and Vanessa had one question to answer as quickly as possible: Did the shrink have it in for her, regardless of what happened during this hour or two, or did Vanessa have room to maneuver?

"For the moment, let's skip over the fact your asset in Prague disappeared seven months ago with a noticeable sum of the taxpayers' money. Some of your *more recent* decisions in the field have been, at the very least, questionable." Dr. Wright held up her slender, manicured index finger. "Failure to obey a direct order to abort a mission, a failure that resulted in the death of your high-level asset in Vienna."

The statement hit Vanessa with a jolt — Chris must have spoken directly to Dr. Wright. Not exactly a shock, but still . . . a shock. Now she did pull halfway out of the damn chair. "As you must know, I was debriefed by the DDO and Chris Arvanitis directly, and it's in my official report — when the order to abort came, my asset was within a few meters of me and I made a judgment call to continue the operation at least long enough to hear if he had actionable intel. He risked his life to meet with me —"

"And died because of it," Dr. Wright finished tersely.

"You don't know that," Vanessa shot back. "My asset was targeted, and it's probable he would have been killed even if I had aborted that meeting, and we would certainly not have his intel now — intel that's driving a vital CPD op."

Dr. Wright raised her pen above the clipboard in her trim lap, but she kept her eyes on Vanessa. "You're right," she said.

"There is no way to know absolutely if your asset would still be alive if you had obeyed orders — but it is possible he would have escaped assassination."

Vanessa suppressed a shudder, only too aware she was under minute scrutiny — body language, vocal inflection, facial expression.

Where the hell did Peyton Wright get off judging the actions of case officers when she'd no doubt spent most of her fifteen-year career in twelve-by-twelve windowless offices, typing up reports based on *soft* science? What the hell did she know about the reality of the ops world?

But Vanessa checked herself sharply. Peyton Wright was *working* her — part of her job as Agency shrink. It wasn't her job to dole out therapy. If you have issues, resolve them outside these walls or don't. The only relevant question in here: Can you do your job or not?

And Vanessa could damn well do her job, so she took a breath and eased her hands to her lap. "No one regrets the outcome of the operation in Vienna more than I do." She kept her voice steady and firm. "First and foremost, I am responsible for the security of the operation and the safety of my assets. Whether I like them or not, I am responsible for their well-being. I am responsible for their lives." Her voice cracked just a little on the last word. She took another breath and finished what she needed to say. "Their safety is paramount. I never let myself forget that. I not only *cared* about the asset who died in Vienna, but I also had great respect for him. With that said, I stand by my judgment call."

While the psychologist put pen to paper, obviously recording her statement, Vanessa stared at her own hands resting in her lap. Her usually blunt, buffed fingernails looked ragged, several of her knuckles scraped, and even though she'd showered that morning, her skin felt as if it were covered with a layer of grime. She held herself straight and steady in the chair — and for a moment even that much energy seemed too much effort against the deep exhaustion that had overtaken her.

She blinked when Dr. Wright clicked the pen and set it against the clipboard. "I've noted your responses. I really do care about getting your side of this, Vanessa. Do you have anything else to add before we continue?"

Vanessa heard an ominous finality in the psychologist's words. She knew she should respond, but all she could do was give a small, reflexive lift of her fingers: *Go ahead.*

"Barely one week after your asset was killed in Vienna, you drove to an open location on Cyprus, and you met with a newly assigned asset. You did this even though, less than twenty-four hours earlier, you expressed concerns for this asset's safety and you requested a surveillance team — a request you made personally to your director of operations."

Vanessa took a breath against the tightness building behind her ribs. She met the psychologist's eyes, honestly trying to set aside her resentment. "There is no rule book, no manual that defines what to do in every field situation. It's my job to make judgment calls — that's why I'm in operations — and making those judgment calls is a vital part of my 'fitness for duty' as a case officer."

"So you made a judgment call to meet, and what did you find?"

Vanessa glanced down, buying a few seconds. Dr. Wright certainly had access to the reports, but no doubt she wanted to interpret and cross-check Vanessa's words in the retelling. SOP for psych evaluations, but still offensive — and evidently effective, because Vanessa had to force the words out. "I heard shots as I was proceeding to the site for the meeting. This was outdoor terrain, very rugged. By the time I reached my asset, he was already dead, but his bodyguard was alive and exchanging fire with the sniper."

"So you took your asset's briefcase that you hoped contained intel he was going to pass to you."

"It did contain intel," Vanessa said flatly. "He'd given me a good indication of what he would deliver."

"And how did this bodyguard react when you showed up?"

Startled when I pulled out my Five-Seven pistol — Vanessa blinked away the thought and said, "After a few moments he recognized me. He was *busy* — returning fire to a point about seven or eight hundred meters from where we were."

"Do you think this is an appropriate time for sarcasm?"

"No, I'm not trying — of course I don't. I was there. I know what it's like to be in the line of fire. Do you?"

Dr. Wright ignored the challenge, instead asking, "So you took the intelligence, and then you left the bodyguard at the scene?" Her voice hardened to a tone Vanessa read as accusatory. "Was he still returning fire when you left?"

Vanessa closed her eyes — felt the warm breeze, smelled her own sweat and Sergei's blood, flinched as she relived the dash from the Queen's Window to the ancient stairway that ascended the ramparts of the castle wall.

"Vanessa?" The psychologist's voice seemed to come from far away. "Was the bodyguard alive when you left?"

She felt the sting of her spent muscles as she crouched on the wall, taking aim on the Chechen, tasting how much she wanted to hurt him — to stop him —

"Vanessa."

Wrenching herself back to the present, she stared at Dr. Wright. After a few more seconds she shook her head. "The bodyguard took a fatal shot just as I retrieved the briefcase." She swallowed past the accumulating lies. Her mouth felt dry. "So I immediately began my descent to the parking lot and my car."

Dr. Wright tipped her head, frowning — you could almost see the circuits running at hyper-speed because she'd sensed missing pieces. Vanessa heard the too-slow heartbeat of a clock hidden somewhere out of easy sight while her own heart seemed to stop and then race to catch up with itself. *Shit — not here, not a panic attack. She'd never be allowed in the field again.* She shifted stiffly in the chair. God, she needed a cigarette. The room seemed smaller now, like a cell.

"Are you feeling all right, Vanessa?"

"Yes." But she felt her head jerk into a nod.

"You've lost color, and you're sweating. I'm concerned, and I think we should break here —"

"*No*. I'm okay" She thought she could detect the shakiness in her own voice. "Let's finish this."

Dr. Wright uncrossed her legs, and Vanessa heard the swish of expensive fabric; at the same time she felt the psychologist's penetrating gaze. How much was she seeing? Vanessa ignored the urge to turn away.

Finally, the doctor spoke. "The loss of an asset doesn't happen every day. In fact, it's extremely rare — especially when he's gunned down in front of you." She nudged the pen on her clipboard. "And when that loss is followed by the assassination of a second asset within weeks, you would be less than human if you didn't experience some emotional whiplash. Even ops officers trained for high-stress extremes may exhibit feelings of guilt and responsibility, even textbook symptoms of PTSD: insomnia, nightmares, day sweats, flashbacks."

For a moment, Vanessa couldn't repress the lightning play of images — Arash crumpling to the ground, Yassi's demand for retribution, Sergei's lifeless body hunched against rough-hewn stones as his frightened bodyguard tried to take aim on his boss's assassin, the Chechen hit man firing at them from his hide.

"And I believe, in spite of your bravado, that every morning you must wake up questioning your role in the deaths of these two assets . . ."

The energy drained out of Vanessa abruptly. Her breath caught. She closed her eyes, scrambling mentally to find a center point. How the hell could she tell this psychologist what it was like to make decisions every day that could affect the lives of one person or hundreds? The same questions that plagued her since Sergei's shooting circled back now. Was she in some vital way responsible for the deaths of both her assets? If so, how? How big was this? Could it be coincidence? But that was unbelievable.

"Of course I feel things," Vanessa said softly, finally, opening her eyes to the light. "Don't you think I've been over it and over it, wondering if there was something I should have done differently? But I can't do my job if I allow myself to become paralyzed with doubt, to second-guess myself — that's like a death in itself."

"Allowing yourself to question your own decisions is not the same as becoming paralyzed with doubt."

Vanessa met Dr. Wright's piercing gaze. "If I don't dwell on things I can't change, I can get on with my job. That's where I put my focus. That's where I can make a difference."

Dr. Wright frowned. "You can't afford *not* to feel."

"*I feel.* And then I move on." Vanessa saw the shrink's green eyes widen. Dr. Wright was watching her closely.

"Well, my job is to make sure you're coping and dealing with the inevitable stress and emotional fallout, so you *can* get on with your job."

Vanessa said, "Fair enough."

"It may not seem like it," Dr. Wright said in a slower, softer voice than she'd used before. "But we're on the same side, Vanessa. I've reviewed your case file and I know what kind of brilliance and courage you are capable of in the field. But I'm curious . . . you've spoken convincingly about your concern for your assets and the risks they take. But you haven't once mentioned the danger you put yourself in."

Dr. Wright pressed forward. "When you disobeyed the direct order to abort, you might have ended up as dead as your asset. *And* there is a very real possibility your security is breached. When I say that, I doubt I'm saying anything you haven't considered for yourself." The psychologist seemed to be waiting for a denial.

But Vanessa met her gaze squarely. "Believe me, I know how serious this is. Not only because of my professional viability, because of the safety of my assets and my colleagues. If my security *has* been breached . . . if I've been pushed out of the hunt for Bhoot . . ."

"Then let's talk about how you're going to cope with the reality of this situation, Vanessa."

"I'll deal." She set her jaw. *I know what needs to be done.*

"Your father was Air Force, a colonel when he retired . . . a pilot during Vietnam, decorated veteran . . . and also, later, he worked in military intelligence. Although much of the record is classified, he did work in a special-operations force designed to investigate acts of biological and chemical terrorism."

Vanessa shook her head, startled by the

psychologist's trajectory shift. "What does my father's record of service have to do with any of this?" She could almost taste the world on the other side of the office door. Heat rushed through her with a dangerous intensity.

"I have no doubt that your father instilled in you and your brother a deep sense of duty, and you've both chosen to serve your country," Dr. Wright said softly. "And you are obviously passionately committed to stopping those who use their power destructively. There is an almost tangible urgency around you to protect the innocent. But it's not your job to save the world alone, Vanessa. Nobody can do that."

Dr. Wright inclined her body forward, a gesture of connection. "You can't talk to friends and family like most people. Ours is a closed world, and you don't have many options when it comes to being able to confide in others." Dr. Wright's voice took on a new energy. "So use me. *Here, now* — what you say stays between us. You don't need to keep everything secret."

Nice offer, but Vanessa knew better — whatever she said would be on the record and used against her if necessary.

The damn clock kept ticking.

Vanessa forced her body to stillness — not

even breathing — punishment until she regained control. When she knew she could speak half-normally, she said, "Are we done?"

Dr. Wright drew her mouth taut. "We're almost finished, yes. Because the reality is, you are not viable for field operations — not at this time. I'm going to recommend that you be called back for consultations at Headquarters for an indefinite period of time."

The words slammed into Vanessa, even though she'd known this was coming and thought she was prepared. She could hardly breathe.

"The life of an ops officer is based on secrecy, we both know that. I know there's more here, and it's really your choice to share it or not." Dr. Wright leaned forward, speaking too quietly now. "But the cost of that secrecy can be acute. I can't count the number of officers who've come through this door with tales of substance abuse, depression, and adultery. Don't let yourself become one of them, Vanessa. My door is always open."

FIFTY-TWO

She stood in the carpeted hallway in front of the elevator, disoriented for a moment. But just as the elevator doors opened and a man and two women stepped out, Vanessa felt someone grip her arm. She swung around to find herself inches from Chris, his dark eyes shining with a manic gleam. "I've been looking for you. I just got a phone call that it's good intel. The analysts are on it, and it looks viable."

"I *knew* it." She felt lifted by momentary excitement. "We need all eyes on this ASAP, we need a briefing now, today —"

"Get in," he said, nudging her toward the elevator. When they were both inside and alone, he said, "Slow down, Vanessa, you're not in on this briefing. You have another job right now, and that's to go back to Nicosia and close up shop."

He pressed the button for the basement quarters of CPD, and the elevator began its

295

descent. Focusing fully on Vanessa now, he said, "Listen, I owe you this because you got us the coordinates. But you should know there's been unusually intense pressure from the 'bomb Iran lobby' to proceed with a military strike."

"That can't happen," Vanessa said. "There would be civilian casualties, and even though the odds of Bhoot showing up may be thin, the whole point of this mission is capture or kill — it's worth the risk, and the SAD team will set back operations at the facility long enough for us to figure out their nuclear capabilities — this is our chance for so much —"

"And because you gave us the coordinates, it looks like we have time to get in and get out and take what we want — including Bhoot." For an instant, Chris's expression softened and Vanessa thought she read regret.

But now the elevator slowed to stop at the fifth floor. A green badger — private contract worker — stepped on.

"Milk run," Chris muttered. Vanessa nodded, but she couldn't stop her thoughts from racing through the million details still to be completed on Operation Ghost Hunt, now that she'd delivered the coordinates. A mission she'd made possible, and Chris wasn't allowing her on the team.

The elevator had barely started to descend before it stopped again at the third floor. The doors whished open, and Vanessa found herself staring at David Khoury. Unshaven, hollow-eyed — looking like he'd been through hell.

Standing too close to him, a wiry man in a white short-sleeved shirt and black suit trousers. *Khoury's handler?*

Vanessa felt absolutely still inside. Something was really off.

Khoury met her eyes, and she saw resignation and apology — as if he had said, *Sorry, but it is what it is* — and then he shut down.

She let out her breath, recognizing again in that moment how very deeply she cared for him . . .

Almost unconsciously she looked to Chris. He was watching her. She looked away again quickly.

She felt Chris take a step back. Heard the ominous chill in his voice as he asked, "Going down?"

Khoury hesitated, but the wiry man stepped toward the elevator. Vanessa couldn't tell if Khoury resisted because he didn't want to involve her in this moment — or if he was resisting his fate.

What the hell was happening?

But David finally stepped forward, too, almost mechanically. This time, as he turned to face the elevator doors, he avoided her eyes.

No one spoke as the doors closed and the elevator descended.

When it stopped again, Chris said, "Our floor."

Vanessa moved first, brushing the lightest touch of her hand against Khoury as she stepped out into the basement hallway. There was only one more floor that could be their destination — the underground parking level. So they were transporting Khoury? *Where?*

The elevator doors closed again and, feeling suddenly helpless, Vanessa looked to Chris. "That guy with David is from security?"

But Chris was already walking, and she hurried to catch up with him. Three steps, and he took her arm, pushing her forward with momentum.

"What the hell, Vanessa? I saw the way he looked at you; I get it now. When were you going to tell me?"

"Chris —"

Still moving, she looked at him, but he shook his head, silent now. Her stomach clenched. Several groups of people hurried past, one or two eyeing them curiously.

A young targeteer, Paula, hurried up, ready to hand off a file to Chris, but he snapped, *"Later,"* and the woman backed away.

As they passed the men's bathroom, Chris pivoted abruptly, pushing Vanessa with him through the door.

A man zipping his pants at the urinal froze. He looked vaguely familiar to Vanessa, but she couldn't keep her eyes off Chris — she'd never seen him this angry before, not like this.

"Get the fuck out," Chris ordered, and the man forgot about the zipper and hurried out.

Chris moved with Vanessa, and she backed toward the door. He pushed his fist hard against it, blocking her exit and anyone who tried to enter.

"Here's what I think," he said, his face close to hers. "You're having an affair with David Khoury. And you are putting everything you care about — your op, your career, him — in jeopardy in a million fucking ways."

The door jerked as someone tried to enter, but Chris pushed back hard. "Use another bathroom," he snarled. "This one's out of order."

He hadn't taken his eyes from Vanessa, and now he pressed even closer. "You're having an affair with David. I asked you to tell me. You didn't. You lied to my face."

"It just happened, Chris, I didn't mean to — it just —"

"I fucking hoped I was wrong." He pushed past her, opening the door.

She blurted out, "Do they know upstairs?"

He froze in his tracks. "Jesus, Christ, Vanessa, you've put us all in jeopardy and that's all you're worried about?"

"I care about the mission, about Operation Ghost Hunt and everything at stake."

He eyed her, cold and silent. "As far as I'm aware, right now, this is between you and me."

He opened the door, starting out. But he stopped, letting the door swing shut. "I've got an operation to carry out, I don't have time for your screwups, but you need to understand that David Khoury is under internal investigation."

"Investigation for *what?*" Shaking her head, Vanessa stared at Chris. "David would never do anything to hurt this Agency or his country."

"That's not how it looks in some people's eyes," Chris said. "All I know, there are concerns about his loyalty, his ties to Hezbollah."

"He's Lebanese American," Vanessa said. "Of course he's got ties to Hezbollah — you and I both know that's part of the reason he was recruited so heavily to join the Agency!"

"Jesus, Vanessa, I don't even want to be in the same room with you right now," Chris said sharply. "Just so you're warned, internal security is all over him and sooner or later they will find the thread to you." And then he brushed past her into the hallway.

For a while she stood, unable to move. Then she walked slowly to the sink. The water ran cold. She washed her hands with soap, splashed her face.

She was reaching for a paper towel when the door opened and a man walked in. He stared at her, startled.

Vanessa didn't react. She couldn't. Inside, she'd gone numb.

She finished drying her face and hands, and then she dropped the used towel in the trash. She stepped out into a hallway bustling with activity, but all she heard was the internal cacophony punctuated by shame and remorse.

FIFTY-THREE

As Vanessa stood restlessly, awaiting the announcement to board her flight from Dulles to Cyprus via Frankfurt, her cell phone buzzed. She almost jumped, thinking it might be Khoury. She'd dared send him only two text messages after their encounter at Headquarters. She used their long-standing trigger phrase — need to chat — which meant "urgent that you contact me." She was terrified by his silence. Did he want to ignore her messages? Or did he have no choice?

But now, when she recognized the number as belonging to Chris from his unsecure line, her pulse quickened and she walked away from the boarding gate to find a more private spot to speak. Surely he would call if he had news of Khoury.

"Yes."

"Change of plans," a voice said. But it was Zoe, not Chris. "You're reserved on the 8:50

Swissair flight to Prague. We've notified them you'll be in country."

"Right." *Them* meaning the COS, the Station Chief. Already scanning the nearest display for the new gate. Nervously energized by a small surge of adrenaline. Ignoring the deep pang of disappointment that it wasn't Khoury or Chris on the other end of the call. She was cut off from two of the most important men in her life, and the third, her brother, Marshall, was stationed in one of the most dangerous corners of a very dangerous world.

"We've had news from Prague police — an unusual John Doe," Zoe said. "We need positive confirmation."

"Check," Vanessa said sharply, her attention abruptly refocused. She couldn't ask questions on an unsecured line. As she clicked off, she steadied herself. The CIA's Prague Station tracked police bulletins closely, and they would be alert to an unidentified, unclaimed body. Her very recent cable to the Prague Station had been timely. The John Doe could mean only that her missing asset from Prague, Jost Penders, had finally turned up.

FIFTY-FOUR

The man traveling as Michel D'Arc, sporting a trim dark mustache and goatee, Alain Mikli titanium-frame eyeglasses, and a dark blue Kangol trilby limped noticeably through the Chunnel terminal at Paris Nord. He steadied himself with an expensive and stylish walking cane. He'd dressed the gunshot wound with fresh bandages this morning, and then he'd taken as much codeine as he dared, needing all his senses to be on high alert. Still, pain from the wound throbbed through him.

With his custom boot insoles, he'd gained just about four centimeters in height. At the security checkpoints, the agent focused on the blue canvas satchel he carried over his shoulder. He set it on the stainless-steel table. The agent gestured for him to open it.

Pauk did. The agent rifled through his wardrobe: two pairs of pants, two shirts, a sweater, pajamas, slippers, boots, and a bag of toiletries, all expensive-looking. He confiscated the new and oversized tube of Elgydium toothpaste. He gestured for Pauk to open the slender document zip case containing renderings and drawings. "For my work," Pauk explained quietly, "as an architectural location scout for a small documentary film company." The agent then asked him to remove his eyeglasses and trilby. He complied, revealing strikingly dark brown eyes and his newly shaved head, always aware that the display was for the security cameras. The agent nodded him through.

And finally he reached the first-class passengers already boarding the Eurostar. But Pauk kept walking until he reached the second-class coach, where the number and economic status of the travelers made them less likely to be memorable to Chunnel personnel.

As he stepped around the food cart and then settled into a seat between an elderly man and a middle-aged woman, he remembered Madame Desmarais's reading last night — she'd insisted on carefully removing her Tarot deck from its velvet bag.

As he stared through the young couple settling into the opposite seats, he once again heard Madame Desmarais suck in a little puff of air, her signal of a confounding card — the Moon. "Deception, fear and conflict, and clouded vision," she'd said, waving her hands.

But next, the Chariot — victory and hard control and bravery, and Madame Desmarais relaxed a bit as she told him the card also signaled a journey.

Appropriate, Pauk thought, as the Eurostar began to roll out of the terminal.

It was the final card — Death — that troubled and disturbed him: the skeletal, armored specter of Death riding a white horse surrounded by the dead and the dying. Madame Desmarais clucked but reassured Pauk that this merely meant transformation of the psyche. Regeneration, she told him. Beneficial.

But Pauk couldn't stop staring at the maiden on the Death card, who, according to Madame Desmarais, represented grief and mourning because the King had fallen in some great catastrophe. Just superstition, he chided himself sharply. There was no way the King represented his mentor fallen in defeat. His mentor stood at the height of his power. His empire grew stronger by the day.

Just a little more than two hours later,

Pauk exited the train at Saint Pancras International station in London. His leg ached intensely again by now, and he moved with an even more noticeable hitch. His eyes burned slightly from the dark brown contact lenses. He kept his blue trilby pulled low, aware of the UK's predilection for CCTV. He still had to pass through passport control before he entered the UK.

Minutes later at passport control, a watchful agent observed a tall, fashionably dressed man — the trendy type, with styled facial hair and a shaved head and a fancy cane, because he had some kind of deformity — pass through and continue toward the escalators that led up to the streets of London. Although the agent doubted he had a match, his attention kept returning to one face on the Interpol watch list, the most recent additions posted on the wall of the closet-size office used by passport control officers. Could it be the same man? The photo was poor quality, obviously taken off CCTV, and the man wore a hat and overcoat and appeared much stockier and younger than the French film scout who had passed through his station minutes ago. The descriptors mentioned a partial tattoo and possible nationality, Chechen. He hadn't

FIFTY-FIVE

Vanessa studied the now mostly decomposed features of the dead man on the
stainless-steel tray. The point at the base of
her throat constricted. She asked the
morgue attendant to pull the sheet down so
she could see more of the body. The attendant complied, but it was a slow process,
because he was careful, especially of the
decomposition. Jost Penders, a fit man in
his early forties, had been proud to show off
a small heart tattooed on his chest just
above his own heart. She thought she saw
the vague outlines now, but she couldn't be
certain — minutes earlier, the attendant had
quietly warned her that the body had been
exposed to the elements and to scavenging
animals before it was covered over with dirt
and debris at a construction site where work
had shut down last spring.

She heard a too-discreet cough — from
the inside officer from the Prague Station,

posing as her friend and keeping his distance from all of them, living and dead. Because Vanessa had not been "declared" to Czech liaison, she had entered the country as a civilian. As far as the attendant knew, Vanessa was here to discover if the body had been her cousin.

She gestured to be able to see the dead man's wrists. When the attendant complied, she leaned closer to examine the right wrist. She could see a white ropey mark — the scar on Pender's wrist where he'd ruefully confessed to attempting suicide at the age of twelve when he realized he was gay.

Her breath caught at a sharp stab of sadness. She squeezed her eyes shut and trapped the inside of her lip with her teeth. After several seconds she nodded to the attendant. *"Ano je to on."* Yes, it's him.

Jost Penders had been executed: two close-range rounds to the head — just like the biker in Vienna.

The biker had been killed in an industrial section on the outskirts of Vienna. Jost Penders had turned up dead in a warehouse district outside Prague. The Chechen was a creature of habit, like most people. Penders had been missing for seven months. If his remains had not been accidentally covered with dirt and debris for those months, he would probably be decomposed beyond identification by now.

She followed the inside officer out of the morgue, a survivor of the catastrophic flood of 2002, when cemeteries were upended and bodies floated through the city streets. A cold, drizzling rain had begun to fall, and beneath her thick woolen coat, the chill reached all the way to Vanessa's bones. But she refused a ride when the officer offered to share a Škoda and drop her at the hotel. She needed to walk, to absorb the shock of Jost Penders's murder, and she turned to follow the short block to the Vltava River.

FIFTY-SIX

Dressed in a dapper charcoal wool tweed and a Christys' black fur felt befitting the gray English afternoon, a middle-aged and slightly overweight man with a walking stick and a pronounced limp slowed as he passed an impressive estate set back from the road in Saint John's Wood.

The gates began opening with a smooth mechanical hiss. A black limousine with MP plates headed out and away from the residence, its windows so darkly tinted there was only a shadowy sense of passenger and driver.

Time noted, the man, Pauk, strolled on in the direction of the park.

Pauk's morning had proven productive. Although his hotel was a flea palace in Earls Court, it was centrally located, and his neighbors were not interested in anything except the overwhelming drama — or boredom — of their own lives.

Pauk's longtime associate had chosen well. He'd also received four packages yesterday without incident. Expressed separately overnight, each contained a nest of metal and plastic parts, including the disassembled pieces of his Dragunov. Now, today, like Humpty Dumpty, it would all have to be put together again.

FIFTY-SEVEN

Sprawled on the soft, billowy duvet in her room in the Hilton Prague, Karlín District, Vanessa stared at the secure scan she'd just received on her laptop — the pages from Sergei's intel that she'd asked Lee in forensic accounting to translate ASAP. They had arrived with a small jpeg of Lee's avatar appearing in one corner — a massively muscled, dangerously spiked warrior zombie. In Vanessa's opinion, the slight, geeky real-life Lee easily surpassed his alter ego.

Pushing back intrusive thoughts — fear for Khoury, and the sadness and a simmering fury at the revelation of Jost Penders's murder — she studied Lee's translated sections taken from the margins of the spreadsheets. The first notation had her completely stumped: a string of thirteen numbers. Not a standard-format eight- or eleven-character SWIFT code — the Bank Identifier Codes, or BIC, used by all banks for international wire transfers. She made a note to return to it later when she had more time, more access to resources.

She moved on. The next entries were familiar: the series of electronic money transfers through one particular account, and Sergei had identified the corporate account owner: Bashir Group General Import-Export, Dubai, UAE.

A front company — importing and exporting nothing legitimate — identified last year by CPD and directly linked to Bhoot's associates.

Vanessa exhaled sharply. She stared at Lee's translations of Sergei's margin notes on this page. Lee had seen through Sergei's string of alphanumerics and he had divided them into date and amount; date and amount; date and amount . . .

Sergei would not have known the significance of the dates, but he had tracked the deposits and withdrawals in the account, and that was enough for Vanessa to put it together.

On March 31, 2011, a transfer into the account for forty thousand euros.

On April 3, 2011, a second transfer into the account for another forty thousand euros. And that same day, all eighty thousand euros transferred out to a separate offshore account.

Vanessa stared at the dates and numbers. She knew what Sergei hadn't known: A Spanish prosecutor had been murdered on April 1, 2011.

Now she raced through the transactions. June 2, 2011, forty thousand euros deposited to the same account, followed by an additional forty thousand euros two days later.

The Russian's Sverdlovsk-45 engineer; according to Sid he'd been executed by sniper on June 3, 2011.

On October 16, 2012, forty-five thousand euros deposited — followed by forty-five thousand more on the nineteenth.

Vanessa closed her eyes, recalling the date Sid had told her the Dutch MIVD officer was killed. *October 18.* Apparently, the Chechen's rate had gone up.

Shit — how much money was the Chechen pulling in? And how many others had he so contemptuously murdered on orders from Bhoot? Because there were more dates, more deposits, dating back several years. But she didn't have time right now to track down the assassinations that might surely be linked to other payouts.

Her pulse tripped over itself as she clicked her way through the virtual pages to find what she was looking for: a transaction for fifty thousand euros on February 1, 2013. She'd last seen Penders in Prague two days later, February 3, when she went to his apartment to look at photographs he'd secretly taken of his occasional lover, the German nuclear trigger expert known as Hans, a suspected player in Bhoot's network. Another fifty thousand euros streamed in on February 4, 2013. All one hundred thousand euros transferred out one day later.

She searched for one more date. She found it on a separate page: one hundred ten thousand euros had flowed in two equal deposits through the same account less than two weeks ago. The entire balance was transferred out on September 18, two days after Arash was murdered.

Jesus — Sergei discovered the money trail from Bhoot to his personal assassin.

She needed to get this information to Chris, but she needed a little more time to decide on a strategy for delivery. She wanted back in on Operation Ghost Hunt.

She sent off a secure cable to Lee, thanking him and requesting the account be tagged with an immediate-priority alert the moment there was any new activity. She hoped it wouldn't occur to Lee to ask if she still had access.

Forty-five minutes later, she heard the ding of her secure version of IM. *Khoury?* Rolling off the bed, she checked her screen.

Bear: hanging in?

Bear was Sid's IM moniker. Vanessa typed a quick response.

V3: whassup?

Bear: chatter up on j-sites

Meaning the chatter had intensified on known terrorist websites and in jihadist chat rooms.

V3: ??

Bear: BOLO on yr guy got a ding

Zoe had sent out the Chechen's picture to Interpol/Europol watch lists — and someone had spotted him.

V3: where?

Bear: london

Some time after Sid disconnected, Vanessa

realized she'd been memorizing plaster patterns on the hotel ceiling. She looked over at the window to see that it was barely daylight outside. She glanced at the clock. She'd been somewhere else for twenty minutes.

Still unsure about her next move and isolated from CPD, she scrolled through secure communications on her laptop. After deleting several cables that qualified as bureaucratic sludge, she held her *ready* finger on the delete key and barely glanced at the next.

Shit. She jerked her finger off the keyboard as quickly as if she'd been scalded.

The bigot list for Operation Ghost Hunt — her demotion happened so quickly, she was still on the CPD distribution list for it.

She stared at a cable from MI5 — sent from Thames House to London Station, where it had been cut and pasted into the cable to Headquarters.

In summary, a sharp-eyed passport officer at border security for the Chunnel terminus in Saint Pancras reported a highly probable match for an individual from terrorist watch list — and confirmation had come via facial recognition software. MI5 was requesting a meeting in London with CPD — "Given mutual concern over security threats to certain high-level targets and Iranian nuclear threat."

Within thirty minutes Vanessa read the confirmation from CPD to London Station that would be forwarded to MI5 — the meeting was on.

She sat down to compose her cable to Chris:

C/O GROVES PLANS TO MEET C/CPD/OPS AT REGULAR SCHEDULED MEETING SITE PRIOR TO MEETING WITH GATEKEEPER AT 1300 HRS ON 28 SEPTEMBER. LOOKING FORWARD TO DISCUSSING OPERATION GHOST HUNT AS C/O BELIEVES SHE HAS VITAL INFORMATION TO SHARE.

What did she have to lose? If she did nothing, she was fairly certain she was headed to the backwater posting of Montevideo via Nicosia and Headquarters. That would be failure, and she couldn't afford to fail; her father had taught both his children at an early age that the strongest have a responsibility to care for those who can't defend themselves.

And ultimately, the thing that drove her to keep pushing her way back in was her

hatred of Bhoot and others like him —
those who dealt death in exchange for
money, power, and ideology. She had everything at stake when it came to stopping the
ghost.

She didn't give herself time to back down.
Instead, she quickly typed the closing to the
cable.

C/O GROVES SCHEDULED TO FLY
BACK TO RESIDENCE ON 28 SEP-
TEMBER. WILL DO SO AFTER RE-
QUESTED MEETING AND PER
HQS CONVERSATION WILL BEGIN
SHUTTING DOWN COVER COM-
PANY AND WRAPPING UP BUSI-
NESS IN ADVANCE OF NEW PCS
ASSIGNMENT.

She sat back and gazed around at the
hotel room, the stacks of hand-scrawled
notes, and the room-service tray of still-
uneaten food.

"Wrapping up" might be a stretch.

The Chechen might be in the UK, the
man who had murdered three of her assets
and possibly dozens of other targets.

With a click of a key she sent the cable,
and then she booked a flight leaving for
London in less than three hours. Chris's

reply came within minutes.

PERMISSION GRANTED FOR C/O
GROVES FINAL MEETING ON OP-
ERATION GHOST HUNT PRIOR TO
PCS DEPARTURE AND TERMINA-
TION OF ANY FURTHER INVOLVE-
MENT WHATSOEVER IN THE OP.

FIFTY-EIGHT

The bore of the Dragunov felt warm and true under Pauk's careful touch. The black steel gleamed from careful tending. He'd always admired the efficient mechanics of the weapon's short-stroke gas piston operation system. After a moment, he set it next to the scope and cartridge case laid out on the bed. Most of it was assembled and ready. He'd removed most of his maps from the walls, folding them into tight rectangles placed one on top of the other. He was quite familiar by now with the most likely locations where he would deal with his target. He was also prepared to encounter more intense security.

He turned, catching a glimpse of his reflection in the chipped and clouded mirror. He stepped closer, gazing dispassionately at his near-naked body, and the abstract pattern of scars that marked his back, ribs, and thighs. Some from the beatings after his mother died and he was taken away to the makeshift orphanage, some from the sicknesses because there was no medicine, others from fighting. But they were all from his childhood. Everything changed when he met his mentor. And when the last war ended, he left Chechnya for good and vowed he would never let anyone hurt him again. After that, the scars became remnants of a distant, ever-fading history.

He looked down at the fluid-soaked bandage on his upper thigh. He'd been taking antibiotics along with the codeine, but still the pain gnawed at him. If anything, it was getting worse day by day. But something else disturbed him more than the pain. Somehow, with this new wound, this new scar-to-be, he had become vulnerable again.

Voices drifted from the hallway, and he looked up, even though he had set the double chain locks and the dead bolt himself.

The room had only one small window, overlooking a trash-filled alley in Earls Court. Last night he stared, sleepless, out at the sickly strays — all the time missing Madame and her cats.

The voices passed, fading, and he breathed.

He wasn't used to being on edge. Everything felt different. He reached for his book on English gardens. He touched the photograph he used as a bookmark and pulled it free.

He'd captured it from the YouTube video — the woman from Cyprus, Vienna, Prague. Somehow she had managed to trespass into his mind. Was it possible he had dreamed about her, he a man who did not dream? The tips of his fingers went to his bandaged thigh. He felt certain he would encounter her again — and then he would deal with her once and for all.

After some time, Pauk realized he had been sitting on the edge of the bed, jaw clenched, hands made into fists. He steeled himself, returning the photograph to its place between the pages of the book. He had a job to do.

FIFTY-NINE

Vanessa took the stairs quickly, descending from Westminster Bridge toward the large wharf complex and the entrance to the London Eye — the great iconic wheel turning slowly against steely river and leaden sky.

On time at 1300 hours, she strode into a brisk headwind that punched up the Thames and made her skin rise with goose bumps. She scanned the waterfront, dreading their initial interaction. *What to say first?* And where was Chris? Had his anger softened?

Thirty seconds later, she saw him near the ticket booth, waiting in the shadows.

And the answer was no — no softening; he stood so ramrod straight in his black overcoat he could have been a palace guard.

Shit. She needed to start strong. She saw him tracking her approach, and she could read the offense in his eyes.

When she was almost to him, he began

walking, taking her arm firmly, moving her toward the ride.

She glanced at him, revealing her surprise, and he held out two tickets. "You wanted to talk." He made it sound like an accusation.

They took their place behind a family of Asian tourists in the queue, a short line for a Saturday. She assessed Chris with a quick glance. Fatigue still deepened the lines on his face, but his eyes were clear and the days-old beard was gone.

She knew he'd taken his own read of her. She couldn't help wondering what he saw. She'd taken efforts to clean up, look professional, and she certainly felt alert. But he gave nothing away as they inched toward the creeping progress of the Eye, where an attendant ushered them forward.

"Keep moving, step aboard the capsule, and catch the view of a lifetime!"

When it was her turn, Vanessa miss-stepped slightly, only to feel Chris steady her with the lightest push — away from the tourists (Vietnamese, she'd realized) to claim the other end of the capsule for themselves.

That was one advantage of the constantly moving Eye, Vanessa thought — nobody joining you once you were a foot above-ground. The disadvantage: She and Chris were now literally caged together.

They sat facing each other in an uncomfortably awkward silence.

However long the ride lasted, Vanessa knew she had to get Chris's attention fast — moving it away from what had happened between them — and refocused on what they could do together to get the Chechen and Bhoot.

She felt a fresh flash of shame for having betrayed Chris's trust with her lies.

The weight of the moment pressed down, along with the gravity of her agenda. She pushed through the silence. "For right now, I need you to put aside what just happened between us at Headquarters. I've got something we need to act on."

He met her straight-on look with his own. He didn't say yes, didn't say no. He wasn't budging, but he was there, sitting across from her, and that meant this was the only open window she would get.

"Let's start with Vienna . . ." Vanessa kept her voice low so she wouldn't be overheard, but the tourists still hugged the other end of the capsule anyway, caught up in the view, their conversations loud and animated, and beyond them, London, in all its centuries-old layered complexity, reaching out in every direction.

"The Prater, September sixteenth, my asset was assassinated," Vanessa said quietly. "On September fifteenth, fifty-five thousand euros are wired into an account at Troika bank. Another fifty-five thousand are deposited on September seventeenth. Both deposits flow from the same account set up by Bashir Group General Import-Export, Dubai, UAE. On September eighteenth, the entire hundred and ten thousand euros are wired to a separate offshore account."

Without moving, Chris had gone still. *She had his attention.*

"Prague, February third, my asset goes missing," she continued. "Two days before, fifty thousand euros dump into our now familiar account; the second deposit, same amount, wires in on February fourth. Again, the balance is wired out, same destination, February fifth. Getting the picture? And the trail goes back even farther — to Amsterdam and Barcelona." She paused for effect, leaning even closer — close enough to see his pupils dilate and contract. She dropped her voice to a whisper now. "There's more, but what matters — at CPD we've already linked Bashir Group General Import-Export as a suspected primary front company for Bhoot. And now, thanks to a brave Russian, we've linked payouts from Bhoot's front company to the hits on my assets and at least three others. There are probably many more if we start looking closely. My final questions, how the hell is Bhoot's batting average so high? How has he been able to target our assets so successfully?" She waited a beat, then said, "And those are all the reasons you need to take me with you to the meeting."

His eyes widened and she kept quiet, waiting for his reaction.

"Excuse me —"

Chris looked up, startled, and Vanessa turned to see a teenage girl standing with camera in hand. A brazen hot-pink streak through her long black hair contrasted sharply with her shy smile. An even younger girl stood a few feet behind her. "You take our picture?"

Vanessa looked to Chris and shrugged — *They don't look like spies, they're kids.*

While he obliged, snapping several photos of the giggling girls, Vanessa watched him, wondering where he stood. Had she persuaded him?

"Thank you, thank you!" Still giggling, the girls dipped and bowed to Chris — and Vanessa, too — before scurrying back to their group.

Chris took his seat again, remaining silent,

pressing the tips of his fingers together. Vanessa couldn't read him.

But, finally, he really looked at her. "Ballistics came back: Vienna and Cyprus are a match." It was a quiet statement that covered a lot of ground. His dark eyebrows knitted together. "But apparently one or two witnesses at Saint Hilarion Castle claim they saw a female shooter . . ."

"You know eyewitness accounts are notoriously unreliable when guns are involved." She gazed at him evenly, aware that the tourists were stirring, their ride winding down, the ground coming at them. But then, abruptly, she pictured the hurt and betrayal she'd seen on Chris's face at Headquarters when he realized the extent of her relationship with Khoury and the depth of her lies. She took a deep breath. "But sometimes eyewitnesses get it right. Do you want to talk more about this now?"

He stared at her long enough she felt the urge to squirm. But then he shook his head. "No, not here. We will have that conversation, but it can wait for later."

She reached out toward Chris to put her hand on his arm. They were close now, their heads almost touching. She said, "It looks like we have a chance to get Bhoot with Operation Ghost Hunt now that you have

331

the facility location. But we can have his minion, too, the Chechen. We can get them both. And it's becoming increasingly clear that they're connected at the hip, and this hit man is *slaughtering* our people for his boss. The links are there — the money trail from Bhoot's front company, the dates of deposit. But what I can't figure out is, how did he know so much about three of my assets?" She tightened her grip on Chris's arm. "Is there a leak? Could there be a mole at CPD?"

Chris stood and Vanessa followed because they were almost on the ground. "I've got a lot to share with MI5, and I think they've got more to share with us. We need to take him down, and I can help you do that."

The automated doors opened, and the teenage girls waved as their group stepped off. Vanessa went next, ahead of Chris. Solid ground felt good, and she kept walking in the direction of Westminster Bridge. She didn't slow until she reached the deserted alcove between the wharf and the stairs. She turned then to see Chris standing a few feet back, where he'd stopped.

When she reached him, he said, "There's something we need to get straight before the meeting. You are smart and driven, and you've had some luck and some successes.

You've also had some tough breaks and close calls and downright fuckups." He wasn't done. "And then you've had some very dangerous lapses in judgment. *You cannot be mixed up with David Khoury.* He is under intense internal scrutiny, security is investigating his family, they're tracking his movements — and I guarantee, if you don't walk away, that scrutiny will fall back on you."

She met Chris's eyes and held his gaze, but her thoughts were scrambling. She thought she'd realized the extent of the trouble Khoury was in — but she was really only beginning to glean the depth.

"I thought you knew this," he said, regretfully shrugging the statement away. "Since you don't — I have to be able to trust what you say. To make this job work, you never lie to me again."

Her mouth dropped open. Even though she'd been trained not to reveal her true emotions, she failed in this moment. But she recovered quickly. She pursed her mouth and nodded to Chris. "Understood."

SIXTY

Vanessa stared down at the man who only vaguely resembled the Chechen — caught on camera by Saint Pancras station's CCTV as he entered the UK via the Chunnel more than twenty-four hours ago. The photo was time-stamped by Interpol and then passed on to relevant agencies. This time he wore a dark blue trilby and sported a mustache and goatee and stylish urban eye frames. The sleeves of his light blue canvas jacket were long enough to cover his wrists. He carried a zippered canvas bag. And he kept his chin tucked — his practiced casualness a posture designed to give away nothing.

But this time we got you, Vanessa thought — in a second CCTV shot from Paris Nord and a camera angled from a distance so the photo showed two-thirds of his face, his hat and glasses off, head shaved clean. She recognized his high cheekbones, narrow, symmetrical nose, and pronounced forehead. She tried to read his face for suppressed pain, hoping she'd done him serious harm at the castle.

Was it really ten days since she'd tagged him from Vienna's CCTV? Her sense of urgency to bring him down had only intensified.

She blinked, looked up, handing both photos to Chris. The MI5 officers — Trevor and Howard — had been watching her. Now Howard shifted the focus of his pale blue eyes to the file beneath his hand while Trevor kept his attention on Vanessa — who had been introduced as Claire. The customary charade of first-name pseudos.

As far as Vanessa could tell, Chris was the only person in the paneled conference room using his real first name — and only because of his rank and the fact that he'd worked with MI5 before.

The surveillance photographs had been Howard and Trevor's biggest contribution so far — to this meeting organized because both MI5 and the CIA were interested in apprehending the Chechen. "He is quite likely responsible for the death of several of your assets," Howard said, with British aplomb, while Trevor added, "And we have reason to believe that he is hunting a new target in London."

Chris coughed. "So why isn't he in custody? Or is he?"

Neither MI5 officer spoke up immediately, and Vanessa said, "You *lost* him?"

Trevor frowned, and Howard said, "We believe we've found the hotel he used. We're checking into all sightings, watching all major hubs and routes out of the city. We may have news on his location any minute."

Everyone was silent for an uncomfortably long moment. Then Chris cleared his throat to signal they were moving on, and he offered up the basic ballistics reports from Prague, Vienna, and Cyprus. "Both long-range rounds were 7.62×54R; the two close-range rounds were Russian-made high-velocity 9×19-millimeter 7N21. An unusual choice, and the link to a number of the other hits."

And Vanessa superficially covered the financial data she'd shared with Chris. The line between sharing too much and not enough was razor-thin.

But she had to push the conversation forward — to get more from the Brits. What the hell was buried in their files? How could she get access to it?

Give some to get some . . . .

"He follows a careful operational pattern, gentlemen," she said, lowering her voice and using body language to pull in both operatives along with the metro police liaison to MI5, a heavy-set man introduced as "Peter." There were advantages to being the only woman in the room.

"We know from ballistics and other sources, instead of a single-shot bolt-action rifle, he's using a semiautomatic Russian sniper rifle, a Dragunov — probably because he learned to kill with one in Chechnya — as well as a Russian military-issue 443-Gratch, for close work. When he snipes, he almost always takes out each target with a single, very accurate, head shot from a range of four hundred to one thousand meters. And he's choosing public spaces — museums, parks, landmarks — locations where his target will be vulnerable and unprotected."

She moved her focus pointedly to the file beneath Howard's spread palm. "Let's not forget that his targets all have links to Bhoot's black-market procurement network — the Dutch intelligence officer, the Spanish prosecutor, and our assets." She spread her bare fingers wide. "These are intelligence and justice targets or targets who have actionable intel about Bhoot's network."

"To put it plainly," the man called Peter

said, speaking for the first time since the meeting had begun, "this Bhoot is ordering the Chechen to take out any bloke who gets him in a lather."

"That's about right," Vanessa said. "We suspect the Chechen was in Vienna for less than forty-eight hours before he took out his target. If we're looking for a temporal pattern, it makes sense that he'd get in and out quickly. My guess, his window in country is thirty-six to forty-eight hours — that gives us at most twenty-four hours to find him in London."

A woman's husky alto came from behind Vanessa. "Sounds like you're telling us we need to get moving on this."

The men all stood. Vanessa turned, taking in MI5's Director-General, Alexandra Hall, who looked as if she were dressed for travel — neutral pantsuit, subtle makeup, and a recent visit to the salon, judging from the highlights and layers in her short cut. Vanessa came to her feet, too.

"Good to see you again, Madame Director," Chris said, stepping forward to extend his hand.

Her expression softened, and she returned the greeting. "Christopher. Thank you for coming all this way. I wish the circumstances were less urgent. This is extremely important to us. Our PM and your president have requested that we work ever closer on these issues of concern to both of us. We have a shared agenda — we have a problem we both need to solve." Her gaze settled on Vanessa, who stepped forward.

"It's an honor to finally meet you in person, Madame Director. I was just going over some of our intelligence and analysis — and stressing the need to move with some haste —"

"As I heard," Hall said. "What you may not know is that we think we have identified the Chechen's next target." She nodded to Howard, and he slid out the file he'd been harboring.

"Your Chechen seems to be staking out our MP Alfred Smythe." She looked again to Howard. "Please share what we've got with our guests."

It had not escaped Vanessa's notice that the file was very thin. So the Brits were sharing — but no doubt only a few of their toys. Certainly not all.

Howard pushed the file across the table.

Chris opened it, and now he tapped it toward Vanessa so she had a clear view. She studied the latest surveillance photo, time and date from the previous afternoon. This time the camera caught a man dressed sportily in a high-collar cardigan, black skinny-leg jeans, black MPTs, olive-green-and-black Polo cap decorated with the familiar pony logo and the numeral *3,* a black-and-white leather sports bag slung over his shoulder.

Vanessa studied the fit, athletic man who looked to be in his mid-thirties. It was him but not him, and his ability to shape-shift sent a chill through her body.

"That's from CCTV outside the Harbour Club in Chelsea," Howard said. "Where the MP plays squash —"

"Every Thursday at four-fifteen," Hall finished.

A detail the head of MI5 punctuated sharply and familiarly, Vanessa thought, taking a closer look at Hall. Why would she know the MP's schedule to the minute?

Chris pushed back in his chair. "I see a CCTV photograph taken outside a sports club with a large membership, where, what, a thousand or so men play squash. What makes you so sure he is after Smythe?"

Trevor gave a nod to Vanessa. "Claire has given us a good sense of the Chechen's patterns, and MP Smythe is a viable match — he's championing a massive bill in parliament: an anti-terrorism bill that will greatly expand the government's power when it comes to surveillance and access to financial transaction records."

Hall said, "A bill that would definitely not endear him to Bhoot. But we're not just betting on hunches. We've picked up more specific chatter from terrorist sites, and we had a tip from a usually reliable asset. And that's why we've had MP Smythe under protection."

Vanessa frowned. "Had?"

MI5's Director-General looked at her Burberry wristwatch. "As of forty minutes ago, he's far from London but still safely under our watch. We're confident the immediate danger has been averted; however, we are as interested as you are in catching the Chechen, and ultimately Bhoot. Believe me when I say that is one of my top priorities. Bhoot and I are old enemies . . ."

Hall held her silence for several moments, her eyes on Vanessa. Finally, she said, "I'm going to share something with you — given the depth of Bhoot's awareness of top-secret intelligence activities, MI5 and MI6 have been concerned for some time about a possible security breach. Has it occurred to you that you may have been targeted by Bhoot because you've been a front runner in CPD's hunt for him?"

Vanessa remained silent, aware of the

unusual nature of this interaction with Hall. How much did Hall know about the events of the past few weeks? How closely was she tracking Vanessa — a CIA NOC — and why? She sensed Chris next to her, registering it also.

"A security breach has occurred to me, yes," Vanessa said slowly.

Hall nodded. "If it turns out this is the case, it is even more imperative that Operation Ghost Hunt is successful in capturing or eliminating Bhoot."

Vanessa nodded. "I understand what's at stake, Madame Director, but I don't understand why you're telling me this now."

Hall said, "I had the opportunity to work with your father on a sensitive operation many years ago. He did me a favor. I feel inclined to keep an eye on his daughter."

Vanessa frowned, trying to absorb both text an subtext. But before she had the chance to formulate her next question, Hall glanced at Howard, and he took his cue almost seamlessly, pushing back from the table.

As he stood, he looked at Chris and said, "We have a hit man to track down, and you have urgent operations to conduct back on U.S. soil."

Trevor and the liaison officer for metro

police both stood, as did Chris.

Vanessa felt abruptly deflated. The meeting was over. She glanced to Chris and then back to Hall, who was nodding at them even as she backed toward the door. "Thank you both again for your cooperation. But if you will excuse me, I can't stay."

"Good luck at the conference," Chris said. It took Vanessa a moment to register that Hall would soon be addressing members of the international intelligence community at the Conference on Terrorism and Cyber Security in Sydney.

"Thank you, Christopher," Hall said. "I'm on a plane in less than three hours, and I still have a rather unique gift to collect for my host. Trevor?"

Trevor, already up, moved with her toward the door. As she stepped out, he said, "The chap at the flea returned our call to say the map is ready and he will close his doors at six p.m. *sharp.*"

The door clicked shut behind the Director-General.

Chris pushed out his chair, and Vanessa stopped him with one arm. "It's still early, and we have more to talk about —"

"We're done here," Chris said, gathering up his jacket. Vanessa heard the finality in his words.

After the briefest hesitation, she nodded. Her reconnection with Chris was still fragile, and there would be nothing gained by pushing for more time after they'd been as much as dismissed by the Brits.

As Howard gathered up the file, Chris said, "Will we have access to the *complete* file?"

Howard blinked. "I'm certain that can be arranged." But his tone said otherwise.

Now Howard focused his pale blue eyes on Vanessa. "We have a full team tracking the Chechen. As the Director-General emphasized, it is one of our top priorities. The other is working with your agency to apprehend Bhoot."

Vanessa nodded. But she couldn't repress a sigh of resignation even as a raw energy coursed through her. In her mind she saw the Chechen in all his guises, eerie in his ability to change his appearance. She couldn't shake the sense that he was here to do a job — a job he would complete very soon.

SIXTY-ONE

"What's wrong with this picture?" Vanessa followed Chris down the faded steps of the old red-brick building that housed MI5's centrally located Headquarters. All the way down the elevator and while they retrieved their cell phones from the security desk and Vanessa grabbed her small roll-aboard, she'd been mentally turning the encounter with Alexandra Hall and the MI5 operatives.

She pulled her slicker tight around her shoulders, chilled by the now-steady drizzle. The darkening of the late-afternoon sky and the icy wind that whipped down the narrow, deserted street made it seem even colder.

"One minute they're talking about the PM and the president, and the next minute they've got it handled, and Hall can't give us the time of day because she's going *shopping*?" She powered up her cell phone,

345

searching automatically for messages and finding none.

"It's very British, you know," Chris said, sounding distracted.

"What's very British, the flea?"

"The gift — and what the hell? Didn't they say there'd be an assigned car waiting at the corner by now?" No-parking signs covered the entire block.

"That's what they said." Vanessa turned back toward the building's unassuming side entrance, but Chris didn't move.

She said, "I'll tell them we're —"

"Let's get a *bloody* taxi," Chris said, grinning like a kid about to pick out a familiar and favorite treat. He took the steps quickly, and she followed him, moving briskly down the narrow street to the corner, where they stood beneath the shadow of one of the building's numerous security cameras.

Within seconds, he'd hailed a shiny, black London cab.

He held the door and Vanessa climbed in first, sighing at the familiar, delicious roominess.

"Head us in the direction of Charing Cross," Chris told the cabbie, who looked as if he could be Dev Patel's twin.

"Right you are, guv," the cabbie said, with a perfect Cockney accent. "A good night for

346

you two to stay inside nice and cozy."

Chris and Vanessa looked at each other, exchanging a smile.

Chris peered out at a world slick and gray as the rain settled in. "I'm guessing you don't have a hotel yet," he said. "I know a great pub at Charing Cross." He raised his voice to be heard above a sudden cloudburst. "We can talk more — and also figure out logistics —"

He broke off speaking while the cabbie executed an abrupt and tight U-turn and quickly cut over to the steely gray chop of the River Thames. When they were heading north, Chris touched Vanessa's arm lightly. "You did good in there. And here's what's wrong with the picture — you don't have it. Or not all of it." He paused to watch a tugboat disappearing under Westminster Bridge.

Then he surprised Vanessa by whispering in her ear — "Alexandra Hall and MP Smythe — he's her ex but not completely ex. It's one of *those* relationships." He leaned toward the seat divider to tell the cabbie which pub, and the cabbie retorted, "Already knew which one was the best, guv."

Chris returned his attention to Vanessa. "You're very quiet."

She frowned, twisting her mouth, still

turning over mental stones. She looked toward the window, but she was picturing the fire in Alexandra Hall's eyes when she said, *We are as interested as you are in catching the Chechen, and ultimately Bhoot. Believe me when I say that is one of my top priorities.*

"It's not adding up." She looked intently at Chris. "It doesn't feel right."

"So . . . this is one of your aha moments? Go on, I'm listening."

"I've been focusing on the pattern, and that's led me to the Chechen — but there's a whole new level to the game when we factor in Bhoot's motivation." Vanessa pulled up straight, as if she might see over something blocking her view.

"This is about retaliation for actions against his network. MP Smythe makes a logical target. He's sponsoring an antiterrorist bill. But what I keep thinking — *he's too high-profile.* The other targets have been practical — eliminating my assets — or they've been intelligence officers, a prosecutor, or someone looking to sell black-market nukes to the competition."

Chris tipped his head. "He could be using a higher-profile target to divert attention from his travel to Iran, the facility . . ."

"Maybe." Vanessa nodded.

"But I'll tell you one thing," Chris said. "It's not Smythe who got the antiterrorist bill through to legislation, it's Alexandra Hall; she's the powerhouse —"

A shrill beep sounded over his words — the alert on Vanessa's cell. She had a waiting text message. She made a face. "Sorry." She gazed down at the phone as she worked her way to the message. After a moment, she sucked in a breath. "Shit."

"What is it?" Chris asked sharply.

She held the phone so he could see the text: E250,000.

"From Lee in forensic accounting — nevermind, I'll tell you later," she said quickly. "But I asked him to tag the account that holds the money transfers between Bhoot and the Chechen. A deposit just set off the alert."

Chris's eyebrows rose above the frames of his glasses. "If that's only the first half of the payment . . ."

"Then this new target is worth five hundred thousand euros to Bhoot," Vanessa finished.

She shook her head in frustrated excitement and alarm. "What if the target was never the MP? What if it's Alexandra Hall? They're sort of a couple; you just told me so yourself. So the Chechen could just as easily have been tracking her. You just said Hall is a powerhouse, she pushed the anti-terrorist bill, and she's not leaving for Australia for another three hours — so the Chechen's still got a window."

Chris was staring at her.

Vanessa shook her head impatiently. "She said she and Bhoot are old enemies. If I'm wrong, bad on me, I'll end up in Montevideo. If I'm right, then this is it. I'm willing to place that bet. The Chechen's window is now. And she's already on her way to the flea market — a public place where she's off her guard. The flea market has to be Portobello, they have at least half a dozen antique-map shops."

Chris went still for a moment. Vanessa felt him deciding. He pulled out his cell phone, and then he leaned forward, sliding the small window open to tell the cabbie, "Portobello, the flea market."

SIXTY-TWO

The cabbie braked hard at the wooden barricade. "Far as I can get you, guv! Sorry, luv, can't squeeze any tighter! They block off the market —"

"Which way?" Vanessa asked, already half out the door and into the drizzling rain — at the same time Chris peeled off several ten-pound notes into the cabbie's hand. She'd already pulled her gray cap low around her face and zipped her slicker to her throat, but the cold cut through to her skin.

"Should be on your left," the cabbie shouted, caught up in their urgency, flapping the money at the rain-spattered windshield. "Straight ahead about two blocks up!"

Bracing with both hands, Vanessa jumped the barricade, almost going down on the slick pavement. She heard Chris close on her heels. He called after her, "I'll try to reach the Station and MI5 — but I'm right behind you."

"Got it," Vanessa called out, as she scanned the street. At least two years since she'd been here, but she recalled a colorful, international wall of makeshift booths lining both sides of the street and, behind those, old shops filled with dust-coated merchandise sold by equally dusty proprietors. Now, as the market loomed, the colors blurred through the constant drizzling rain. Where the hell were the street numbers?

Vanessa looked toward the row of shops on her left. *It would be one of those —*

The main street was crowded and noisy — two drummers carrying their doumbeks out of the rain while a third musician wailed away on a saxophone. And a few booths beyond, a guitarist and a singer performed a folk song. On top of all that, canned music. And the babel of languages matched by the heavy and exotic smells coming from an equally international array of food vendors.

She stepped wide around a mother chasing two toddlers and a Scottie dog. She scanned the market and the street, evading what was right in front of her, while she strained to catch a glimpse of Alexandra Hall or the Chechen.

She pictured the latest CCTV image, jacket and hat and the way he held his face at an angle. But she registered her silent question: *What do you look like today?*

"Map shop!" Chris said, startling her — and she felt his hand gripping her elbow for an instant before he let go. Then she saw the shop almost hidden behind a booth draped in brightly dyed fabric covered with African designs and its sign: *Map of the World, number 118* in print barely large enough to read.

Chris entered, leaving the door ajar. Vanessa stood outside, splitting her focus between what was happening on the street and Chris. He talked animatedly with the proprietor, a stooped elderly man.

"Yeah, Miss Alexandra was here, but she left," the man said, and Vanessa heard his sharp, nasal complaint clearly through the open door.

"Said she wanted to look at my competition, even though I sell the best and been here the longest and she knows that."

"Who's your competition?" Chris barked. "We need an address."

Vanessa tensed at a sudden spurt of rapid-fire percussion — but almost instantly she identified the sound as drums, not firearms.

The old proprietor shook his head.

A tiny dog pulled its leash taut, walking its short, obese owner.

A boy kicked at bits of trash stuck to the dark, wet pavement.

Several men caught her eye because they were slender and wearing hats — but not one of them was the Chechen.

"Show us!" Chris almost shouted, stepping out of the shop. The old man stopped at the door, shrugging, pointing, "Open your eyes! She didn't say which one!"

Vanessa stared at the line of shops, squinting at their signs closely now, as if they had just sprung out of nowhere.

Rare and Vintage Maps and Charts.
Ye Old Mappe Shoppe.
Here Be Dragons.

"Damn." Chris was beside her, trying and failing to wipe rain from his face with the wet sleeve of his overcoat. "Who knows how many there are?"

"I'm on this side," she said, already moving. "You take that side."

They split up, and she hurried to a shop, peering in to find it empty. When she tried the door, it was locked. As she dashed to the next shop advertising antiques, books, and maps, she caught a glimpse of Chris on the other side, heading for a shop with a great pink sign: *Antiquarian Maps.*

When she reached the door to Ye Old Mappe Shoppe, she noticed movement, and she stuck her head inside. "Have you had any recent customers?"

A round woman in a housedress dashed her cigarette in the ashtray. "Come on in, darling, you're soaked —"

But Vanessa was already moving on.

A flash of dark blue caught her eye when she stepped from behind a booth. A man in a blue raincoat. Walking away and up the street. *Right height. Hat pulled low. Carrying a pack slung over one shoulder.*

For a startling instant the sun appeared from behind clouds, skies drizzling and the light suddenly blinding. Vanessa blinked to adjust her eyes. But she didn't see Chris anywhere, just the blue raincoat moving farther from her, and she couldn't afford to do nothing. So she followed.

He waited up the street three hundred meters from the map shop, inside which his target now shopped. Leaning with his weight on his good leg against the small counter at the food stand. The hip of his injured leg propped against the stool reserved for customers. The wound burned like hell. A sudden ray of sun oddly illuminated the bratwurst and roll on a paper plate in front of him. Coffee steaming from a paper cup. His Dragunov carefully assembled and pressing against his right side, beneath the overcoat.

A young woman passed so close he could reach out and touch her wet, dark blond hair. A shudder ran through him — *it had to be her.*

But the woman put her arm out for the black man walking with her, and they laughed and kissed quickly before breaking into a run.

With his left arm, he reached for his coffee, shocked to notice a slight tremor as he sipped. The anxious fluttering in the pit of his stomach, the rock-hard knot between his eyes, the unsteadiness when the pain became almost unbearable — all of this so completely foreign, a feeling heightened by the strange, underlying sense of the inevitable.

He drank more coffee, spilling this time so the dark liquid stained the left cuff of his dark green Crombie overcoat. He dabbed with a napkin, forcing himself to take care. All the while his rifle pressed hard against him. Then, when he dropped the napkin into a trash can, he let his gaze slide to the shop — number 121 — and the clear signs of movement behind windows. She'd been in there for the past seventeen minutes. So she was buying. As he set the coffee down again, he surveyed the street, the flea-market vendors and their customers — always with 121 in his peripheral vision.

SIXTY-THREE

Vanessa lengthened her stride to gain on the blue raincoat. If it was the Chechen, she needed to make the identification now.

But crowds had thickened here, and rain made the oily street slick and slowed everyone. She slipped once but caught herself and kept moving. Staying parallel and gaining on him a bit at a time.

What the hell would she do if she verified it was him? Should she call Chris? Her almost-numb fingers reached for speed dial. Had he gotten through to the COS London?

She hesitated when he turned away suddenly, down a small alley.

Damn. It looked like a dead end, but it might cut through. *Follow?*

She did for roughly half the block — until he raised his head, as if to check his surroundings, and then he pivoted abruptly in her direction.

It's not the Chechen — not him —

Adrenaline ripped through her, trailed instantly by knife-sharp frustration and a deep sense of relief.

So maybe she was wrong about all of this, and that was fine, that was good . . .

She turned, checking for Chris, retracing her steps along the alley. But at the intersection, all she saw was another map shop down the street — number 121, windows smeared with a film of dust and rain that made it impossible to see anything or anyone inside, at least from this angle.

She started toward the faded blue doors, inset with frosty glass panes, stopping mid-street to pull up abruptly as a skateboarder raced past.

Someone yelled, "Get off the street!"

Someone else — *"Cuidado!"*

Vanessa turned her head, drawn toward the voices.

That's when she saw him.

The Chechen.

Standing beneath an umbrella at a food-stand, maybe two hundred meters from her.

He wore a dark green overcoat, his right sleeve tied off as if he only had use of his left arm — so he was holding his weapon in ready position under the coat. He'd tugged his hat low across his brow. As he surveyed the scene, apparently casually, his attention kept returning to the blue shop door down the street.

The moment froze for her, the world reduced to a triangle with the Chechen at one point, the door to 121 at the other, Vanessa in between, at the apex.

Also present — the ghostly sense of Arash and Sergei and Penders pulling the air from her lungs.

Chimes rang out, and Vanessa caught the flash of movement as the faded blue shop door pushed open — roughly seventy meters to reach it.

The door opened, and Pauk readied himself for the unfolding. The black-suited body-guard glanced out the doorway, checking the street, while the woman who ran MI5 waited a few paces behind, still sheltered in the shop. Pauk's target.

Beneath his coat, his right hand gripped the Dragunov's trigger frame, his right index finger on the trigger. As soon as his target stepped into the doorway, he would swing his rifle up and onto his shoulder in firing position.

But he froze when he spotted the dark armored Range Rover inching down the street toward the shop. The privileged head of MI5 getting door-to-door service, and she and her bodyguard had slowed and were now waiting inside the shelter of the shop and out of his clear sight.

He almost stopped breathing while the vehicle approached the doorway. But the Range Rover slowed a good five meters before the shop. Pauk felt eyes on him, believed he'd been made by the driver. He raised his rifle swiftly through the front slit of his coat to his shoulder — heard someone cry out, "Gun!" — and he fired through the windshield of the Rover and into the driver's head.

Vanessa was closing the distance — only twenty-five meters more — at the same time she noticed the black Range Rover advancing slowly through the rain toward the shop. And then she saw movement in her periphery and turned just as the Chechen raised his rifle through the front of his coat.

"Gun!" Vanessa shouted, flinching at the sharp sound of gunfire. The Range Rover's windshield exploded.

As the Chechen sighted on the doorway of the shop for his next shot, Vanessa made a dash to reach the cover of the still rolling Range Rover. Because the Dragunov was a semiautomatic, the Chechen had no need to shift position and he could fire continuously until he used up his magazine.

Crouched and moving with the car, she peered around the rear wheel and caught a glimpse of Hall's bodyguard in the doorway as he pushed the director of MI5 down to the floor with one arm — the map sliding from one end of the document tube in Hall's hands.

When she looked back to the street she saw the Chechen's rifle gleaming in the rain. And about twenty meters beyond him, Chris crouched behind a wall. *Trying to catch the fully armed Chechen off guard and from behind.* As Vanessa watched, he managed to close the distance by a few steps. What he was trying to do was insanely risky. If the Chechen spotted Chris, he could slice him to pieces in a matter of seconds.

The Chechen fired again, and Hall's bodyguard groaned, falling back into the doorway, hit. Vanessa stayed low, lunging around the inside of the still coasting Range Rover, hunching as she moved with the vehicle, shielded by the front-left tire. As far as she could tell, the Chechen had his focus on the wounded bodyguard and hadn't seen her yet. The bodyguard was down, but he still seemed capable of firing his weapon — as soon as the panicked clutch of pedestrians cleared enough so he could fire without collateral damage.

Vanessa pressed her shoulder against the car and gripped the rain-slicked latch. Her fingers slipped off. Was it locked? She tried again, and this time the latch gave. Apparently the MI5 driver, a member of Hall's security team, or Protection Command, had unlocked it in preparation to pick Hall up in the rain.

Vanessa opened the door and leaned her body into the Range Rover, stretching the short length of the front seat to reach the driver.

Slumped behind the wheel of the idling vehicle, his foot still resting against the pedal, he was obviously dead. She slid one hand under the lapel of his jacket, around his left ribs. Her fingers closed around the butt of the weapon in his shoulder holster.

A Glock 19 high-capacity 9-millimeter pistol with a round in the chamber and a full thirty-magazine of Plus-P cartridges. The driver never even had a chance to fire. But she thanked God the Protection Command used high-performance ammunition. It would make up for the 9-millimeter's slow ballistics. It gave her a lethal range of one hundred meters — a fighting chance.

A gunshot echoed outside — the bodyguard's Glock.

Vanessa flinched at the unmistakable report of the Chechen's rifle as he returned fire. She raised her head just enough to look out at a blurry world through the shattered, rain-soaked windshield. *Fuck.* She'd never see anything if she didn't leave the shelter of the Range Rover. But she had to get closer to the Chechen before she could take a shot.

The Range Rover's engine hummed softly. Vanessa shook her head — what the hell, she would drive. She took a deep breath, waiting, sweat pouring off her now. She knew what she had to do. She wiped her hands dry as best she could, silently apologizing to the dead driver for the use of his jacket.

Peering out just above the dashboard, she pressed down on the dead officer's boot. She kept the pressure light and nothing happened at first. Then the Range Rover began to move again, very, very slowly.

She tried to count seconds and factor distance. She guessed she had only moments before the Chechen focused on the vehicle and mowed it to pieces with his Dragunov.

She released her hand from the dead officer's boot, and the Range Rover slowed to a stop.

If she had all the luck in the world she had only one chance to make her shot. Had she closed the distance enough so her target was within range? The momentary silence outside spooked her.

She slid back toward the door and readied herself to exit quickly. She almost sensed it was coming — another round from the bodyguard, who was a distance behind her now and apparently still trapped and injured in the shop doorway.

The Chechen fired.

And that's when Vanessa moved — propelling herself out of the Rover, crouching again just long enough to orient herself, the Glock gripped in both hands.

The Chechen had changed position, advancing another ten meters or so toward the map shop. He was within Vanessa's range, and she locked his forehead in her sights. She slowed her breathing, readying to stand and leverage herself against the vehicle and fire — all within a second or two. With the faint hope the element of surprise would work in her favor.

Without taking her eyes from the Chechen, Vanessa sensed Chris making his move. But if he tried to get closer, he would be completely exposed.

Vanessa saw the slight slackening of the

Chechen's body and knew he'd sensed Chris. She stood to full height — aware of the gleam of the Chechen's rifle as he turned and fired at Chris. Then swung the rifle at her.

Almost at the same instant, she took her shot.

And missed.

Unconsciously, she braced for the impact of his bullets —

But nothing happened.

It took a very long moment to register — her bullet had struck the Dragunov's gas tube just above the barrel.

Just as the Chechen felt someone behind him and twisted seventy-five degrees, the woman rose to standing next to the black Rover. He recognized her even with the hat and the rain slicker — her weapon raised and ready.

In that instant, he hesitated just a fraction of a second before firing at the man.

Just as he turned back to her, he felt the impact of her first shot. It missed him but hit his rifle.

Incredibly, she'd disabled the Dragunov's semiautomatic operating system. He could not fire without manually resetting the bolt's operating lever.

For those moments it seemed they were locked together, staring outside of normal time, each finally looking into the eyes of the other.

He saw the muzzle of her weapon flash. Heard her second shot. Felt nothing at all as her bullet entered his brain.

Vanessa slumped against the Rover, but she had to move, had to get to Chris where he'd fallen. Was he alive?

She barely registered Alexandra Hall pulling her bleeding bodyguard back into the safety of the shop doorway.

"You okay?" she tried to call out to Hall. Her voice seemed trapped in her throat.

"Yes, yes, yes," Hall answered in a stunned sort of way. "But you're bleeding."

Vanessa refocused on Chris and crossed the distance toward him. She glanced at the Chechen — he was dead.

When she reached Chris, his eyes were open and he seemed alert. The blood seeped from his shoulder, turning his light gray rain slicker black.

"You got him," Chris whispered as Vanessa knelt beside him. "And you're hit, you're bleeding."

"No, Chris, that's your blood, but you'll be okay. We killed the bastard."

A siren rose up sudden and sharp in the distance.

After what seemed like a very long time, she saw black leather boots. *Shit* — her left arm was beginning to burn like hell. Beneath her jacket her skin felt warm and wet. Best she could tell, she'd managed to reopen the gunshot wound from the Chechen's bullet on Cyprus.

"Stay down, we'll get you to hospital," a male and very British voice commanded sharply. "You're okay, we've got you."

SIXTY-FOUR

The nightmare invaded her sleep again — the Kurdish children and their kitten sprawled dead where they had fallen after the cloud of white poison drifted from the sky. She wanted to save them. Still, the toxic snow drifted down, and Vanessa tasted the ripe sweet death on her tongue, felt the heat singe her skin. She dropped to her knees, crawling forward.

But the nightmare shifted to a familiar darkened hall filled with shadows and the murmur of voices. The soft, occasional croon of her mother, but mostly the harsh, broken whisper that she barely recognized as her father. *Home again to the base after one of his endless tours of duty.*

Vanessa didn't call out — "Daddy!" — she knew instinctively that she wasn't supposed to overhear what he was telling her mother. So she crouched low, her fingers gripping her flannel PJs, making herself tiny in the hallway outside the door of her parents' bedroom. And she heard his words, and something terrifying in his voice she had never heard before: *helplessness.*

"— we saw so many bodies — children, women and the babies, old people — some of them frozen as if they'd died in the middle of a gesture or a word, others contorted, agonized, covered with their own vomit, men and women who died trying to shelter their children, their tiny babies. My God, Lois, some children were still alive, and we tried to help but it was too late —"

Her father broke off, and Vanessa heard the sound of choking and she pulled into a ball, wondering if her father was dying, too?

Now, these many years later, she knew it was the only time she'd heard her father weep.

SIXTY-FIVE

Vanessa opened her eyes to find she was reclining inside the dimly lit cream-colored cabin of a Gulfstream IV, one of a fleet belonging to the British government. Outside the porthole windows, the jet raced across pale dawn skies over a bank of soot-gray clouds.

"Apparently you needed sleep."

Vanessa looked toward the deep, female voice to see Alexandra Hall seated across from her in a beige leather VIP chair. "Madame Director." She began to pull her body up to a seated position and almost instantly a steward appeared in the aisle to adjust her bed back to a chair. "Thanks," Vanessa murmured, stifling a yawn and pressing her fingers deep into the buttery soft leather.

"An upgrade from travel in a C-17, isn't it?" Hall smiled, the skin around her eyes creasing, her mouth turning up slightly higher on the left side.

"How long was I out?" Vanessa asked, looking uneasily at her watch — but her wrist was bare.

"Forty-five minutes, give or take." The director of MI5 glanced at her wristwatch. "At the hospital I believe they stored your personal items safely in a pouch, and that's probably in your carry-on. It's 0500 hours, and we'll begin the approach to D.C. within minutes."

"It's Saturday — the twenty-seventh —"

"Going on two in the afternoon in Iran," Hall said. "Operation Ghost Hunt is under way so I suggest you enjoy a good cup of coffee while you still have time." Her focus shifted to the aisle behind Vanessa.

Turning, Vanessa nodded gratefully at a second steward, who offered her very hot coffee in a porcelain mug. "Thanks," Vanessa said, taking her first sip. As the steward served tea from a translucent bone china pot to Alexandra Hall, Vanessa took a moment to gaze around the jet's interior. She and the director occupied the back cabin, and a bank of three monitors were set between windows on the other side of the aisle, one tuned to BBC news — where they were packaging yesterday's Portobello Road shooting as a domestic dispute — and one other to CNN, where a well-known political correspondent told her story from in front of the U.S. Capitol. The volume down, Vanessa read the choppy thread of closed-captioned narrative: ". . . with mounting tensions and pressure from conservatives to take military action against Iran — not a new story, Wolf, but one to watch . . ."

Satisfied she hadn't missed any breaking news while she slept, Vanessa pivoted now, the seat spinning with her, to see into the middle cabin. Two men and one very serious-looking woman, all in black suits, occupied three of the four seats. Chris was seated on a couch, propped against several pillows, staring intently at the screen of his laptop. Last night, while they were being patched up at the hospital, he'd found the heart and the moment to ease a small bit of her misery around Khoury. "David knows about this," he told her quietly. "We got word to him that you're safe." She didn't have to ask her next question, because Chris kept going. "He wants you to know that, considering the circumstances, he's all right." Vanessa didn't dare ask for more information, and, anyway, she didn't believe Chris knew anything more than he'd shared.

"Thanks," she said, touching his left arm lightly.

Now, illuminated by the first light through the G4's windows, he had his jacket off, and the hospital bandage protecting the wound in his right shoulder made him look asymmetrical. Hard to believe that it had been only fourteen hours since she'd shot the Chechen. Instinctively, Vanessa's fingers slid up her arm to her rebandaged biceps, and she sucked in a breath in reaction to the sting of pain. *We make a pair,* she thought, and, as if he heard her words, he glanced up, tipping his head in a quizzical nod.

She raised her eyebrows and puffed out her cheeks, more than ready for an update on Operation Ghost Hunt, but he wagged one index finger and shook his head. She took a breath and told herself they would be on the ground soon, in gear, and catching up on the operation's latest developments. The thought of returning to Headquarters triggered a montage of images, most of them disturbing: her last encounter with Khoury, the resulting confrontation with Chris, the session with the OMD psychologist. Dr. Wright, with her sanctimonious insight — *It's not your job to save the world alone, Vanessa.* Now Vanessa's mouth pulled taut as she caught the vivid image of the Chechen lying dead in the rain. *Not the whole world, no . . . but I can do my best to keep a small part of it safer.*

"Your military has begun tracking an unidentified jet flying in Iranian airspace," Alexandra Hall said.

And Vanessa jerked around in her seat abruptly. "For how long — where is it now?"

"Flying over southern Iran." Hall took a sip of tea.

Vanessa frowned in sudden frustration. "*Where* in southern Iran — that's an area of about three hundred thousand square miles."

"Southeastern Iran."

"Bhoot?" Vanessa's spine stiffened. "Heading toward the facility?"

Hall arched her brows. "In the past thirty minutes, our SAT analysts have isolated what appears to be a rudimentary airfield roughly one hundred fifty kilometers due west of the facility. Other sources are leading us to believe retired Iranian general Abbas Nazemi may be on his way there, traveling by land."

"Shit," Vanessa murmured. "It's happening." And just then she felt the first pull of the jet's descent.

"It may well be," Hall said. "I'm sorry I

can't stay and play — but I will be following events closely."

Vanessa saw an expression of genuine if
fleeting regret on Alexandra Hall's face,
pushed away so quickly by her customary
mask of fierce intelligence that Vanessa
almost doubted she'd seen the deeper
emotional layer.

"Seat belts, please," a passing steward
said. "We'll be landing shortly."

Her thoughts racing now, Vanessa tightened her seat belt gingerly. When she looked
up, she met Alexandra Hall's gaze and held
it. She sensed Hall's curiosity, and she
almost expected a question and yet the
silence between them lengthened.

"You said you knew my father," Vanessa
said finally, surprising herself with the
prompt.

"I said I worked with him." Hall nodded.
"He wasn't an easy man to know. But he
was certainly one of the toughest SOBs I've
ever met. Stubborn as hell and driven."

Vanessa looked away from Hall to focus
on the yellowy-gray clouds pressing against
the windows. Butterflies took off in her belly
— the shift in cabin pressure and the pre-
mission jitters. She heard Hall's matter-of-
fact words. "He was also one of the best
officers I've come across."

The plane dipped below the clouds, and sudden swaths of ocean, earth, and city seemed to press up toward the sky. Vanessa turned back to Alexandra Hall and began to speak quietly.

"If the mission fails somehow — if we don't get Bhoot or even if we do — I need to find out if there's a breach, a mole, and I need to deal with him or her."

"Yes, you do." Hall's mouth pursed, and her focus shifted to some point in the near distance. "I told you I owed your father a favor." She refocused on Vanessa, and her brows pulled together, eyes narrowing. "It now seems I'm in your debt. Call on me when you need to."

SIXTY-SIX

There was barely time for the briefing in CPD's makeshift war room. The lead-up to Operation Ghost Hunt was over, and all teams were about to go live. They had one small window to review the impending operational sequence — even while they all knew anything could and might end up FUBAR.

From her perch on the edge of a cluttered conference table, Vanessa watched as Chris covered ground as quickly as possible. "The goals of this operation are twofold. Capture or kill the black-market nuclear arms dealer we call Bhoot. Disable the secret underground facility and set back any nuclear ambitions in the real world. After that we see what we have — gathering any and all intel in all the ways we know how. Operation Ghost Hunt is ambitious, and that's an understatement. There has already been intense pressure to proceed with military options. But we in the intelligence community know the real value is taking down Bhoot, preferably alive, at the same time we sabotage their ability to produce anything resembling a nuclear weapon at this facility. We clear on that?"

There were nods and general noises of agreement around the room.

Now Chris acknowledged one of the youngest and greenest imagery analysts, who stood a bit shakily. "We have confirmation the unidentified jet the military has been monitoring has landed at the closest thing resembling an airfield anywhere near the facility," he said, speaking so quickly his words ran together. "We're tracking a convoy of SUVs, and they still appear to be heading for the airfield. Our guess, to pick up human cargo, as in a passenger." As he sat down, he finished with: "We'll update as we know more."

Vanessa felt her muscles contract from the tension. Would Bhoot really show? Would they get him?

Chris looked to the back of the room, singling out a lanky, dark-haired man who Vanessa recognized from SAD, the CIA's version of special ops. He was so muscled, he barely seemed to fit in his chair, and he chewed gum at warp speed.

Eduardo, the muscled man, sat up straight, taking his cue. "The timing is tricky, and we're using two teams. Team one will be kill-capture, and their operational goal is to ambush and take down the convoy, contain collateral damage, and deal with whoever they find." He shrugged, still working his gum. "Team two will be divert-disable. We're providing cover for team one at the same time we need to actually disable the facility." He smiled, nodding. "So what we came up with is using carbon fibers to drape over the power lines. Done right, it would completely and permanently disrupt the electrical grid, cut the lights, cause havoc and confusion."

"Do you have to get inside the physical facility?" Chris asked.

Eduardo shook his head. "Nope. That's the beauty. It's all done outside, to the power lines leading into the facility. And with any luck, it will look like an accident. Because the power goes down and by the time they look at the lines, the carbon fibers have blown away in the wind."

"So the team goes in on the ground at dark?"

"Yep." Eduardo nodded. "SAD team one is in place right now, about sixty klicks east of the target. On alert, ready to get the job done and then get to a safe house. Team two is even closer, about forty klicks away. We go in, we go out — like they don't know what or who hit them."

"And we've been monitoring activity at the facility from our satellite and with a high-altitude observation drone," Chris said. "They are definitely gearing up for something unusual and apparently big."

"So that tracks with outside open-source chatter about Bhoot visiting the facility," Sid said. Seated behind Vanessa, he leaned forward now and whispered in her ear, "Most of these guys have no clue what you did to the Chechen, but word leaks around." He patted her awkwardly on her shoulder blade. "The way I hear it, you were fucking awesome."

Vanessa glanced in his direction, but she didn't turn, and she saw Chris looking at the clock on the back wall. She shifted restlessly — her stomach turning with anxiety around the op and all that was at stake. *Time to get moving.*

Sid stood, signaling his intention to speak with a low cough. "I've already let Chris and Vanessa know I have an asset who might be able to insert himself into the efforts to repair the facility after SAD's through mess-ing with it. I can get with you for details later."

Chris moved a few paces restlessly. "Obviously, if we can pull that off with your asset, it's golden. Zoe?"

Zoe nodded, uncharacteristically excited. "That's good, that's great, that will leave Iran's procurement network in place and it doesn't scare them off. We're getting really close to nabbing him."

Vanessa glanced at the latest aerial recon photo as Layla gave the team a quick update: on the safe house, the translator's flight to Afghanistan to support the SAD teams, and the transfer of currency from Ankara Station. It was money they would need to pay sympathetic locals on their way out of Iran.

"Bottom line," Chris said, "the clock is ticking. An asset gave his life to get this critical information to us, and he would not have been so persistent if he didn't think time was running out. And we all know how much the military boys will want to play with their guns." He nodded several times for emphasis. "You have all shown remarkable skills at pulling this together. Thank you for your work so far. Now, let's go do it."

SIXTY-SEVEN

Six glowing dots of light moved across the otherwise black screen inside the National Counterterrorism Center situation room at Liberty Crossing in (the ever-expanding) Tysons Corner, Virginia. Vanessa pressed back hard in her seat at this view of SAD team one moving into ground position one-half mile from the Iranian underground facility.

On a second screen, a convoy of three SUVs kicked up threads of dust visible in their headlights as they raced across the Iranian moonscape just miles from the facility.

On a third screen, the glowing dots of SAD team two spread out awaiting the convoy's approach on a dirt road that was made visible only because of faint, snaking tire ruts.

Twelve people, two teams, taking on the risk thousands of miles away while their respective crew chiefs commanded from Pakistan — and Vanessa and the others watched the live-action feed of Operation Ghost Hunt via satellite relayed by AWAC, the USAF's Boeing E-3 Sentry.

1710 hours in D.C.

0140 hours in Iran.

The dots of team one, clustered until now, began to spread out.

On track so far — twelve minutes and counting.

A burst of static chatter caught the room off guard, and Vanessa wasn't the only one who flinched in the small theater. On her left, Zoe sat rigid except for the manic vibration of her foot. To her right, Eduardo, charged with running the video feed, focused intently on his netbook. The DDO had his spot front and center. The palpable collective tension made it hard to breathe.

There was nothing any of them could do now but watch.

An hour ago, Chris had entered the room, staking out a seat on a corner desktop, after moving two bursting-to-the-top burn bags to the floor. He'd looked for her in the group.

On the first screen, the six dots of team one kept moving, and in her mind, she heard each officer's controlled breathing and the muffled crunch of their boots on sand.

Folks were putting themselves on the line, and it was too late to think about Bhoot, if he was actually in one of the convoy SUVs rapidly approaching the team two ambush site. So she sucked back her anxiety and focused on the lights of team one as they spread out, roughly delineating a forty-five-degree angle along the facility's power supply.

Instinctively, Vanessa pulled up straight, her fingernails driving into the white binder on her lap. Without fully breaking focus from the action, she noted the time — 0145 hours in Iran.

Still on track — seven minutes until they hit the power lines.

The rightness of the mission rushed through her — *Arash gave his life for this.*

Finally, they would realize his intel. This was their chance to get Bhoot — what a coup that would be — and their break to get an inside view of the facility, its technology and equipment. They could get answers to so many questions. Had the Iranians resurrected the program using UD3, uranium deuteride, to test a neutron initiator? If so, how close to full production were they? And was Bhoot in a full and unprecedented business partnership with a powerful member of the Revolutionary Guard?

It wasn't every day that reason and subtlety won over military shock and awe.

Both teams had pulled close to their final positions, moving in, now roughly a quarter-mile away from their actual targets — the facility power lines and the road. In less than six minutes, if everything stayed on track, each member of team one would be using a modified bow and arrow to shoot carbon fibers up and over the lines. Objective: to completely blow out the facility's electrical grid. Team two would use IEDs to create a section of temporarily impassible road.

Her heartbeat accelerated, and she noted just peripherally the quickening of Zoe's breathing. She found herself looking toward Chris — this was a great moment for all of them, regardless of what had happened between them. She saw him lean down to catch something from the DDO, and when Chris glanced around the room, his sharpened features revealed high-wire energy.

A second burst of audio fractured the silence — the crew chief's flat, hard voice ordering: *"Abort. Abort. Repeat — Abort."*

Vanessa pushed up against the arms of her seat, her body rigid.

She heard the DDO ordering NCTC's communications officer: "Get me SecDef."

She thought she heard Zoe's agonized whisper: "What the hell!"

On-screen, the tiny lights of the SAD teams drew back and away from their targets — and then they dimmed abruptly to black.

Seconds later, new lights streaked across the screen, and then the black ignited with the unmistakable heat of massive explosions.

In a moment of stunned silence, the realization slammed through Vanessa — *My God, they're bombing!*

She bolted to standing, aware that Chris and the DDO were on their feet — the others, too — unable to resist the pull to watch the unthinkable drama unfolding on-screen.

At the same time, a chorus of phones began ringing simultaneously.

The entire screen lit up as bombs obliterated the facility. *Where the hell were the SAD teams? Were they safe? And who was bombing?*

Without warning, all three screens went to black — communications shut down.

And then a harsh voice next to her amid the confusion — Eduardo hissing, "Is it Mossad or us? What the fuck just happened?"

Vanessa couldn't take her eyes from the screens, and she could barely breathe. *Where was Bhoot? Had the convoy turned back, or had they been annihilated, too?*

Three hours and fifteen minutes later, Vanessa and CPD learned that the Pentagon had authorized a tactical U.S. air strike against the underground Iranian facility. Both Agency SAD teams had managed to safely retreat — and they had already crossed the border out of Iran. Those behind the strike considered it a great success.

No word yet on how many in the facility were killed, how much "collateral damage." No way to know if Bhoot was among the dead. Iran's defense minister was blaming Israel and the United States for "invading Iranian airspace and attacking a target inside Iran's Baluchestan Province." The attack set off the anticipated condemnations not only from Iran but from its allies, Russia, Syria, and Lebanon's militant group, Hezbollah.

Over the coming hours and days, all parties would be paying very close attention to the fallout from the attack.

Deputy National Security Adviser Allen

Jeffreys and his militant bomb Iran lobby in the Pentagon and its allies in the militant think tanks around Washington had won the round.

EPILOGUE

Vanessa nudged on the accelerator of the rented Mercedes coupe convertible until she felt the smooth burst of the 400-horsepower turbocharged V8. Traffic on I-95 had been unexpectedly light on her return trip from a town in the middle of Long Island. She'd gone to visit Arash's widow and daughter. Zari had lit up when she saw Vanessa and the plush toy kitten she'd brought. Yassi's welcome had been cooler. But now four and a half months pregnant, she had softened in many ways.

"You and your baby are good?" Vanessa asked, and Yassi's smile stretched so her delicate, perfect teeth glistened in sunlight.

"A boy, and his name is Arash," Yassi said. She blinked back tears when Vanessa gave her the embroidered silk bag she'd bought to hold Arash's personal possessions — finally released by Agency analysts. But when Zari was showing off her cartwheels on the lawn and the women were seated together in wicker chairs, Vanessa quietly delivered her message: "The man who killed Arash is dead."

Yassi's expression shifted then, altered by a quickening of emotions — fierce satisfaction, the constancy of grief, and, at the same time, profound release. "You were there? You saw this for yourself?" Yassi asked, her eyes never leaving Zari, her hands clapping for her daughter's somersaults.

"I was there," Vanessa said — and somehow Yassi heard the message beneath the words. She reached out, took Vanessa's hand, giving it one almost painfully strong squeeze.

Later, when it was time to leave, Vanessa gave Yassi a heavy package wrapped simply in brown paper and twine. Zari did the unwrapping honors, and then her mother carefully took out the beautifully illustrated first-edition signed copy of the Shahnameh, the Khaleghi-Motlagh edition.

"I imagine Zari's already read it in Farsi," she said, only half-joking. "But this is a beautiful translation, and thanks to Arash, it turned out to be key to our operation."

As Vanessa drove away, Yassi was playing with her daughter on the lawn. *They will be okay,* she thought. But she was relieved that

Yassi hadn't pressed her to say more about Arash's assassin; she'd killed the man who pulled the trigger, but she was still tracking the man who ordered the hit.

As she neared Route 267, she eased in and out of two lanes, wind whipping her hair, sun on her skin. It was October, and the leaves on the sugar maples cast their fiery red-golden glow over this edge of the world.

Vanessa was on her way to Dulles to catch her flight to Nicosia, where she had a job to do. But this time she wasn't under directive to close up shop. For the past three weeks since the shocking end of Operation Ghost Hunt, she'd spent hours in the subterranean Agency archives, going through boxes and examining their dusty contents: accordion files stuffed with documents, floppy drives and cassette tapes, photographs with hand-written notations — old bones of the previous century's intelligence.

As far as the Agency and CPD were concerned, Bhoot was presumed dead.

Or he was missing. To date, they'd had verification from an asset on the identity of three sets of human remains found in the rubble. Two of the dead were from the facility's night maintenance crew; the third had been an engineer working late. There were more victims to be found — at least five workers unaccounted for — but three Iranian families had been notified about their loved ones.

As for Bhoot, Vanessa believed he was alive.

She'd spent most of her hours tracking the link between the Chechen sniper and Bhoot. She learned that the Chechen had gone by the name Pauk. And her persistence had paid off.

Now on Route 267 to Dulles, she passed a DOT exit sign for Clarks Crossing Road, a stop she needed to make before continuing on to the airport. She guided the Mercedes onto the exit ramp, before turning sharply onto Clarks Crossing Road to a large, almost deserted commuter parking area.

A dark green Chevy Impala sat idling near the center of the lot. She guided the Mercedes toward it carefully, until she could clearly see Khoury through the open driver's-side window. She circled around him, and then she pulled parallel, nose to tail, their windows facing each other with only inches between them. She reached out first, and he didn't hesitate — he took her hand and held it.

She felt the weight of the distance between them, and she tried to bridge it, keeping her voice and words light. "You look better than you did the last time I saw you at Headquarters."

"That's because my polygraph isn't scheduled until this afternoon. This is the third poly in as many months."

"Damn it, Khoury, damn them, they have no grounds." Vanessa's throat tightened in anger that the Agency would attack her lover, her friend. She knew the reality — the cloud of suspicion and accusation ruined careers. There didn't need to be truth behind any of the rumors and innuendo. The damage could get done with lies.

"Why didn't you tell me you were under investigation?" she asked, almost pleading.

"I tried." With a shrug, he let his fingers slide from hers.

"Cairo," she said, knowing the exact moment. "I'm sorry — I let it go."

"I know." He waited to continue while a jet passed overhead. When the engine noise faded, he spoke quietly, without heat or accusation in his tone. "But you were fine asking me to take risks for you, Vanessa. It's not the same for me, and it never will be — I'm Muslim, my parents were born in Lebanon, some of my cousins work with Hezbollah or else they're sympathizers.

There's no way you can truly understand that."

"Then why did you agree?" As soon as the childish words were out, she knew the answer. He loved her, and he would do almost anything because of that fact. It was her job to recognize the line between what she could ask and what was forbidden.

She heard him say, "I've got to go. Polygraph."

She reached for his hand again and caught it. She said, "They are worse than fools to doubt you in any way. They're stupid, and they abuse their power, and it's wrong —" Her voice broke, and tears were hot behind her eyes.

"Hey, we'll get through it," Khoury said.

His hand felt warm and strong, and she twined her fingers through his. A car turned into the lot, cruising past them slowly. "Khoury, when will I see you?"

He shook his head. "We'll figure it out." He pulled her hand gently toward his window, leaning out awkwardly to attempt a kiss. But his lips smacked air. It made her smile.

He let go of her, settled behind the wheel, and shifted. As the Impala inched forward, he said, "I'll contact you when I can. We have to be very careful."

She nodded, still leaning her head out the window to watch him go. She called out, "I love you," and thought she saw him turn to look at her once more. And then he was gone.

In the business-class lounge at Dulles, Vanessa claimed a seat off in a corner, away from the fairly busy flow of travelers coming and going. Her flight had already been delayed for forty-five minutes. Not a good omen. At least the lounge attendant had promised to keep her updated.

She'd picked up some magazines at a kiosk — airports were the only places she gave in to magazines like *Vogue* and *People*. She'd save her copy of *Gourmet* for the flight. But even as she thumbed through the glossy pages, she scanned the room with habitual vigilance.

When they announced her flight would be pushed back an hour, she knew she should get into gear and book a better flight on another airline. But the exhaustion of the months seemed to pull her down like an anchor. She closed her eyes, just for a few seconds . . .

"Miss?" Someone was tapping on her arm. Someone — she bolted up.

"Oh, I'm sorry I startled you." One of the lounge attendants was watching her with concern.

"What time is it?"

"They are just calling your flight," he said, and she heard the faintest Oklahoma panhandle accent, just barely. "It's ten after seven."

"Thanks for waking me," she told him, already on her feet. She hefted her carry-on with her good arm and headed for the exit.

"But you've left something, Miss."

Vanessa pivoted to see the attendant holding a bookmarked paperback.

She started to shake her head — but something stopped her. "Thanks, I'm not awake yet."

She held the book gingerly, stopping at a row of phones on the concourse to examine it. *Great Expectations* by Dickens. When she tapped open the cover, the bookmark slipped out. It was a ferry ticket from Turkey to Cyprus, dated two days before Sergei's murder. A candid picture of her had been glued to the other side. At first she didn't recognize the location. Then it came to her. The photo had been taken in London — a shot of her standing on the steps of MI5. Beneath the photo, a message had been written neatly, in small, careful script:

Hello, Vanessa. I feel it is time that we get to know each other. You will hear more from me soon.

~ Bhoot

Seventy minutes later, seated on board Lufthansa's flight 4536 to Paris, Vanessa stared out at the night sky. She hadn't touched dinner. Instead, she sipped a Bourbon. A worn manila folder rested in her lap. When most of her fellow passengers were asleep, she picked it up carefully. And still she kept the contents sheltered by the half-open folder. Inside, a photo from CIA Archives: Chechnya, 1996, legendary resistance leader Ibn al-Khattab astride a downed Russian Mi-8 helicopter; he is flanked by three other fighters, two of Middle Eastern descent (their AK-47s raised in the air), the third a scrawny, young Chechen, barely out of his teens. (She was almost positive the boy was Pauk: his Slavic cheekbones, the long-distance stare.) A fifth man, fit and muscled, stands aboard the helicopter's runner, his weapon held at his waist. His face has been cut from the photograph.

But what caught Vanessa's eye the first time she pulled it from a box she'd dragged from behind at least six other boxes down in Archives were his hands. Pale and delicate, fingers long and tapered, the hands of a musician or an artist, not the weathered hands of a rebel fighter.

What happened to you, Bhoot? How did you find your calling to sell massive death and destruction to the highest bidder? And, most important, what have you set your sights on now?

She slipped the photo back inside the folder on her lap. She took a final sip of the whiskey and set the glass on the empty seat next to her. She closed her eyes, letting the faces and the voices come to her — the people she'd lost in the last few months, and the people she loved, the ghosts and others from so very long ago. A child's soft wail rose up, and then almost as quickly fell away to silence — but it wasn't a cry from her dreams. It was a child and mother, seated a few rows away. Vanessa settled back into her seat, but now her eyes were open. She was awake.

ACKNOWLEDGMENTS

From the authors

This project never would have gotten off the ground without the encouragement and belief from the extraordinary David Rosenthal. You have our respect and loyalty.

Thank you to Elyse Cheney, whose judgment and professionalism have come through in spades, time and again.

Deep gratitude to Theresa Park, for your unflagging guidance, wisdom, and friendship.

Aileen Boyle, despite having to drag us kicking and screaming into social media, we think the world of you and your staff for your help, your smarts, and your bountiful enthusiasm.

With admiration to Vanessa Kehren, who asks the most astute questions and whose composure and calm direction kept us on the right track.

■ ■ ■ ■

We would like to acknowledge and express our sincere appreciation to the following friends, who have given so generously of their time and knowledge to help make this book a reality.

To Jane Baxter, for your sweet friendship and suggestions for WDC watering holes.

We owe a deep debt to Paul Evencoe, whose generosity with his encyclopedic knowledge of weapons is truly impressive.

If I'm ever in a bar fight, I want Larry Johnson to have my back. Thank you for your help in many ways.

To Porchista Khakpour: we are indebted to you for your unique assistance in unraveling the veiled mysteries of ancient Persian literature. To Catherine Oppenheimer and Garrett Thornburg for your friendship, support, and knowledge of fine wines.

To Howie Sanders, whose enthusiasm and suggestions kept our forward momentum.

Thank you to David Smallman; your wise counsel helped me navigate stormy waters many times.

With gratitude to Kathy and Chris Tone, for their friendship, wit, and help with Russian swear words.

With love and thanks to the best big brother I could ask for, Robert Plame.

With love to Joe Wilson, Samantha Wilson, and Trevor Wilson. Thank you for your patience with me. My world begins and ends with you.

Peter Knapp, Rachel Bressler, and Park Literary for always taking care of business with style and grace.

Natasha Powers, for basic weapons training 101.

Carole Poland, for your grounding humor and patience — our thanks for letting us know how bad guys clean up dirty money.

Juliette Lauber, for your grand heart, gentle wisdom, integrity, and friendship — and for your knowledge of all things French!

John Stroud: we are grateful for those street racing tips and kind corrections.

Ben Allison: your steadfast legal guidance was the beginning.

Cindy Shearer, for your heartfelt loyalty, wise words, and faith.

Fred Brown, for your unerring pendulum and your balance sheet.

Bill Geraghty: your money smarts helped keep the Lovett house afloat.

Maggie Griffin, for your friendship, humor, honesty, knowledge of everything bookish — and for insisting I buy the right shirt!

Beth Chitwood: the research stacks are a little neater because of your organizational skills.

Gay and Jenni Knight: you kept Pearl on the ground in NYC!

Alice Sealey and Suz Johnson, for all the years of good advice, laughter, and love.

Alexandra Diaz, for your wit, your laugh, and your sweet care of Pearl through the longest hauls.

Lupe Baca — twice a month you bravely fight back the chaos.

Pat Berssen, for your friendship, discretion, and amazing aplomb — you keep this house in order!

ABOUT THE AUTHORS

Valerie Plame's career in the CIA included assignments in counterproliferation operations, ensuring that enemies of the United States could not threaten the country with weapons of mass destruction. She and her husband, Ambassador Joseph Wilson, are the parents of twins. Plame and her family live in New Mexico.

Sarah Lovett's five suspense novels featuring forensic psychologist Dr. Sylvia Strange have been published in the United States and around the world. A native Californian, she lives with her family in Santa Fe, New Mexico.

The employees of Thorndike Press hope you have enjoyed this Large Print book. All our Thorndike, Wheeler, and Kennebec Large Print titles are designed for easy reading, and all our books are made to last. Other Thorndike Press Large Print books are available at your library, through selected bookstores, or directly from us.

For information about titles, please call:
(800) 223-1244

or visit our Web site at:
http://gale.cengage.com/thorndike

To share your comments, please write:
Publisher
Thorndike Press
10 Water St., Suite 310
Waterville, ME 04901